Memoir for the *Wasp*

For my wife, Terry,
whose encouragement kept me going

Memoir
for the
WASP

Enda McLaughlin

THE GLENDALE PRESS

First published 1989 by
The Glendale Press Ltd.
1 Summerhill Parade
Sandycove
Co. Dublin

British Library Cataloguing in Publication Data

McLaughlin, Enda, *1924-*
Memoir for the wasp
I. Title
823'.914 [F]

ISBN 0-907606-55-5

Cover Illustration by John Robbins; Design by David L. Murphy.
Typeset by Wendy A. Commins, The Curragh, Co. Kildare.
Make-up by Paul Bray Studio.
Printed by The Guernsey Press, Channel Islands.

Contents

To forget them completely would be
ungrateful and dishonourable

Acknowledgement

To David Ashby of the Naval Historical Library, MOD, London, for pointing me in the right direction and to Commander Rodney Preece BA RN, who read, corrected and advised me on the early draft, I gratefully acknowledge the help freely and generously given.

1   The Log

The summer I found the diary was the summer of my accident. Not that there was any connection between the two events, it was just sheer chance that one event led to the other.

I had been at work as usual that June morning with nothing more immediate on my mind than how I was going to talk my boss into letting me borrow his 24' sloop for the weekend to take my girl friend sailing in the Channel. Maybe even as far as Jersey, if the wind and weather held up.

Perhaps I should have been thinking more about my job at the time than about the delights I fancied were in store, because seconds later I was lying on the ground with a broken leg.

My job? I am in the Navy. The Stores branch to be precise, and I drive an elderly desk in the accounts department on which I follow the path of invoices, requisitions and stores issue notes, from one totally uninteresting office in Portsmouth to other equally uninteresting offices in any one of half a dozen bases around the country. The only justification for my job, I firmly believe, is that it keeps me out of sight, and therefore out of mind, of senior officers who couldn't care less whether I exist or not.

I suppose the only interesting things about me are that I'm approaching twenty eight years of age and my name is Stephen Roberts.

Be that as it may, on this particular day, approaching the weekend, I was walking across the famous dockyard at Portsmouth, where the *Victory* sits safely in her concrete berth, on my way to a supply office which had somehow managed to mislay several thousand toilet rolls, when a car came from behind a parked lorry and hit me.

When I recovered my senses I was surrounded by a mixed group of curious and sympathetic Navy personnel, male and female, service and civilian, who appeared disappointed when they saw my eyes open. For some seconds I just lay there wondering what on earth I was doing stretched out on the cobbles, then I tried to sit up. As I did an elderly petty officer leaned down, put a hand on my shoulder saying 'Stay where you are, mate, the ambulance will be here in a minute. I think you've hurt your leg.'

From then on I lost control of the situation. The ambulance arrived, I was bundled onto a stretcher and whisked off to hospital where my leg was put into plaster and then we were both − my leg and I − deposited in a small ward befitting my rank and injury. I found that I had lost all interest in the whereabouts of the missing toilet rolls and drifted off to sleep. Doped to the ears, no doubt.

Several hours later I was wakened by a rather homely but very efficient nurse with a cup of tea, who told me that my CO had arrived to see me. As he was a lieutenant, like myself, I wasn't too impressed, but being my first and only visitor to date I levered myself up in bed to show that I was paying attention when he spoke. A moment or two later he breezed into the room.

'So this is where you've got to? Lolling around, being waited on hand and foot by gorgeous nurses. . .' he glanced at my angel of mercy who simpered coyly . . . 'when you should be working. I just don't know where it will all end. What is the Navy coming to?'

This was delivered with a broad grin, then followed up quickly with 'How are you? Does it hurt? Is there anything I can get you?'

With what passed for a roguish look the nurse left the room.

On being assured that I didn't need anything he pulled up a chair and sat down. He had been making enquiries and knew all about the accident and, more importantly, knew that following a few days in hospital I would be free to go on sick leave. I hadn't even considered this.

'Sick leave? I'm not entitled to sick leave. I'll be up and about in no time at all. As a matter of fact I was wondering could I borrow your boat this coming weekend, but perhaps I'd better make it the following weekend, just in case? May I?'

'I'm afraid not, old son.' Seeing my look of disappointment he continued. 'Don't you know that your leg is broken in two places? You won't be sailing for a month or so. You're ashore at least until you're walking with a stick. Now lie back and enjoy that prospect.'

As he was speaking I could feel my leg beginning to ache and lifting up the sheet peered down to see what it looked like. The plaster felt cold and heavy and looked enormous. I realised that he was right and groaned in frustration.

'There's no need to be like that. Look on it as a small blessing. When you get out from here you can lie in the sun, doing nothing but enjoying yourself thinking up ways of spending your unearned pay. My God, you've got the luck of the Irish. I could use a few weeks off in this weather.'

Such cheerfulness was beginning to jar. My bruises were starting to hurt and, although I knew he meant well and was doing his best to cheer me, I felt a bout of self-pity coming on.

'I suppose my suit was ruined too?'

"Fraid so, but it could have been worse. You could have been in uniform and had that ruined. The Navy won't mind your suit being ruined, there isn't any paperwork involved in getting a replacement. Isn't that good? Everything is working out well.'

All I could do was to laugh at this outrageous view of things. Then another thought struck me. 'Sick leave, you said? Where can I go on sick leave if I can't sail?'

'Now that is a problem. Let me think.' I waited while he sat with his eyes closed, as if in thought. Ten seconds later he opened them. 'I've got it. Where else would you go on sick leave but home? You have a home, I take it?'

'Of course I have a home. In the Irish Republic,' I added. 'And now that you mention it, it has been rather a long time since I was there. On the other hand, I don't fancy making the trip to the far north west corner of Ireland hauling half a hundredweight of cement firmly attached to my leg. I think it might be better to take the ferry to the Isle of Wight and check into a guesthouse for the duration. With a bit of luck I might even find one with a beautiful daughter just dying to nurse a heroic naval officer back to health.'

'You should be so lucky. That isn't on at all. In fact, the more I think about it the better I like the idea of you having a long leisurely rest at home. Where you can't pick up the phone every time you feel like bothering me. Consider yourself under orders to report to your dear old Mum as soon as they let you out from here, and I'll make all the necessary arrangements.'

He was as good as his word. A fortnight later I was loaded on board a naval communications aircraft at Lee on Solent, which two and a half hours later landed at Ballykelly airfield outside Derry. My parents had been advised of my arrival and met the aircraft. An hour later I was safely back in the family home outside Rathmullen in Co Donegal. Tired, hungry, irritable and impatient at the way I was being fussed over but, in a way I couldn't express, glad to be home after being away for so many years.

The days following my return took on a pattern which I had almost forgotten. Over two or three weeks I felt myself slow down and pick up old threads of country life. When I had progressed from crutches to a walking stick it was still early August, and as I strolled down to the village in the mornings to pick up the newspapers fresh in from Dublin and Belfast I would stop to look out over the calm waters of Lough Swilly, totally empty of shipping, and compare it with the busy polluted waters of the Solent, to the latter's disadvantage. I was becoming rusticated and enjoying the process.

My mother made no secret of the fact that she was glad I was back home. A steady stream of visitors visited the house during the first few weeks I was there, then it trickled off as my leg improved and I ceased to be an object of either interest or entertainment. Eventually there was only one person who called every day, someone I hadn't seen for years although we had been at school together, still unmarried like myself. Her name? Joyce Campbell.

When I say that we had been at school together I do not mean that we had been in the same class and were more or less the same age. Joyce was younger than me, I think she was a mixed infant when I was a worldly senior of eight or so, but since our families were friends we knew each other growing up. In fact our relationship was never more than a nodding acquaintanceship. But looking at her now I wondered why I had never noticed before just how attractive she was. It was the highlight of each day when she arrived to see me and I found myself looking forward more and more to her visits. My mother noticed my interest in Joyce and encouraged her to stretch out the time she spent with me, from an initial fifteen minutes or so to a couple of hours by the end of the second week, with afternoon tea laid on.

This suited me admirably. Having been away from home so many years I had few friends left in the area who were prepared, or even able, to spend time with me because of marriage, social and business commitments. I understood this but time would have hung heavily on my hands had I been depending on them. Joyce, however, was enjoying the long break from the southern university where she worked as a lecturer and researcher during the academic year. And we had one major interest in common. We both loved sailing.

This interest came to light early on when we were getting to know each other again. We had been talking about Navy life and I mentioned summer sailing in the English Channel, exploring the French coast, and the longest voyage I had completed to date, from Portsmouth to Inverness in Scotland. She was interested in this and sympathised when I explained how it was to be a round Britain voyage but had been brought to an early end by bad weather, which necessitated leaving the boat in Scotland over the winter months and returning to base by train.

I must admit that I had been laying on the rigours of the trip to impress her. Then, rather smugly, I asked had she taken her boat, which was lying at anchor off the long Rathmullen pier, anywhere interesting.

'I've been to sea a couple of times and hope to take another trip before the university reopens. I've been lucky though and haven't had to leave the boat anywhere like you did, touch wood. That must be maddening.'

Thinking that perhaps she had been down the coast to Galway or around the north coast of Ireland to the Clyde, or even the Hebrides, I pressed her for details. I was sorry I asked.

'I've been to the Azores twice and took part in the Admiral's Cup once. I didn't fancy that very much as it meant having a crew and I much prefer single handing. It is far easier not having to worry about someone else all the time.'

'You did the full Admiral's Cup? Including the Fastnet?' I asked in disbelief.

'Of course. As I said, I had a full crew, and since that was part of the series we did it all. It didn't amount to very much and we only came in fourth in our class. But it was an experience.'

She looked innocently at me and I couldn't decide whether she was having me on or not.

'What do you intend doing this summer? Another trip to the Azores?'

'Not this year. As you may have heard, Dad has become rather frail and I don't want to be too far away from home. Mum has told me not to let that stop me but I know she would be glad of my support if anything happened. Besides, there is a lot of water around Lough Swilly which I've never explored. When your leg gets a bit stronger how would you feel about crewing for me? Or do you object to sailing with a girl skipper?'

'Not at all. Some of our WRNS are very capable skippers and I've sailed with them happily. But I must admit I don't know any who have single handed to the Azores. Even once.'

It was obvious by then that she had been telling nothing but the truth, the plain unvarnished kind, and I found myself looking forward to exploring the twenty five miles long inlet with her. From then on we talked about boats and crews and the oddballs one invariably meets in strange harbours, until my mother arrived with a tray of tea things.

About a week later Joyce announced one afternoon that she thought the following day would be ideal for sailing. The long, hot, dead calm weather seemed to be breaking and light Force Three winds were forecast for the first time for almost a fortnight. So it was decided. When she had left to return home my mother asked had I any foul weather gear with me.

'I didn't know that I'd be getting in any sailing while I was here, but it is hardly likely that I'll need it tomorrow. I rather think that we'll be sailing in bathing costumes.'

'Perhaps not, but it is possible that the westerly wind will bring some rain with it. Anyway, it isn't a big thing to have some dry clothing on board, is it? I would take oilies, especially since you've been laid up for over a month now.'

Did I mention that my mother is inclined to fuss a bit, but she lived there and as it was quite possible that she knew more about local weather than I did I decided to go along with her. Calling her an old fuss-pot I agreed, then asked where I was likely to get a set of waterproofs in the village. I had a feeling that I'd have to go further afield.

'Not this time. I was in the attic about a month ago looking for curtain material in a trunk up there and I opened a bag, like a big kitbag, and saw waterproof clothes inside. I didn't take them out. If they fit you I think it would be no harm to take them with you.'

I was intrigued by this as I'd never heard about this cache of old equipment before and asked her where she thought they had come from. She vaguely remembered someone having left sailing gear many years before but couldn't for the life of her remember who it was. Nobody had ever enquired about the equipment and it had been relegated to the attic a long time ago for convenience. She assured me that it was most unlikely that the owner would call about it the following day and that it would be quite safe to borrow whatever I needed. I decided to go up to the attic, there and then, to see what was there. Taking a torch I made my way up.

When you have been in one attic you know what they all look

like. Water tanks, rolled up carpets, old sports equipment and mysterious boxes everywhere full of abandoned, mislaid and forgotten debris of family life. This was no exception. Swinging the beam of the torch around it didn't take long to spot the bag which my mother had mentioned. Made of white waterproof material it was indeed considerably bigger than a kit bag, more like a sail bag, and it proved to be quite heavy when I dragged it across to the trapdoor.

Although it was bulky it wasn't too difficult to manhandle and a few seconds later I followed it down onto the bathroom floor. It was dusty but a quick wipe with a damp facecloth took care of that. Then sitting on the edge of the bath I opened the knotted string at its neck and tipped it out on the floor.

The bag did contain someone's sailing gear. There was a suit of oilies, trousers and jacket with attached hood, and a pair of yellow wellies. There was also an inflatable lifejacket, safety harness, a torch – which didn't light when I pressed the button – binoculars, and a sheath knife on a lanyard. There was also a book with a black leather cover which was held closed by several turns of sail thread wrapped around it.

Putting the book to one side I tried out the oilies for size. They fitted me reasonably well, certainly well enough to keep me dry should the rain my mother was expecting decide to come. The wellies were a bit tight but I prefer wearing sneakers or runners on board anyway. The equipment was in good condition, hardly worn and certainly far too good to be abandoned. There wasn't a name to be seen anywhere to identify its owner which was unusual. I had another look at each piece, searching for some clue as to where it might have come from, then repacked it all into its bag.

Taking the bag and book I crossed the landing to my room and left the bag there where it would be available the following day. Then I took the book downstairs where I could examine it at my leisure over a cup of tea which my mother had just announced was ready.

On closer examination the book proved to have not one but two covers. The outer one was, as I had thought, either sheepskin or leather, black with age and stiff as if it had been soaked in sea water, then allowed to dry out. I had to cut the sail thread which held it closed as it was impossible to open the knots. Inside this cover there was another, made of canvas, which had been sewn into the shape of an envelope and folded closed. This was easily unrolled and inside I saw a neat packet of handwritten papers.

My mother, who had been watching me open the 'book', now showed interest in what I was doing and came to sit beside me on the couch. Putting her hand over mine she told me to take care as the whole packet looked very old and it would be a pity to damage the contents through a moment's carelessness. I agreed and slowly slid the papers out from their canvas cover. We both looked at the top sheet on which was written, in very black ink, 'The personal log of Geo. H. King, RN'.

Mystified I looked at her. 'I don't know who this man King is, or was, but I'm sure of one thing. He isn't the owner of the gear upstairs. This looks as if it was written sometime in the last century and the stuff in the sailbag can't be more than five or six years old. Are you sure you can't remember who left it here?'

'I've been racking my brains about that and just can't remember. I have an idea though that it could have been left by a young man who stayed with us one night some years ago. He came to join friends who were to arrive on a yacht, but something went wrong and they didn't arrive. As he was hitchhiking back to Galway he asked could he leave a bag here for a few days and would return to collect it. I agreed. We never saw him again. If that isn't the man who left it I don't know where it came from. I don't know his name, nor am I sure he even came from Galway. He could have been a university student and in that case he might have gone on anywhere. Maybe he was a relation of this George King? Let's see what the log says.'

At some time in its past the 'book' had been subjected to considerable pressure and the sheets were almost bonded together. I was afraid that if I attempted to pick them apart I would tear them and explained this to my mother who went into the kitchen, returning with a cook's palette knife.

By now we were seated at the table under a strong overhead light and taking the knife from her I very carefully slid the thin blade between the top and next sheet of paper: a few nervous seconds later they were parted.

At first sight the paper was covered in a closely written, beautifully formed, copperplate handwriting. There was a date at the top of the page, 17 July 1884, followed by the word Queenstown. Next there was a space of one line, then the script began. 'Arrived here this morning having reported to Admiral Lethbridge in Cork that I am ready to take up my appointment as navigator of HM gunboat *Wasp*. The *Wasp*, being presently at sea, I was ordered to report to the officer commanding this base, Captain Whitehouse, and await further orders.' . . .

I looked at my mother, feeling the hairs at the back of my neck prickle.

'Do you know what this is? It's the diary of an officer who was on the *Wasp*. Remember the *Wasp*? Wasn't that the ship that sank on Tory Island under mysterious circumstances?'

'I believe it was. How very interesting. Do you think this might be important?'

'I don't know, Mother. But one thing I'm sure of, we're not going to risk damaging this log until we know a lot more about both the *Wasp* and the officer who wrote it. Now who around here would know?'

'Why don't you ask Joyce's father? A lot of his family served in the Navy in the old days and they lived in this area since long before 1884. He would be a good man to start with I think. Joyce herself might be able to help too, you never know.'

Carefully rewrapping the log in its canvas envelope I put it away in a steel cashbox. Further questions could wait until the following day.

Shortly after nine o'clock next morning Joyce and I transferred our gear and food from the dinghy into her boat. Being used to the cramped confines of the 24' sloop I usually sailed I was more than impressed by Joyce's Mirage 30. With three cabins, a centre cockpit and a 20hp diesel engine tucked under the floor I had no doubts that I was moving upmarket and as I watched her casually but confidently prepare the boat for sea I shed any reservations I might have had regarding her seamanship and ability to take on a single handed voyage to the Azores and back. Or anywhere else for that matter.

The weather forecast had almost got it right, the F3 breeze hadn't actually arrived but we could see the catspaws ruffling the water. Half an hour later everything was stowed away, the sail covers were off and the halyards loosely looped around the winches. We were ready to weigh anchor, only needing a little more wind to carry us off shore into the middle of what is generally considered to be the best deep water port in the whole of the British Isles and Ireland. From there we could expect enough wind to take us right down to the sea more than twenty miles away, even if the hoped-for breeze never arrived.

'Enjoying yourself?'

I turned to look at Joyce who was soaking up the already warm sun on the cockpit cushions behind me. While I had been unpacking the sails she had changed into shorts and bikini top and I had to smile as I thought of the foul weather gear stowed in the bag on my bunk below decks. She put on a face when she saw me and asked was I laughing at her.

'No, no. Of course not.' I moved over and sat down on the starboard seat opposite. Starting to explain about the oilies I remembered the log which I had found and decided to start my investigation there and then. When I had finished telling her how far my mother and I had got with it she was sitting up listening very intently to my story.

'And your mother has no idea at all who could have left the bag at your house?'

I explained about her vague memory of the man who might have been from Galway, then brought up the bag from below and took everything out once more to search pockets and examine the clothing in greater detail and better light than we had had the night before. At the end of fifteen minutes as I was repacking everything, having discovered nothing fresh, I looked up at her from my position on the cockpit floor.

'I didn't think we had missed anything. Did you notice anything which might be a clue?'

She looked thoughtfully at me. 'No, I'm afraid not. It looks exactly like any other foul weather gear I've ever seen. What do you know about the *Wasp*? I've heard the stories, many times over the years, but everyone seems to have his own version of what happened to her. I must admit though that I wasn't very interested and it did happen a long time ago. Still it would be a pity not to follow it up now that it has been dropped into your lap, as it were. Agreed?'

'Agreed. But where do we begin? I take it that you'll help?'

'Of course I'll help. Don't forget, research is the largest part of my job at the university and who knows, perhaps some of my long gone relations were on her? It's unlikely but even so I'd like to help with it.' She glanced up at the small burgee atop the mast, watching it slowly swing round in the light airs. 'I'll give this some thought during the day. But for now, get the jib up, then stand by the anchor windlass.'

There wasn't any doubt who was skipper on this boat.

For the rest of the morning we drifted slowly down the lough, occasionally helped along by infrequent puffs of warm air until about mid afternoon I felt the sleek Mirage lift to a slight swell and looked up at the mainsail which had silently filled. Joyce sitting totally relaxed, her arm stretched along the tiller, holding the boat on a steady heading, appeared unaware of the change.

'Are we going to get the "fresh breeze" we were promised by the weatherman?' I asked of no one in particular. There was silence for about half a minute.

'Did you say something? I'm sorry, I was thinking about the *Wasp* and the poor man who wrote the log. What did you say?'

Feeling slightly foolish I repeated my inane remark.

'I don't think so. At least not today. But I thought it might interest you to come here, where the lough meets the sea. If you use the glasses you might see Tory Island off to port in about ten minutes when we clear the headland. You won't see much as it's thirty miles off, but it is where it all happened and we can date the beginning of our research from this moment. Everything has to have a starting point, ours should be at sea.'

'Agreed, Joyce. And can I say I'm glad to have you aboard, if that isn't a pompous remark since the boat is yours anyway. But you know what I mean?' I finished anxiously.

'I know. Thank you. Now look out there. Way down on the horizon. That's Tory, if you can see it in this haze.' She gave me about three minutes to scan the horizon and convince myself that the light cloud at one point was, in fact, the island. Then she called, 'Ready about. . . . Lee Oh', and it was back to work as she brought the boat about, heading for home.

Joyce certainly took her work seriously. The next morning before nine o'clock, she was knocking on the front door and calling up to my window. A couple of minutes later she was talking to my mother in the kitchen and I was shuffling downstairs, unshaven, half awake and sporting an old worn woollen dressing gown which had seen better days. I came into the kitchen, annoyed at having been wakened for no good reason. My annoyance didn't last long.

'There you are. Good show,' she greeted me. 'I thought an early start would get our little project under way, but I was delayed unfortunately. Still, better late than never.' Suddenly noticing my appearance she put on a concerned look and asked if I was all right. 'Not sick, or anything? Still, you'll probably feel better when you have had a shave and something to eat. I thought that we would divide the work in two. Unless, that is, you have any other ideas?'

Taking the cup of tea which my mother had handed to me I assured Joyce that any ideas she had would be quite all right with me. After all, she knew far more about conducting a project such as this than I did.

'Good. Now I want you to take the logbook into Derry this morning, to a firm which deals in old and rare books. I've already been on the phone to the managing director who is an old friend and he will look after you. In the meantime I'll start asking questions about the loss of the *Wasp* and find out what the locals know of the story. If we're lucky the information will be the same from both sources. If we're not . . . well, we'll cross that bridge when we come to it.'

An hour later I was on my way to Derry driving Joyce's mini. The rest of the day was spent with her friend, Cecil Wheatley, who certainly knew and appreciated old manuscripts like the one I handed him. When he took it from me he literally caressed the blackened leather cover, then smelt it and turned it over very gently in his hands. I had to explain to him what I had done to try to open it up. This caused him to 'tut-tut' in a mildly shocked manner but he didn't make any further comment. Instead he picked up the house phone and called in his works foreman who was equally interested.

For a few minutes I sat and listened to them as they discussed the problem. It wasn't new to them, I could see, and shortly afterwards I was seated on the opposite side of a workbench watching the two enthusiasts go to work.

After they had established that the pages were merely pressed tightly together by compression and were not stuck together with an adhesive, the work progressed smoothly and satisfactorily. Page after page was sprayed with a liquid which penetrated and then loosened it from the one beneath. As they parted, each page was placed in a small calorifier to dry, then carefully slid into a clear plastic cover to protect it and allow it to be handled without being touched.

By early afternoon the job was finished and I was on my way back to Rathmullen having stood my two new friends the best lunch we could find in Derry. This was the only payment they would accept. The way they saw it they could not take money for such a simple and satisfying task.

That evening when dinner was over Joyce and I spread the now protected pages on the dining room table to examine them. From the first entry on 17 July until the last on 20 Sept., sixty eight days elapsed with an entry covering each day. The entries differed in length, some were very brief, often just a record of the weather, while others took up a full page, or even two.

On our first reading we merely skimmed the surface of the story Lieutenant George King had to tell, then Joyce decided to set it out like any other project, taking a day at a time and relating it to events as she uncovered them.

On the following pages I have set out the path our project followed. And the unexpected results.

2   HMS *Wasp*

Lieut King's Log   17 July 1884 Queenstown

Arrived here this morning having reported to Admiral Lethbridge in Cork that I am ready to take up my appointment
as navigator on HM gunboat *Wasp*. The *Wasp*, being presently
at sea, I was ordered to report to the officer commanding
this base, Captain Whitehouse, and await further orders. I
hope that I do not have to wait too long as the accommodation found for me is of poor quality and at an inconvenient
distance from the base.

The town of Queenstown, close to the mouth of Cork harbour
and sixteen miles downstream from that city, existed to serve
those who made their living from the sea and its ships.

The principle feature of the port was Spike Island, lying to the
south of the channel which cut upriver to the city. The island
was fortified, its fort mounting a battery of guns sited to completely cover the entrance to the river. In addition to this main
armament, further firepower could be brought to bear on shipping from the buildings along the shore on the opposite, north
side of the channel. These buildings housed the stores, accommodation for transient personnel, the administration staff and
the barracks of the Royal Marine Light Infantry.

Originally a fishing village the town had grown during the
Napoleonic War when the Lords of the Admiralty decided that
an unprotected harbour was an invitation to the French fleet,
and had fortified it. From then it had grown until its present
garrison was more than 15,000 men and the original fishing fleet
had moved to a smaller and quieter harbour further along the
coast.

The threat of war long since passed, the base had become the
headquarters of the Royal Navy in Ireland. It also served as a
way-station for packets en route to and from America and Canada
and as such, coaling facilities were established to feed the bunkers
of the coal burners which were using the harbour more and more
frequently.

These packets were, of course, civilian vessels. The Navy was only now beginning to convert in large numbers to steam and there were some members of the Admiralty in London who viewed the transition with the deepest suspicion and distrust.

Steam, they said, had no future. Warships couldn't afford to give up vital space to coal when the space was needed for men and stores. Where, they asked, would the *Victory* be if Nelson had to leave two hundred men ashore so that he could take on coal when the battle of Trafalgar was about to be fought? Besides, everyone knew how unreliable steam engines were. The whole idea was preposterous.

Leaning on a wall high up on the hill overlooking the town, George King wasn't at all worried about these and other problems currently besetting their Lordships. It was a hot summer day with very little wind to be felt down at the jetties, but up where he now was, two hundred or more feet above the river, a light breeze cooled him pleasantly.

He had walked up here to get a bird's eye view of the harbour and to remove himself from the eye of the harbour captain who was always on the look out for spare people, to whom he could delegate some of the work which needed to be done, but for which nobody ever seemed to be available. It was the same everywhere. King, who had recently arrived from Portsmouth, had expected it and wasted no time making himself scarce. Now he was determined to enjoy his unexpected freedom. Idly letting his eyes sweep the harbour he considered taking the ferry upriver the following day to sample the delights of the bigger town, then ruefully decided that he could hardly afford it and dismissed the thought.

The scene below was interesting however. As the new navigator of HM gunboat *Wasp* it was important that he make himself familiar with the harbour, its islands, channel and fortifications since this would be his home port in the future and he would be expected to know it blindfolded. There wasn't any better way of getting to know strange waters than from a height like this on a clear day. An hour spent studying the whole panorama was better than four times that length of time poring over a chart. He took out a notebook and roughed in a small sketch of the waterway, making notes of points and bearings to be plotted later on a full size chart.

As he worked, part of his mind thought of his new appointment and he congratulated himself on his luck.

The ship he was joining was less than four years old, it had already earned itself a reputation even as far away as Portsmouth. Her young captain's name regularly appeared in the columns of the *Times* in connection with harrowing reports of starving peasantry to whom he brought food and help, frequently at considerable risk to his ship and her company.

That this was not due to any magnanimity on the part of the Admiralty, King was well aware. But because they believed that acts of apparent generosity, particularly those which didn't cost the exchequer anything, enhanced their own reputation with parliament. They had allowed a practice to grow over recent years, of hiring out Her Majesty's ships to organisations connected with the public good.

Bringing relief to destitute people, whose condition frequently was the result of the actions of the same parliament, was an example of this. The Quakers had hired a number of vessels from the Navy, of which the *Wasp* was one, and since coming on this station she had been busy taking food into small harbours and ports right up the west coast and as far round as Belfast.

It wasn't going to sea 'Navy style', but in the absence of a war to be fought it was a lot better than swinging around a buoy or being tied up to a jetty. And for a navigator he could see that it would be a very interesting experience and test of his skill. There was always the possibility of a good chase after smugglers as well. All in all, life could become quite exciting when the *Wasp* picked him up.

Aged twenty four, King was the son of a widow whose husband had been lost at sea returning from America some years earlier. From childhood he had been determined on the Navy, joining the training ship *Brittania* at the earliest possible age. Since graduating from midshipman to sub lieutenant he had spent the intervening four years between Portsmouth and Plymouth doing relief duties for officers sick or on leave. Each ship he had joined he had hoped would accept him permanently, but it never happened until now. So, fourteen ships later, he was about to join his very own first ship. And he was determined to make this posting a memorable one, come what may. If only for his mother's sake.

Straightening up from the wall on which he had been leaning his attention was caught by a flash of white sail coming into view from behind the fort. He paused. Even at a distance it looked familiar. He waited until the vessel was fully visible and then there wasn't any doubt. The sleek lines could only belong to HMS *Sea Witch*.

Known to everyone simply as the *Witch*, it was one of the last of a generation of sailing ships to be ordered by the Admiralty. From now on, no matter what the die-hards maintained, sail would be replaced by steam totally. Which was a pity. Watching her slip silently and seemingly effortlessly through the lines of moored shipping, wondering could the manoeuvre have been better carried out had the small frigate been steam powered, he felt the conviction growing that there was only one captain who could handle a boat in such confined waters with such panache and skill. His old friend and classmate on the *Britannia*, Milo Hannon.

King had seen enough. Making his way back down the hill he knew that the *Witch* would be safe and secure alongside the jetty long before he was back at sea level, so he didn't hurry. But there was an expectant smile on his face and a new spring in his step as he made his way along the dusty, rutted road. If Hannon was based in Queenstown too the posting here could have some very pleasant times ahead for both of them.

Reaching the main road which ran beside the river, he passed along the red brick wall surrounding the dockyard until he reached the open, high wooden gate which served as the entrance. Guarded by two marines who were busy inspecting and directing the constant flow of traffic and horse drawn vehicles through in each direction, he paused until a break gave him a chance to enquire where he might find the ship he was seeking.

To his surprise, the marine to whom he was speaking asked him to wait for a moment while he called his sergeant to deal with King's casual enquiry. A few seconds later a marine sergeant stepped out from an open door, saluted King, then politely asked to see the lieutenant's dockyard pass.

As he was searching for it King glanced at the stream of people passing in and out without hindrance and, slightly annoyed at having been singled out apparently for no reason, asked why he was receiving such attention.

'Sorry, sir. You're new here, aren't you?' the NCO asked.

When King agreed that he was, the marine continued, 'All the people going through the gate at this time of day are known to us, at least by sight. Next time you go through you won't be stopped either but for now we have to be sure that you are who you seem to be. There's some very peculiar people around here, sir, people with no love for the Navy and we can't take any chances.'

He handed back King's pass and nodded to the nearest guard who had stopped him. King was interested. He hadn't fully realised that the differences between England and Ireland were wider than just geographical, but the gate wasn't the place to pursue his enquiries.

Thanking the sergeant, he returned the salute, moved inside the gate, crossing the cobbled yard towards the jetty where he could see the *Witch* already secured for harbour routine with a sentry posted. Minutes later he was on board being greeted by his friend in the tiny cabin reserved for the captain.

Although both men were very much of the same age they were totally dissimilar in appearance and temperament. Where King was tall and looked slightly under weight, with a clean shaven face and a demeanour of friendly interest in everything about him, Hannon was stocky and very much the outdoor man with face tanned, where it could be seen behind his beard, from long exposure to the elements. His uniform too looked as if it had experienced much more severe wear than King's well pressed coat and almost new hat, but Hannon made no comment on this. Instead he greeted his friend boisterously and with every appearance of pleasure and delight at meeting up again so far from Portsmouth.

While Hannon was finalising his reports and signing requisitions for the purser and chandler who had come aboard behind King, they managed to exchange some local gossip, bringing each other up to date on the activities of various mutual friends.

King then explained his own presence and to his surprise Hannon greeted this news with silence. It was as if Hannon's pleasure had suddenly evaporated and King couldn't feel but disappointed. He waited for a few moments longer and when there was still no comment asked his friend outright was there something wrong, something that he didn't know about.

'What do you know about the *Wasp*?' Hannon answered.

'Very little, now that you ask. But I've been reading about her in the *Times* for the past year or two. Although she does most of her work with the harbour commissioners and fisheries people, she has been on famine relief around the coast and it would seem, has been doing a good job of work. Apart from that, nothing. Why?'

There was silence as Hannon carefully signed some papers,

then laid down his pen and screwed the lid tightly onto the ink well. When this was done to his satisfaction he looked straight at his friend.

'It's not for me to criticise a fellow captain. Especially one who has been doing, as you say, good work. But there is something wrong about the *Wasp*. I don't know what it is and I don't suppose that anyone else does either, especially if they haven't sailed on her. But I can tell you to be careful and to keep your eyes open.'

Further questioning by the now perturbed King eventually induced Hannon to enlarge upon his cryptic and disturbing remarks.

'Look George, I'm sorry I said so much because I don't really know what is wrong. John Nicholls is by way of being a friend of mine and he is a top rate captain. I know that you'll like him when you meet and there is no doubt at all about his ability, but some very odd stories are circulating about the *Wasp*.'

He paused as if considering how much further he should go while King sat in anxious silence. Making up his mind, Hannon continued, 'If you were anyone else I'd say no more, but I at least owe it to you to pass on what I've heard. Then it is up to you to make up your own mind.'

King nodded in both agreement and encouragement.

'All right then, George. The *Wasp* has been based here since she joined the fleet. When she first came here she had another captain, then following her engines being fitted in the spring of '82 Nicholls was appointed captain that summer. Until then, and for nearly a year afterwards, the *Wasp* and her new captain were the pride of the station. They were clean, smart, efficient, and what their Lordships would call "a happy ship". I envied John Nicholls a bit myself because, no matter what the old timers tell you, a ship like the *Wasp*, with its engine, has many advantages over the *Witch*.

'Before you say anything, I know that coal is dirty and that it takes up a lot of space, but if it means being able to go into action no matter how wind and tide are conspiring to prevent you, or more important, extricate your ship and crew from a situation which can result in the total loss of both, then I'll take steam every time. That's not to say that I'd change from the old *Witch*. Her fighting days are numbered, I'd say, but while she floats I'll be proud and happy to command her. I joined the Navy to see action, like yourself I suppose, and since the *Wasp* has a better chance of that I envy Nicholls his opportunities. Or, at least I did, until recently.

'About a year ago people started noticing changes in the *Wasp* and her officers. They were small changes. But, I suppose, looking back now they were significant. For instance, she began being late at rendezvous points. Up to then, when Nicholls said he would be at a certain place at a particular time one could rely absolutely on his being there. Then he started being hours late, up to ten or twelve hours, which could have had very serious effects had we been at war and due to meet or intercept an enemy ship. Then it went to being two or three days late and eventually he was summoned to appear before Admiral Lethbridge who wanted to know just what was going on.

'For a time after that things got better as far as timekeeping was concerned. But other things were going wrong. For instance, there was endless trouble with his engine. It got so bad that other captains told him to tie a rope around it and use it as an anchor, half as a joke but half in earnest, and the problems continued until the ship was docked and a full inspection carried out. Nothing was found to be wrong with the engine after all that. I can tell you that his reputation didn't gain much when the dockyard engineer put in his report on that occasion.

'All this was beginning to tell on Nicholls. I had a night or two out with him in Cork and he told me how worried he was. I could see it was true. He had lost weight and his confidence was badly shaken. He even had a slight tremor in his hands. This, as you can appreciate, is very bad for the captain of any ship. What he told me then was that he knew things were going wrong and his crew were becoming difficult to handle but he couldn't put his finger on what was causing it. He had tried every way he knew, questioning the crew, surprise inspections, increasing punishments for defaulters, but nothing worked. The *Wasp* wasn't either happy or efficient any longer. Rumour had it that old Lethbridge was even considering relieving him of his command. However, by then the *Wasp* was contracted to the Quakers to carry out famine relief and there wasn't another captain on the station who knew the coast and the tiny harbours as well as Nicholls, so no action was taken. Then an odd thing happened.'

Pausing, he took out a pipe and silently packed it with black tobacco from an old pouch. King waited. A few moments later Hannon, his pipe going well, continued.

'Everything started going right for the *Wasp* again. It took some time for this to be noticed here as the ship is temporarily based in Westport, halfway up the west coast, and the supplies she was delivering were being brought by train from Galway and Dublin. But as members of her crew, some of whom live here, came home on leave so the story spread. It was like hearing about a different ship, or as if a curse had been lifted — not that I believe in such things myself, you understand? — but it was like old times again.

'About then I had a letter from Nicholls. Why he should have written to me I don't know. We were never sufficiently close to write to each other, but there you are. It was an odd letter, about two pages long and rambling with no point to it. The gist of it was, however, that we, the English, were responsible for the state of the peasantry of Ireland and that, according to the Bible, we would have a terrible price to pay later for our treatment of these poor souls.

'I know the Irish have had a very hard time ever since the famine years of '46 and '47. Emigration and starvation are terrible bedfellows and it will be a long time before the country recovers fully from those years, if it ever does. But when he starts blaming us, and quoting the Bible for good measure, I think the influence of the Quakers must be affecting him. It can't be that he has been too long at sea since he spends more time in port than on blue water. And blaming us for causing the inhabitants to starve is nonsense. Has he forgotten that this is an island and the seas around it are teeming with fish? I don't know what to make of it all. But I intend to find out what's behind it when I see him.'

'When did this letter arrive, Milo?'

'Let's see now.' He closed his eyes, thinking. Moments later he opened them and stretching out an arm took a thick ledger type book from a cupboard over his bunk. He flicked rapidly through its pages.

'Here it is. I got the letter when I came back from a patrol down to the Channel Islands and the French coast, and that finished on 10 May, so it was about two months ago. Why, is it important?'

'I don't know,' King replied. 'Remember, I don't know the man at all, but it does seem extraordinary behaviour for a naval officer. I'll think about it and when I've met him, and been to sea with him, I'll let you know. In the meantime, thanks for the cautionary tale. Now let's talk about something more cheerful.'

'A good idea. Forgive me. All I can say is that living alone must have made me forget totally my manners and gentle upbringing.' He bellowed with laughter at his own joke. 'Now then, what will you have to drink?'

He pulled a sea chest from beneath the bunk, opened it and took out two pewter cups which he wiped with a slightly grubby towel, then unrolled a uniform jacket to reveal an unlabelled bottle. Setting the bottle on the desk he carefully pulled the cork, then poured two very generous measures into the cups.

Unsuspectingly King took a deep swallow, then gasped for air as his body was suffused with heat, warmth, and a feeling of well-being.

'My God, what is it?' He sniffed at the remaining liquid in his cup and glanced up at his friend's grinning face. 'I've never tasted anything like it before.' He looked again at the bottle. 'It smells like rum, a bit, but certainly doesn't look like it. More like gin. But it has a wonderful taste.'

'It is rum. White rum, they call it. And you'll know just how good it is in a few minutes. I get the occasional bottle from ships on their way back to England from the West Indies. One of the perks of the job, you might say.'

Two hours later the two friends came ashore and made their way to the large hotel beside the railway station where they had dinner and then spent the remainder of the evening playing billiards with fellow officers whom they met.

George King didn't give Captain Nicholls another thought for the rest of the night.

Lieut King's Log   20 July 1884 Aboard the *Wasp*

At last I am aboard my first ship as a full member of the wardroom. I do hope that everything goes well and that I meet the expectations of all my friends, relations and myself. The last three days in Queenstown have seemed the longest I have ever spent, torn as I was between impatience and dread. Impatient to join the *Wasp*, yet fearing what it would be like and if I would measure up. Milo's tale about the ship and her captain was something I could have done without but in a way it prepared me for the task which Captain Whitehouse has given me. What makes it so bad is that my first impressions have been favourable and my fellow officers have already made me welcome. The ship is small but comfortable and my quarters are certainly better than those I suffered, I won't say enjoyed, ashore in Queenstown. I am sharing a cabin with John Kerrigan, the gunner, with whom I think I could be friends. I will ask him about Milo's tale in a few days, as he has been on board for more than a year and he may have knowledge not in the file. What dirty tasks one can be given when ashore. I am looking forward so much to the next twelve months at sea.

The following morning George King was called early from his bed in the small house where he lodged. The landlady banged on his bedroom door shortly after seven to tell him that a messenger had come to say that Mr King was to report to the harbour captain's office within the hour.

As he shuffled out of bed and looked, red-eyed, at himself in the small fly speckled mirror he wondered did he look as close to death as he felt. It had been a heavy session in the hotel when the games of billiards finished and the boisterous party went down to the bar, where Hannon and himself had remained until all the others had left and the night porter told them that he had used up all the stock which the proprietor had left out for him.

In the cold light of day King thought that such an excuse was distinctly improbable but at the time it seemed reasonable enough. He only wished that the porter had thought of using it several hours earlier but it was water under the bridge now.

Washing and shaving in cold water didn't take too much time and he left the house following a plateful of porridge and a cup of strong black tea, which slightly eased the headache he could feel developing, with twenty minutes in hand to get to the office of Captain Whitehouse on time. He made it with three minutes to spare.

An hour later, from where he was seated on an ancient horsehair stuffed armchair, he watched the arrival of the captain. Ten minutes later he was invited to present himself in that worthy's office.

'Ah, King. There you are. Did you want to see me for something? I noticed you waiting as I came in.'

'No sir. I mean I don't want to see you. You sent for me, sir.'

'I did? I wonder why.' The harbour captain was a man in his middle fifties who projected an air of bumbling incompetence which King had been warned was totally false. Nothing went on in his domain which Whitehouse wasn't fully aware of. King wondered now was he being punished for having absented himself from the work for which the captain had earmarked him. He stood in silence as the senior officer aimlessly moved papers around his desk, apparently looking for one in particular.

After half a minute or so, during which the elusive piece of paper continued to evade the captain, while King watched in growing fascination, he realised that he was being studied from head to toe. The man behind the desk was not in the least interested in the papers which, now that he saw his little charade had been uncovered, he brushed to one side. King assumed an air and posture of respectful attention.

'I have no idea, sir.'

'No idea? What are you talking about, man?'

'No idea why you sent for me, sir.'

There was a further silence while Captain Whitehouse thought about this admission. Then he sat back in his chair, the better to study Lieutenant King.

'Very well, Mr King. Let me enlighten you. I understand that you are temporarily attached to this station awaiting the arrival of HM gunboat *Wasp*, which you are to join as navigating officer. Is that so?'

'Yes, sir.' King wondered what was coming next.

'Good. And during the waiting period you are free to assume any temporary duty which I, or other senior officers, might find it incumbent upon us to have you undertake. Correct?'

'Yes, sir.'

'Better still.' He looked silently at the younger man still at attention for a few seconds as if considering what to say next. King's feeling of unease suddenly assumed massive proportions. Finally having made up his mind, the captain sat forward putting his elbows on the desk.

'You will leave here the day after tomorrow to join your ship in Limerick where it will be loading famine relief supplies. Until then we have about 48 hours and I have a task for you which you are ideally qualified to carry out. In fact, you are the only person qualified to carry it out. But before I tell you what it is I want your assurance that what you hear from me, or what you will learn during the next two days, will go no further. Do you understand?'

Puzzled, King agreed.

'Very good. Now relax, man. Sit down on that chair and pay attention.'

When King was seated, more worried than ever, Captain White-house produced a thick folder from a drawer which he placed in front of himself without opening. Putting his right hand on it he leaned forward, looking King straight in the eye.

'I assume that your friend, Lieutenant Hannon, told you some-thing of the recent history of the *Wasp* when you were catching up on old times last night.' He held up his hand to silence King seeing that he was about to speak.

'I do know what goes on in my command, or at least some things, and four people have already told me how much Hannon and yourself had to catch up on. I fully understand and approve. But did he tell you how much this history of the ship and her crew has concerned us all? Did he tell you, for instance, that we had occasion to take the ship out of service, raise her for a full inspection, set up a court of enquiry into certain actions of the crew, and, having found nothing at all amiss — refloat the ship? Did he tell you that Admiral Lethbridge was so worried that he considered relieving Captain Nicholls of his command a short while ago? Did he tell you that the *Wasp* inexplicably changed from being a happy, efficient ship into a slovenly, semi-mutinous, disgrace to the service, did he? Speak up man.'

'He did say that the ship was having a hard time, sir. But to tell you the truth we didn't discuss it very much more than that,' King stammered.

He was at a total loss, not understanding why he was seated in the presence of a captain, discussing the conduct of an officer with his own command. This was so unthinkable that he didn't know what to answer. The harbour captain, if he noticed King's indecision, ignored it.

'Well, I suppose that was natural enough. This folder contains all the reports which have emanated from the *Wasp* since she came onto this station. In addition it contains the findings of all the enquiries made about the ship, its crew, its performance at sea. In fact, everything that anyone has written about the *Wasp*, or reported during the last two years is in here. What you are going to do is take it away from here, read everything inside it and then tell me your conclusions. I said that you were ideally qualified to do this, now I'll tell you why. You are approaching this problem totally without prejudice. You don't know the ship or anyone on board her . . . or do you?'

King shook his head silently.

'Very good. That makes you the only person on this station capable of making a totally objective assessment of the ship, her crew, and the events which led to the deterioration of both. Your assessment will be based solely on these reports, which are, of course, the result of studies carried out by others. But you have one major advantage over the people who wrote the reports. Do you know what that is?'

Dumbly, the now bemused King shook his head.

'Your advantage is that, having read everyone else's reports, and having then discussed them with me, you will actually join the ship, as a member of the ship's company. Nobody else has been able to do that. The officers and crew of the *Wasp* are expecting you to join them, have been for a considerable time in fact, so they will think of you as one of themselves and not one of us. You are just an ordinary junior navigating officer who has arrived in the usual way to join his ship. They will expect you to know nothing of the ship's history – other than some rumours you, like everyone else, has heard – apart from that you will be as ignorant as a babe in arms in their eyes. But in reality, with complete knowledge of the background events and the people concerned, you will be able to determine the reasons why the *Wasp* was almost lost and the captain's career ended.'

He paused, looking at King who sat opposite him in petrified silence wondering if he had gone mad. Then rising to his feet he went across the office to a glass fronted cabinet and took from it a bottle and two glasses. Without speaking he poured two measures of its ruby contents and handed one to King.

'I think you'll like this, Lieutenant. It has quite remarkable curative properties. A French captain on a trader which calls here occasionally gave it to me. Drink up.'

He returned to his seat and sat down, sipping from his glass. King took a swallow and as the firey spirit slipped down his throat his shocked senses slowly stabilised. Another swallow, sighing he put the glass on the edge of the desk and opened his mouth to speak. The captain's upraised hand stopped him.

'One more thing, Mr King. While you are in possession of this folder do not remove, or show to anyone else, any document which it contains. That goes without saying. When you have read it you will return it to me personally, exactly as you were given it and any questions you may have at that stage you will address to me. The reasons for this secrecy will become apparent to you during the next two days. Finally, until you are released from this undertaking by me or a more senior officer, in person, you are on the personal staff, on temporary duty, of Admiral Lethbridge. In addition, of course, to being an ordinary serving crew member of HMS *Wasp*.

'Now, unless you have any questions about this conversation so far, I suggest that you return to your quarters and begin work. Report back to me here at eight o'clock on the morning you leave for Limerick.' He smiled mirthlessly. 'Don't worry, King. I'll be here on time, be sure you are.'

King shook his head as if to clear it. He had some time earlier stopped trying to make sense of what he was hearing. There was an air of total unreality about everything he now found himself part of. Being asked to spy on fellow officers . . . worse, being ordered . . . was unthinkable. But then sitting drinking spirits with a harbour captain at ten-thirty in the morning was also unthinkable. As was a sudden and mysterious appointment to the Admiral's personal staff. He stood up as it penetrated his bewilderment that he was being dismissed.

Captain Whitehouse also stood up. Surprisingly he held out his hand for King to shake.

'I'm glad that you agree, King. And having met you I'm sure you'll prove to be the right man for this job. I have every confidence in you, as has the Admiral. Just remember, be discreet and don't mention what you are doing. To anyone. Anyone at all.'

He picked up the folder and passed it across his desk. King took it, put on his hat, saluted and left the office. Then in a daze walked out through the outer office and lobby and downstairs to the street door. Outside he mechanically turned towards the main gate and walked slowly along the dusty cobbles while trying to bring his confused thoughts into order.

Some time later, he never knew how much, he came back to reality when hailed by the driver of a laden dray trying to pass him on the narrow roadway. As the shouting registered he moved to one side, barely in time to avoid being run over by the pair of huge horses struggling to pull their load up the hill. He looked around.

To his surprise, he was on the road which he had used the previous day, leading to the vantage point from which he had seen the *Sea Witch*. To his left there was a gate, partly open, into a field. He walked across to it, entered the field and sat down behind a low wall overlooking the harbour. From this position he couldn't be seen from the road.

Opening the folder he skimmed through the contents, noting the many and differing styles of writing used in compiling the reports, then glancing at the sketch maps and drawings which were also included. As he flicked the sheets of paper over he felt his interest quicken, and when he reached the end his lethargy had completely vanished. Returning to the beginning again he started reading, this time with full attention and curiosity.

More than an hour later he closed it, placing a stone on it to prevent the light breeze taking any of the papers, and sat back against the wall. There was a puzzled look on his face. Taking out a handkerchief he mopped his forehead in an automatic reflex action as his skin was quite dry. He stared in silence and unseeingly at the activity on the water in the estuary below.

The reason for his puzzlement was quite clear. He was puzzled. He had missed something. Something important, but couldn't put his finger on what it might be.

All the reports and opinions, and even the rumours which had been noted and then vainly followed through to an inconclusive ending, were in agreement. There was something badly wrong on board the *Wasp*. But what? And, more importantly, why?

The ship was in commission. Her officers were capable, the crew seemed to be loyal and competent. And yet they were beset with not just one but several series of crises and minor disasters which started up, then ended a few weeks later, leaving the crew demoralised, the ship almost ineffective, and the Admiralty totally baffled and enraged.

Getting to his feet he walked down the sloping field to where it ended in another dry stone wall, then turned making his way back up to where the folder lay, thinking about what he had read. It did no good. Nothing seemed any clearer. He decided to return to his lodgings and read through the reports again in the hope that next time he would come across something new which might explain the mystery.

During the next day and a half he worried the problem in his mind endlessly. Slowly, methodically and making notes as he went through the folder, over and over, he approached the problem from every possible angle. He suspected mechanical problems as being the cause of the ship's trouble for a time, but this wasn't borne out by the engineer's reports which found nothing at all wrong with the engine. Similarly with the sails and standing rigging there wasn't anything wrong, but the fact remained that the *Wasp*, on more than one occasion, couldn't make sufficient speed, under ideal and even favourable conditions, to keep a rendezvous.

Later he considered that perhaps the crew had been struck down by a mysterious illness, all at the same time and to the same degree, leaving them with no recollection of what had happened. This was so patently absurd that he dismissed it, but not before he had searched for something, anything, no matter how trivial, that might lend credence to his unlikely theory. But there wasn't anything.

For a while he seriously considered taking Milo into his confidence and asking him to go through the folder with him in the hope that it might jog Milo's memory, releasing some recollection which, in turn, would provide some answers. But then he remembered his assurances to Captain Whitehouse and gave up the idea.

As a result, it was with a feeling of having failed an important test, through lack of preparation, that he made his way back to the harbour captain's office before eight o'clock on the morning he was due to leave for Limerick.

This time he didn't have to wait. As he entered a rating, who had obviously been waiting for him, stepped forward and saluted.

'Lieutenant King?' He didn't wait for a reply. 'Captain Whitehouse is waiting for you, sir. Please follow me.'

On entering the office he was surprised to see another man there with the harbour captain. A man dressed as a civilian, though he looked as if he might have been more comfortable in naval uniform than in his present clothes. Both men watched as he came to attention in front of the desk and saluted. The salute was acknowledged by a nod from the captain.

'At ease, Lieutenant. Please sit down.' He motioned toward the man beside him. 'This is, 'er, Mr Carrington. He is also interested in the report on the *Wasp*, and is aware of the task which you have undertaken.' He paused for a few seconds, waiting for King to be seated, then continued.

'First, have you any questions regarding the reports which I gave you?'

King hesitated, then decided that it was better to be truthful even if it made him look an idiot. And if that caused the captain to relieve him from the 'task', as he called it, so much the better.

'Well, yes, sir. I have a feeling that there is something missing from the folder. I don't know what it is, but there isn't enough information here for me to come to any conclusion. I have some theories, but not enough information to substantiate any of them. I'm sorry, sir. But although I have racked my brains for the past two days, and gone over and over everything in the folder, I must admit that I don't know what might be wrong with the ship.'

The two older men glanced at each other, then settled back in the easy chairs which they were occupying. King still sat stiffly, as if at attention, waiting for the scorn he expected to be poured over his head. It didn't come.

'What would you say, Mr King, were I to assure you that there is nothing missing from the folder? Nothing at all. That is the full and complete record of all the information the Navy has about HM gunboat *Wasp*.'

He turned to look at Carrington who had asked the question.

'I don't understand, sir. When things go wrong on a ship there is always a reason. Sometimes it isn't immediately clear what that reason is, but if one looks long enough signs will appear which at least point in the direction to follow to find the answer. That is normal procedure. I appreciate that my experience is limited, or perhaps it is that I haven't spent enough time going through these records, but I didn't see any signs which might tell me why problems were arising. Everything seems to be normal, yet it obviously cannot be. I'm sorry, sir. I'm afraid that I cannot help you. I don't even know where to begin.'

Again the two men looked at each other in silence, then Carrington gave a heavy sigh. There was another short silence before Whitehouse picked up a ruler from the desk and thoughtfully slapped it against the palm of his other hand. King waited. Ten or twelve slaps later the captain laid down the ruler and folding his arms looked at King.

'There isn't any need to be sorry, King. I didn't expect it to be otherwise. In fact, both, 'er, Mr Carrington and myself would have been very surprised indeed had you solved our problem from merely reading the contents of the folder. But do you remember why I said that you were uniquely qualified to help us?'

For a moment King was puzzled. Then it came back to him.

'You said that because I was joining the ship I would be treated by the crew as one of "us", not one of "them". In that way, and having read all the reports, I'd find out what was wrong and be able to report back to you.'

'Exactly, Mr King. That's exactly what I said. I saw at the time that you didn't like what I was saying, and I fully sympathise, but perhaps you now see the reason why I recruited you?'

'I think I do. In case something like this should happen to other ships, it is important to know why. And since outsiders haven't been able to find out, the only method remaining is to infiltrate the crew with someone acceptable who is knowledgeable about the earlier events. In other words, forewarned being fore-armed.'

'I couldn't have put it better myself, Mr King. Don't you agree, com . . . I mean, Mr Carrington?'

From that point on the discussion revolved around the matters to which King would pay particular attention, both at sea and ashore, the likely behaviour of the other five officers on board, and the behaviour of the ship under the different conditions which might be experienced.

As far as King was concerned, apart from the ethics of report-ing the behaviour of his fellow crew members, which he wasn't too happy about, the task was both straightforward and simple. He was in agreement with the Captain and Mr Carrington, whom he now suspected was a Commander, about the necessity to find out what was behind the mysterious events which had befallen the *Wasp*. And since it didn't seem to be any reflection on him-self that he hadn't been able to solve the mystery from the documents in the folder, he felt more confident as he boarded the train which would take him to Cork on the first leg of his journey.

From Cork, where he changed trains, he travelled to Limerick Junction — another change there, then four hours after leaving Queenstown he hailed a hansom cab outside Limerick station and told the cabby to take him to the naval dock.

When the cab was stopped by the policeman at the dock gates King enquired how far it was to where the *Wasp* was lying. On being told it was just a few hundred yards he paid off the cabby and picked up his valise to make his way on foot to the ship. The policeman agreed to hold the rest of his luggage in the hut until a sailor came to collect it later.

His first sight of the *Wasp* was both reassuring and a surprise though, as he told himself, he didn't really know what to expect.

The gunboat was a composite of wood and iron construction, 125' in length, 23' 6" wide and drawing 10' of water. This much he knew from having looked it up in the dockyard engineer's office before leaving Queenstown. She had three masts, with the funnel midway between the main two, and a smaller mizzen mast between the end of the deck housing and the stern. The funnel served the single shaft reciprocating 440ihp steam engine which could drive the ship at nine and a half knots.

From the stem a bowsprit jutted out about twenty feet. Lying port side on to the jetty he could see two boats slung neatly in their davits, and knew that two more were similarly slung on the starboard side. Directly in front of the funnel, overlooking the forrard deck and main gun turret, was the small open bridge with a young man in sub-lieutenant's uniform standing on it. He appeared to be in charge of a work party, engaged in manhandling sacks and boxes on board, and it was evident that he wasn't satisfied with the rate of progress the party was making as he frequently shouted abuse at the sweating men.

Standing on the jetty King couldn't hear the precise words but it didn't take much intelligence to guess what they were. Most of the work party just ignored the abuse. One or two were annoyed though there wasn't much they could do about the situation. King watched the activity for a couple of minutes until the last of the sacks had been carried across the gangway and lowered through a small hatch into the vessel's hold, then made his way across the jetty to board the ship.

Before reaching the side of the gunboat he was aware that the young officer had seen him approach and was watching him with some curiosity. Ignoring him he was about to step onto the gangway to board the ship when the young man leaned over the side of the bridge and shouted at him.

'Stop where you are, you there, and state your business.'

As King was less than twenty feet away, and the sub was shouting at the top of his voice there wasn't any way that he could be ignored. All the work party on deck suddenly stopped what they were doing to see what was going on.

Divided between amusement and irritation, King carefully put down his valise and looked up at the figure on the bridge.

'Are you addressing me, son?'

Since there wasn't more than about three years separating the two, there was a loud chuckle, quickly smothered, from the sailors. King continued . . . 'Because, if you are, my business is with the man in charge. Run along and tell him, like a good lad.'

The furious young man flushed bright red and struggled to get the words out while the work party froze in anticipation and expectant silence.

'Damn your impertinence, man. I'll have you know that this is a ship of the Royal Navy and I can have you arrested for trying to come on board without permission.' He turned and shouted down to the work party, 'Andrews, take two men and arrest this civilian immediately.'

Nobody moved on the foredeck. Again he shouted at the group of men barely six feet below him. 'That is an order, Andrews.'

A man wearing a petty officer's badge on the sleeve of his shirt, who was at least twenty years older than the arrogant youth on the bridge, stepped out from the group, answering, 'Aye, aye, sir.'

King decided it was time to bring the charade to an end.

'Just a minute, Andrews,' he called. Then turning to the youth on the bridge, asked in the crisp tones of one used to giving commands, 'How do I know this is a ship of the Royal Navy? All I see is a bum boat with a group of stevedores loading cargo. There is no sentry on the gangway, the bridge is being used as a promenade deck by someone who could be either a passenger or crew member, naval discipline is non-existent.' He looked aft to where the ensign staff flew a filthy coal stained white ensign. 'Even your ensign is a disgrace, unless of course, you are from Morocco or some such place where black flags are common. Are you?'

Taken aback by the unexpected attack the youth cast his eyes towards Andrews who was standing still, obviously waiting further orders. However, before he could think of anything to say, King stepped onto the deck and addressed Andrews.

'Petty Officer Andrews. Please arrange for someone to collect my luggage from the policeman's hut at the main gate. My name is Lieutenant King and I am the new navigator reporting on board. Is the captain on board?'

Barely concealing a grin Andrews came to attention. 'Sir. I'll have your luggage collected right away. And no, sir, the captain is not on board. Sub Lieutenant Guppy is officer of the watch. You have already met Mr Guppy.'

'I see.' King turned and coldly looked Mr Guppy up and down as he stood open mouthed and disconcerted on the wing of the bridge. The development during the past few seconds had been so totally unexpected that he was at a loss as to what his next action should be.

King put him out of his misery. 'Please join me in the wardroom Mr Guppy, at your convenience.' He looked around for his valise to see that a rating had already picked it up and was waiting for him to follow.

The wardroom, to which the rating led him, was located below the main deck, almost directly over the engine room. It was about fifteen feet from front to back but stretched the full width of the ship. Here all the officers ate, relaxed, entertained visitors when in port, and generally used it as their living room when not otherwise on duty. It was comfortably, if not luxuriously furnished, with dining facilities on the port side and sitting room facilities on the starboard. Midway along the aft bulkhead a closed hatch indicated the location of the pantry where meals were plated and served, and the steward kept the small bar stock. The general layout was so familiar that the one sweeping glance King gave when he entered told him all there was to know about it. Even the picture of the Queen was exactly the same as those on every other ship he had been on. It was like being home, he thought.

Almost on his heels as he entered came Sub Lieutenant Guppy, wearing such an expression of chagrin that had it not been for the earlier display of ill mannered arrogance he would have taken pity on the young man. As he pulled out a chair from the dining table and sat down, however, with memories of his own days as a sub still fresh, he decided that some lesson needed to be administered.

'That was quite a performance you put on for the amusement of the crew and myself, Mr Guppy. Is it your practice to arrest people wearing civilian clothes who attempt to come on board?'

'No, sir. I'm sorry, sir. I didn't realise that you were the new navigator we've been expecting.'

'I don't suppose you did,' King remarked dryly. 'Are you the only officer on board?'

'Yes, sir. The captain, Lieutenant Nicholls, is with the harbour captain at a meeting. Mr Kerrigan, the gunner, and Mr Browne, the surgeon, are arranging for relief supplies to be delivered later today or perhaps tomorrow, and Mr Hudson, the engineer, is somewhere around the dock workshop. They will all be back on board for dinner at two bells I expect.'

'I see. Which cabin have I been allocated, do you know?'

'Oh, I believe that you are sharing with Mr Kerrigan. That is cabin No. 4, just off the portside passageway from the wardroom. Shall I show you the way, sir?'

'I think I'll be able to find it myself. But what you can do is change into working rig. This ship is a disgrace to the Navy. I want is cleaned up before the other officers return and you're just the man to do it. But before you do anything get a marine posted on the gangway and draw a clean ensign from the bosun's stores so that passers-by will at least think we're part of the senior service. Now, jump to it. There's work to be done.'

Two hours later the change in the ship's appearance was noticeable. King, who had changed into uniform, had spent most of that time inspecting the ship while managing to keep an unobtrusive eye on the arrogant Mr Guppy. However he had no cause to complain. Petty Officer Andrews had taken charge and given leadership to the men which the Sub had followed, and had worked as hard as any of the crew getting the ship cleaned up. The deck had been scrubbed, a fresh ensign flew at the stern, and all the crew who could be seen from the dockside looked alert and properly dressed in clean working rig. An armed marine was on duty at the foot of the gangway, and a signaller and assistant bosun were on duty at the top.

Leaving the deck to go to the chartroom King could see Guppy listing the contents of the paint locker and getting it tidied up as if ready for an inspection by the captain. Andrews had just complemented the Sub for something and the young officer looked delighted with himself. Making a mental note to himself that the petty officer's leadership worked upwards as well as downwards, and that the Sub had some potential after all, he entered what would be his own domain to familiarise himself with the ship's paperwork.

Before he could do more than glance cursorily around, he heard the sound of a bosun's whistle outside and stepped over to a scuttle from which he could see the bottom of the gangway.

Standing on the quayside, looking slightly nonplussed, was a haggard looking man, slightly older than himself, wearing uniform. As the whistle stopped he stepped onto the gangway and a voice called out, 'Cap'n coming aboard.' The marine came to attention. Returning the salute the captain came up, leaving King's area of vision. He waited, knowing the other man would probably come straight to the bridge and chartroom when advised of King's presence.

Seconds later the two stood face to face, inspecting each other.

King was the first to speak. . . 'King, sir. Reporting for duty. My orders are in my cabin. If you will excuse me I'll get them.'

'Never mind. I'll see them later. I've been advised that you would report when we arrived in Limerick. Glad to have you on board.' He held out his hand which King shook. 'By the look of things you are just the man we need.' He nodded towards the open door. 'I suppose that you are responsible for the sentry and deck watch which greeted me?'

'Yes, sir. Mr Guppy was busy when I arrived and I helped with a few suggestions.'

'I rather thought you had. Good, good.' He looked around the chart room as if wondering where he was, then came to a decision.

'Good, King. I'll leave these things in my cabin and then I'll introduce you to the others who should be back soon. I'll see you in the wardroom in about half an hour when I've cleaned up.' With that he turned and left before King had time to answer.

To say that he was shocked would put it mildly. From the reports which he had read and comments made by Milo Hannon and Captain Whitehouse about Lieutenant Nicholls, George King had expected to meet someone totally different from the indecisive, absent-minded, haggard and untidy person who had just then greeted him.

Good officers, and he had been led to believe that Nicholls was one, were positive and courageous. They ran their ships in a calm, controlled, effective manner in which young officers and senior ratings knew their places. More importantly, they never, ever, accepted an unknown on board without at the least, immediate sight of his orders.

The guards on the main gate at Queenstown didn't do that, he reflected.

But even this basic rule had been ignored, and the state of the ship and crew had him wondering if the captain was 'all right'.

He wasn't quite sure what 'all right' actually meant, but officers who were 'all right', in his admittedly limited experience, would never permit the leniencies Nicholls tolerated in dress and discipline. Good officers were 'all right', bad ones were not.

Suddenly he felt apprehensive, without knowing why. The concern Captain Whitehouse had expressed for the *Wasp* and her captain became a reality, and Hannon's warning to 'take care' now was something more than a casual expression of friendship.

But before he could let it affect him he resolved to find out more. A hasty, ill advised decision on his part wouldn't be fair to Nicholls or Whitehouse. And there would be plenty of time to make his mind up in the months ahead.

He picked up one of the ship's manuals and opened it as he heard the first of the other officers return on board.

3   Westpark Manor

Lieut King's Log   24 July 1884 Aboard the *Wasp*

The past three days have been busy preparing the ship for
sea. Despite our bad beginning young Guppy and I seem to
be becoming friends, at which I am pleased. The surgeon
and the engineer, being the oldest members of the wardroom tend to keep to themselves. I haven't had a chance to
speak to my cabinmate, Kerrigan, about the story I was given
by Milo, but there is an odd and disturbing atmosphere on
board, of which I have slowly become conscious. This is
apparent throughout the ship and is hard to identify. The
only way I can describe it so far is to say that while the crew
seem to be competent and able, they are unwilling, and that
this is not a happy ship. I hope that I am wrong.

When the chartroom clock told him that thirty minutes had
passed since the captain had gone to his cabin King closed the
manuals, replacing them on the shelf over the plotting table.
He had been disappointed at not finding the deck log as he was
curious about the mishaps which the ship had suffered and hoped
to learn some of the details concerning them. Deciding that it
probably was in the captain's cabin he carefully worked his way
through the remainder of the books without coming across anything unusual or of great interest, so it was with a feeling of anti-
climax that he put on his cap and made his way below to the
wardroom.

The buzz of conversation stopped abruptly as he entered.
Four faces turned to inspect him. He glanced around hoping that
the captain would be there to introduce him but there wasn't
any sign of him. He stopped in the doorway, waiting for someone to speak. To his surprise it was Sub Lieutenant Guppy.

'Gentlemen, allow me to introduce the newest member of the
wardroom, Lieutenant George King, our navigator.' There was a
general movement towards him when he entered and Guppy
introduced each in turn as they shook King's hand. Within a few

moments he was surrounded by the others, with a large pink gin in his hand, answering questions about how things were in Queenstown and Portsmouth. He quickly found that the others and he had many mutual friends, and as George sipped his drink, whatever feeling of strangeness he had, had quickly evaporated. When the captain entered some fifteen minutes later to take his place at the head of the table for dinner, King already felt that he had been accepted, and relaxed in anticipation of a pleasant evening ahead.

It wasn't to be. The meal was eaten in almost total silence and the earlier conviviality was lost. At the table the captain only spoke twice to say 'I see that you have all met Mr King. Good, good,' and ten minutes later 'What time will the remainder of the stores come on board tomorrow, Mr Kerrigan?'

When told that they were expected at six bells he nodded, said 'Good', finished his meal silently and without even saying 'Good night' returned to his cabin.

Following his departure the atmosphere lightened a little and King and Kerrigan chatted together for a while. The surgeon, Otway Browne, and the engineer, Bill Hudson, tried explaining the mysteries of three-handed whist to Guppy at the end of the cleared dining table until he brought it to an end by saying that he was still officer of the watch and had rounds to do. The two older men left shortly afterwards, presumably to retire, leaving King and Kerrigan alone.

'It is my practice to have a short stroll before going to bed. Would you care to join me, King?'

Glad of any excuse to get outside King rose to his feet and the two crossed to the jetty, turning right to walk along the left bank of the river Shannon, which was about two hundred yards wide at that point. For a minute or two, until they were well out of earshot, they strolled in silence. Then Kerrigan spoke.

'I expect you're wondering what sort of ship the *Wasp* is?'

'Well, 'er, as a matter of fact this is my first ship. Up to this I have only been a relief, so I don't really know what to expect. Is there anything you think I should know?'

Kerrigan looked sharply at him, but didn't answer the question.

'I think you'll find us harmless when you get to know us better. I take it that you haven't served in a 'composite' before?'

When King agreed that he hadn't Kerrigan continued, 'Well, the main difference between us and the old fashioned sailing ships is purely one of efficiency. We are the forerunners of the new fleet.'

He continued in this strain for the next twenty minutes, detailing the superior performance and reliability of the *Wasp*, its efficiency and the small crew needed to get into action, but never once mentioned the many problems which King knew to be causing so much concern back in Queenstown. It was as if Kerrigan was serving in another ship and, of course, King couldn't mention them either, since he wasn't supposed to know about them. Fascinated, King listened to Kerrigan talk his way round them all as he told his listener about incidents which had taken place during the year or so he had been on board.

'Have you had Captain Nicholls with you since you joined?'

'Yes, of course, and a better captain you would go a long way to find. What did you think of him?'

Sensing the defensive shielding behind the question, King's answer was carefully worded.

'I didn't form any definite opinion of him, other than he doesn't seem to talk very much. Is he always so quiet?'

'No, he isn't. In fact it is only recently that he has been like this. Before, he was, if not exactly the life and soul of the wardroom, a more cheerful and outgoing person. But recently he seems to have a lot on his mind. The rest of us are glad you've arrived as you'll be able to take some of the load off him. Perhaps he is just tired. I'm sure that you'll get on well together when you know him better.'

'I hope so.'

They walked on in silence, King considering what he had heard, and strongly doubting Kerrigan's diagnosis of tiredness being responsible for Nicholls appearance and unsociableness. He decided to pry a bit further.

'The fact that I haven't had to produce my orders, although I've been on board now for nearly six hours, has surprised me. I'm not surprised that the Sub forgot to ask me for them, even though he is OOW, but it is odd for a captain to let a stranger on board with all the talk that's going around about Fenians. Do you agree?'

Kerrigan laughed. 'I heard about you and the OOW and I can't imagine a Fenian behaving as you did. But I do agree. You should have presented your orders by now and I'm surprised that Nicholls hasn't asked you to. He must have things on his mind. Once we go to sea I guarantee he'll be different when you see him at work. He knows the west coast like the back of his hand. In fact I'm sure he could work this coast without a navigator on board at all. No offence, old man,' he added hurriedly.

Shortly after this they returned to the ship and went to bed having told the duty hand to call them at four bells in readiness for the arrival of the stores.

'Not that they'll be here at seven, or maybe even eight o'clock if I know this place. But we had better be awake when they do get here,' Kerrigan told him. A few minutes later King watched the glow from the quayside lamps through the scuttle for a short time before he slipped off into sleep.

For the next two days it was a case of snatched meals during daylight hours as the *Wasp*'s own stores of food, clothing and ammunition were loaded and stowed. King, to the relief of the others, took his turn as OOW and managed to bring the charts up to date by doing extra duty after dinner each evening.

By the morning of the third day, following a final inspection by the captain, with Guppy in tow, the cargo was pronounced safely loaded and secured. A quick detour to the coaling berth followed, and some hours later, when everyone and everything was filthy from the coal dust, the bunkers were shored up and closed and the *Wasp* headed down the estuary on her way to the sea.

For the first thirty miles the *Wasp* proceeded under steam. Then the fires were banked and the sails shaken out as the bow lifted to the first swell rolling in from the Atlantic. For a few minutes all was action on deck, sheets were tightened and halyards secured while King completed his first fix and the engineer, William Hudson, stood behind the captain waiting to be told, 'Finished with engine.'

With a last glance at the chart table King straightened up as the captain turned towards him.

'Course, Mr King, please?'

'West south west, sir.'

'Very good. Steer west south west, bosun.'

Slowly the *Wasp* turned towards the west south west and steadied up, the sails filling and bow wave gurgling as the speed increased. The bosun turned to call out to the captain what he had just been told through the voice pipe from the wheelhouse, 'Steady on west south west it is, sir.'

As darkness fell the small ship sailed steadily on its selected heading. The watch changed at midnight and again at 04.00, and by six o'clock she was being gently berthed at Smerwick Harbour on the extreme west tip of the Dingle Peninsula.

Within half an hour a line of men had appeared and work was under way unloading food and relief supplies to the desperately poor peasants on the quay. It went on for most of the morning, the stores being taken away on carts, horseback, and even on the backs of the people for whom they were intended.

Initially King was shocked at the sight of the people, barefooted and in rags with emaciated bodies. It was far worse than he had envisaged, but it wasn't until the officers sat down to lunch that he had his first opportunity to question any of the others about the sight. Again it was Kerrigan he sought the information from.

'Some places are even worse than this, George. Wait until we get up to Mayo and Donegal. That's where you'll see poverty. If it wasn't for our efforts, and the stores and money provided by the Quakers, most of these people would be dead. I agree it is bad, but most of it is the fault of the politicians in London and Dublin who neither know nor care what is going on here.'

'Don't know? Does nobody tell them? Are we the only ones helping out?'

'Well, no. There are other relief schemes, naturally, but few as well organised as we are. Some of the big landowners help their own workers and the churches help their parishioners where they can. But it is all very piecemeal and pockets of people are left with nothing, either because they don't hear when food is available or, worse, because the food runs out before their turn to get some arrives. It would break your heart to see the despair on their faces when that happens.' He lapsed into silence as he obviously relived at least one such occasion. King waited silently. A moment later his friend continued. . . 'But would it surprise you to learn that this is the good side of our job?'

He looked questioningly at King who was baffled by the query. Then continued before King could say anything.

'That's right, the good part. When we aren't helping starving people, like we're doing today, or patrolling the high seas for enemy ships, which we have been trained to do, we are regularly engaged in helping to evict people from their homes because they haven't the money to meet the rent being charged by their greedy landlords. Most of whom are Irish, like themselves.'

'Evicting people? I can hardly believe that. That's not the job of the Navy,' King said incredulously.

'I assure you it happens.' Kerrigan's voice was bitter and King noticed the heads of the others at the table, who had been listening in silence, nod in agreement. 'More often than you might think too. When it does it makes us feel as if we are robbing the dead because the hovels in which these poor wretches live are virtually the only possession left to them in their near-dead state.' He took a drink of water, then put it down quickly as his hand was visibly trembling.

'It makes all of us very angry, particularly as there is little we can do. The landlord takes their money as rent, then lets them starve when they can't buy food because they have no money, and finally throws them out of their homes because they haven't the strength to work because they have no food. Whole families at a time. And it is all done legally, with the help of the courts which are run by the same landlords and their friends.

'The ironic thing is that the natives have got elected representatives of their own for more than fifty years and things have just got worse. I don't understand it myself, but then I'm not a politician, just an ignorant sailor like you.'

As he spoke the ship's whistle sounded recalling the crew to work and it was a very thoughtful King who went back to checking the lists of supplies being unloaded.

By three o'clock all the stores to be unloaded were ashore, the hatches secured and the ship again ready for sea. The mooring lines were singled up and some of the crew idled on deck waiting for the command to cast off, but apart from a thin wisp of blue smoke rising into the still afternoon air from the grey funnel, there was no activity to be seen.

King, as navigator, waited on the bridge for the captain to appear and give the commands which would bring the ship to life and get her under way.

So when he heard steps coming up the ladder leading to the bridge he was surprised to see the red face of the surgeon, Otway Browne, appear.

Browne was a sailor of the old school, a man who had spent most of his life at sea and claimed to know every port from the China Station to the Barbary Coast. How he had finished up on the west coast of Ireland on this tiny gunboat was a puzzle to King, but having watched him working all day in a makeshift clinic on the quayside, treating wives and children of the peasants working with the crew, he was glad he was aboard.

There wasn't a lot the surgeon could do, but what practical help he could give was appreciated. He seemed to know most of his patients because they greeted him with friendliness while they kept their distance from the other crew members. Browne's usually jolly face was sombre now and he was quieter than normal as he came to stand beside King on the wing of the bridge, looking down on the deserted quayside.

After a short silence he spoke without looking at King. 'I hope it isn't going to be like the last time, Mr King.'

King waited for an explanation of this cryptic remark and when none was forthcoming, put his hands on the rail and said, 'What do you mean, surgeon? What happened the last time?'

'The last time we were here, about two months ago, we had to help with an eviction in the Dingle area. As John said at lunch, it is a horrible business when you have to do it, one that's not easy to forget, and it leaves the whole crew disturbed for days afterwards. I've got a feeling that we are waiting now for a message telling us we are required to do the same thing again.'

He took a small silver flask from his pocket and uncapping it offered it to King who refused. Then he took a long swig himself and carefully replaced it in his pocket. 'I take this purely for medicinal purposes, you understand.'

'Of course.'

There didn't seem to be anything else to say and the pair stood watching the sun slide slowly down to the horizon. Some twenty minutes or so later, when Otway Browne seemed to be about to leave the bridge, there was a noise from the shore end of the quay and a man driving a horse and trap came around the shed used by the local fishermen. The horse had clearly been driven hard and was blowing when it pulled up alongside the ship.

'Is the captain there?'

Captain Nicholls had heard the arrival of the man and had silently come up behind the two officers who were taken aback when they heard his voice behind them.

'I'm the captain. What do you want?'

'I've a message for you, your honour. From the police inspector in Dingle.' He waited.

'Here's a sovereign. What's the message?'

'The inspector said that you won't be needed this trip. There's nothing else.' The man touched his cap with his whip, muttered 'Thank you' and turning his horse and trap around, made his way back along the quay.

King heard the other two slowly let their breaths out, then suddenly realised that the deck had quietly filled with crew members while the conversation had been conducted between the captain

and the messenger. Everyone had been listening to the exchange
and were now looking up at the captain in expectation.

'Stand by navigator to put to sea.'

Suddenly everyone was smiling on deck as the men heard the
command and moved to their positions.

'Aye, aye, sir. Stand by to let go, bosun.'

For the next week the *Wasp* moved slowly up the coast, calling into the small harbours it passed, sometimes to offload food
and clothing needed by the near starving natives, other times to
carry out work for the harbour commissioners who were responsible for the upkeep of the jetties and breakwaters.

During this period King took careful note of everything that
transpired but nothing untoward occurred. The captain was
indeed a skilled and capable navigator, as Milo had told him, the
gunboat was an ideal vessel for the work it was engaged on
because of its size, the crew were cooperative and cheerful, all
of which left him more puzzled than ever.

Even Kerrigan's forecast of the change to be expected in the
captain once he was back at sea proved correct. From being
indecisive, taciturn and untidy, within a few days he was the
epitome of the best captains King had served under; exact, con-
cise and neat, in full control of his ship and crew. Even his
haggard look was gone and while he still wasn't the life and soul
of the wardroom, meals weren't eaten in silence. Instead he
insisted that everyone contribute something of use, or of interest,
or of entertainment to the conversation during dinner so that
the meal became the highlight of the officers' day.

If this was normal behaviour there didn't seem to be any
reason at all for the extraordinary series of mishaps which had
been plaguing the ship and crew for almost twelve months.

Lieut King's Log   2 August 1884 Aboard the *Wasp*

Tomorrow we berth in Westport which is our home-from-
home on this coast. From what I hear its accommodation
falls far short of Queenstown, much less Portsmouth, but
it will be a break to spend a few nights alongside a jetty
and the crew are looking forward to relaxing ashore. All
the officers are invited to an afternoon tea party at Westpark Manor on Sunday, I hope my uniform passes muster
by the local gentry. This will be my first social contact with

the upper class so my mother should find my next letter home more interesting than usual. Which reminds me. My first report to the mysterious Mr Carrington in Queenstown is due. I'm afraid that I'm going to be a disappointment to him as I have no idea at all what is behind the peculiar happenings which befall this ship. Maybe something will become clear when we are ashore.

With the last of the relief stores safely on the pier at Leenaun, Nicholls piloted the ship back down the fiord-like Killary Harbour to the open sea.

The prospect of the weekend ashore lifted spirits among the crew. Even the captain was relaxed and when the surgeon, Otway Browne, stepped off the bridge ladder asking permission to come onto the bridge, he smiled and said, 'Of course.'

Looking slightly disconcerted at this unexpected, and for the captain, effusive welcome, Browne looked closely at Nicholls for a second or two before he advanced to stand close to the weather screen, on the starboard side of the bridge. He took off his peaked cap to wipe the perspiration from his forehead with a large, not too clean, handkerchief.

'What a day,' he announced to no one in particular. 'If I've had a hundred patients I wouldn't be surprised. And the sad thing is that none of my medicines could do any of them as much good as a solid meal.' He looked at the coast slipping past. 'But this makes it all worthwhile. I've waited all day just to see that mountain up ahead. That's Mweelrea, the highest point in the Sheffrey Hills. Did you know that Mr Guppy?'

Guppy, who at that particular moment was taking a practice bearing on the mountain, under King's supervision, muttered under his breath.

Ignoring him, Browne continued. 'Lieutenant King, you probably didn't know that, being a newcomer to these parts, but the sight of that mountain means we are on our way home. Or what we are pleased to call home when in these waters. Isn't that so, captain?'

'That's right, surgeon.' He spoke to both Browne and King, 'Of course we sometimes have to call to the islands out there and occasionally to Roonah Quay, but this time we will proceed without delay to Westport. It seems that Lord and Lady Mulrany, for reasons which totally escape me, have asked that the officers of this ship present themselves on Sunday — that's in three days time for those of you who may have lost count — to enjoy the delights of afternoon tea on the lawn of Westpark Manor. I trust that you all remember how to use a knife and fork correctly?'

'Good Lord, has that come around again?' Browne turned to King, 'This is the annual highlight of the social calendar every summer in Westport. Lord Mulrany gives a tea party on the lawn for all his friends and, of course, the Royal Navy is invited to add a little class to the event. Some of the local garrison from Castlebar are invited too, but nobody pays much attention to them.' He paused and looked thoughtfully at the captain.

'I take it you'll be with us, sir?'

Nicholls' lips spread in a wide grin. 'Well, actually, no. As a matter of fact, as soon as we berth I have to catch a train to Dublin, and as I'll be away for a few days I will, most regrettably miss the party. I am desolate, but there you are.'

Browne groaned theatrically and looked back at King. 'I should have known better than to ask a stupid question. Every year our gallant captain is desolated because events conspire to prevent him attending the party. Last year he went climbing the day before, slipped and hurt his leg, and despite all my ministrations and vast experience, it didn't get better until the day following the party. Very puzzling it was. The year before it was something else.'

The light hearted exchange continued with King taking part when he could, and it was obvious to him that there was a general release of tension with the regular crew getting into a happier and much more companionable state of mind. As dusk fell and the captain and Guppy went below for dinner he pondered on the wisdom of taking advantage of this unbending by trying, as subtly as he possibly could, to find out what the lower deck thought about the mishaps. The petty officer quartermaster was sharing the watch with him.

Deciding there wasn't anything to be lost by trying, he moved across the bridge to stand alongside the PO.

He carefully swept the horizon through his telescope, closed it and broke the ice. 'I really think, Mr Rattenbury, that the world wouldn't come to an end if we had a mug of cocoa while everyone else is at dinner. Do you think it could be arranged?'

'Of course, sir.' He turned to the helmsman on the wheel, 'Dunn, a mug of cocoa for Lieutenant King. I'll take the wheel while you are away.'

As Dunn released the wheel King held up his hand, 'Just a

minute, Dunn, I meant cocoa for all three of us. Bring up three mugs and if the cook — what's his name? Hutton? — can manage it, get three good sandwiches as well. I'm sure each of you could down one.'

As Dunn disappeared below the quartermaster who was now on the wheel, spoke to King. 'That is very kind of you, sir. We were both hungry and it is a long time until the end of the watch. There is nothing like hard work shifting stores to work up an appetite.'

'I know.' He raised the telescope to his eye and slowly traversed the horizon again, then snapping it shut he looked at the quartermaster. 'How long have you been on the *Wasp*, Rattenbury?'

'Since shortly after she was commissioned, sir. Just over three years.'

When it was obvious that nothing further was forthcoming King knew that he would have to draw the man out.

'Well, what do you think of the ship? Have you served in a coal burner before?'

'No, sir. A lifetime under sail, but this isn't so bad. At least we don't spend all our time under a cloud of smoke, like some ships' companies have to. And I've served on worse ships than the *Wasp*. Take Mr Nicholls now, you would go a long way before you met a better captain or a finer seaman than Mr Nicholls. He has taken the *Wasp* into harbours along this coast that I wouldn't try to enter in a longboat, and never even got a scratch on the paintwork. Everyone on board feels the same way, as you'll find out when you've been longer on board, sir.'

'That's good to know and it bears out my own opinion exactly. In fact the whole company impressed me very favourably when I got to know them. I must admit that the day I joined in Limerick I had some doubts but first impressions can be misleading. I suppose you heard about that little incident?'

A smile appeared on Rattenbury's serious face. 'Yes sir, I did. And if you don't mind my saying so, everyone was grateful to you for what you did. I wasn't there myself, but the lower deck spoke of nothing else for days, and everyone agreed that you were right. The ship was a shambles and who knows what might have happened had you not come along when you did. Mr Guppy hasn't been the same since.'

Discussing another officer with a crew member was getting close to thin ice. King backed off very quickly.

'Well, that's over and done with. Let's hope that we don't

have any more of the mishaps that have been occurring, for the rest of this voyage.'

'Mishaps, sir?' Rattenbury enquired innocently.

'Mishaps, accidents, call them what you will. I've heard some odd things have been happening on board during the past few months. Would you not call them mishaps?'

'Well, yes, sir. I suppose mishaps is as good a word as any. You're thinking about the time we got lost when on patrol? That was a rum do and no mistake. Mr Nicholls was very upset about that. But it wasn't his fault. The whole crew was vexed that he got into trouble, but there wasn't anything we could do about it.'

'Oh. What did happen then? I've heard stories, of course, but they all differ. You are the first person I've spoken to who was actually there at the time.'

For a few moments Rattenbury was silent as he thought about his answer. He had never, in all his service, spoken to an officer man-to-man like this and he wasn't quite sure what it might lead to. It could even lead to trouble for someone if he wasn't careful. He decided to just give the bones of the story.

'You understand, sir, that I wasn't on the bridge when the captain first realised that the *Wasp* had gone and got lost?'

King nodded and made reassuring and sympathetic sounds.

'Well it was Andrews who told me how it all started. We had been at sea for a week, patrolling about a hundred miles south west off Kerry, and on this particular day we were to meet up with a ship coming in from America. From a place called Galveston, I believe. Anyway, the story was that she might have fever on board and we were to stop her and bring her into quarantine. Some of these merchantmen will go anywhere and spread any disease, just as long as they make a profit, and it was our job to see that this particular one behaved herself.'

'I see. So what happened?'

'When we arrived at the place we were supposed to be, there was no sign of the American, so we waited. The day was overcast and the navigator wasn't able to get a good fix. Next day it was the same, solid cloud and no sign of the ship. The following day was a bit better and the captain got his fix. That's when the trouble really began. We were miles away from where we were supposed to be. I wasn't on duty then, but I heard that the language used in the bridge nearly took the paint off the funnel.

'Anyway a new course was plotted and off we went, "with

the utmost despatch" as they say. Ten hours later, when it was dark and overcast, we arrived at another position, and again we waited. Next morning the sky cleared and the navigator got the fix he wanted. I was watching him when he rose from the chart table, white faced. It wasn't hard to see something was badly wrong. The captain was called and came up, half dressed, with a face like thunder. When the navigator told him that we were, once again, nearly seventy miles from where we should be, I thought he would throw the navigator overboard, but of course he didn't. By that time all hope of meeting up with the American was gone, so it was a stroke of luck for us that it didn't have fever on board after all.

'Well there was a right to-do, I can tell you. The charts were inspected, the bridge log was examined to see that the right courses had been steered and all was in order. Then the captain decided to examine the compass.'

He stopped speaking as Dunn returned to the bridge carrying a tray with steaming mugs of cocoa and three 'doorstep' sandwiches. King took his mug and placed it on the weather screen ledge, giving the other two men time to get their snack safely arranged on suitable and convenient locations. Dunn formally advised the petty officer that he was taking the wheel again, repeating the heading which the ship was on before Rattenbury relinquished the wheel. Relieved of the duty he then moved to the wing of the bridge, carrying his food with King close behind.

'I don't know how long it was before the captain thought to check the compass, or why he did. Perhaps it was because everything else had been examined and was in order. Anyway, he took it from the binnacle and himself and the navigator examined it very carefully. Then they decided to take the whole binnacle to bits and had the carpenter lay out each piece on the deck. When the binnacle was totally dismantled they stood looking at it for a few minutes. Then the captain told the carpenter to put it back together again and that was when the mystery was solved. Lying on the deck was a lump of tar with three or four big metal washers embedded in it.

'The navigator saw it first and picked it up. But it was Mr Nicholls who knew what it was and when he turned over the pieces of the binnacle we could all see where the tar had been stuck just close enough to the compass to let the washers distract the needle. That's why we were finishing up in the wrong places, the compass was distracted and nobody noticed it because we were nearly two hundred miles from land under an overcast sky.'

'So what happened then?' prodded King, who knew the outline of the faulty compass story from the report he had read in Queenstown, but hadn't seen any suggestion anywhere that the compass might have been deliberately interfered with.

'Well, for the next few days it was the talk of the ship. The captain had every officer and man in front of him, one at a time, to be questioned, but he never found out who the culprit was. He was sure it had been done deliberately, and so was everyone else for that matter, but that was all. Even when we were back in Westport we couldn't find out who put the washers beside the compass and as far as I know it is still a mystery. I can tell you, sir, the crew took a very poor view of it all and had we found out ourselves who did it the villain would have been for the deep six. But I don't suppose we'll ever know now.'

There was a silence as both men thought about the story which Rattenbury had told, but before King could ask him anything further Dunn raised his voice to advise them that it was time to alter course. From then on no further opportunity arose to pursue the matter.

The following three days passed very quickly. The first task was to get the ship cleaned up, ready to take on more relief supplies, all of which had to be sorted, assembled according to the needs of the people for whom they were identified, loaded and secured. Then came the provisioning and refuelling of the ship herself and finally a badly needed and very welcome 'make and mend' day for the ship's company.

During this period Nicholls was absent, attending to his business in Dublin, and King, being first lieutenant, was acting captain. It was a job with more problems than prestige, but having been a general dogsbody on several ships before joining the *Wasp*, he had learned certain survival routines along the way which he was now able to put to use. As a result the work was accomplished without too many problems and the ship's company didn't create any more difficulties during the work than might reasonably be expected.

By now he was learning that the ship's company wasn't a major problem at all. Through some mysterious chemistry which he hadn't so far identified the men swung from cheerful and willing cooperation to grumbling, time wasting and delaying

activity. Then back again without any apparent cause. He had
seen this happen before and knew the cause was quite simple
usually. Anything from a badly cooked meal served up to them,
to a feeling of being put-upon by the officers could do it, but
finding the actual cause and dealing with it was the real problem. He wasn't experienced enough to do that though he suspected that Sub Lieutenant Guppy might have had something to
to with it. He also wasn't long enough on board to have earned the
confidence of any of the crew who might have helped by drop-
ping a quiet word in his ear to warn him of impending trouble.

The matter of the distracted compass bothered him. As he
worked it kept coming into his mind, but no matter how he
approached the problem there wasn't any aspect of it he could
use as a starting point. Someone had deliberately interfered with
the navigation of the ship, but who or why remained a mystery.

The fact that it could have been an officer, while almost unthinkable, meant that he couldn't discuss it with anyone on
board. And the time was quickly approaching when the authorities in Queenstown and the shadowy Mr Carrington would expect
to hear from him with some results. Somehow or other he would
have to take action which might precipitate events and point
him in a more positive direction than he presently was taking.
He was beginning to profoundly wish that he hadn't accepted
this assignment, but it was too late now to back out.

Sunday afternoon came, a glorious, hot, summer's day with
the smallest wisps of cirrus cloud high in the sky and a light
warm breeze which caused the bunting on the marquee in front
of Westpark Manor to flutter, giving a holiday appearance to
the scene.

When King and the small party of officers arrived at the top
of the curving drive, having walked the short distance from the
quay, a cricket match was in progress on the lawn. They stopped
to survey the scene. He was accompanied by Otway Browne
who was already perspiring and held a handkerchief in his hand
to continually mop his forehead; Tom Guppy had adopted an
air of bored disdain under the impression that this was how the
upper class – of which he believed himself to be a shining
example – appeared when forced into contact with the peasants;
and John Kerrigan, who looked as if he was thoroughly enjoying
it all. The only absentee was Bill Hudson who had stayed behind
to act as officer of the watch and to see that some essential maintenance work was properly carried out on his precious engine.

All four were in their best uniforms, showing the creases which had accumulated while being stored in boxes for the past few weeks. But they were perhaps more conscious of this than the civilians were. Sailors, in general, were no novelty in Westport. The *Wasp* considered the town almost as its home port. But not many of the townspeople knew any of the officers to speak to as they lived on board and hadn't got a shore base like soldiers, in which social functions could be held. As a result, when they were noticed standing in a group at the edge of the lawn, and drew the attention of one or two of the players, there was a general movement of the onlookers towards them in greeting.

After a quick glance of inspection to make sure that all his officers were at least presentable, King led them towards an elderly gentleman leading the onlookers with hand outstretched.

'There you are at last. Good of you to come, gentlemen. We don't see enough of our gallant mariners. You are very welcome. I'm Mulrany.' By this time he had reached the party and King proceeded to introduce himself and his colleagues.

'What a pity Lieutenant Nicholls couldn't come. We were looking forward to meeting him this year.' The speaker was a remarkably attractive young lady in a light dress who had positioned herself directly in front of King. 'Has he hurt himself in another climbing accident?'

It was patently obvious that she didn't believe a word of the excuse Nicholls had sent the previous year and was teasing King. Caught unawares, both by her charm and the way she was watching him, he struggled to make the current, and true, explanation sound at least partially convincing. As he launched into the excuse she held up a white gloved hand.

'It is perfectly all right, Mr King. Or do I call you Lieutenant?'

Not having the faintest idea who this lovely creature was he looked around for help which wasn't forthcoming. The others had joined little groups and were moving back onto the lawn to watch the cricket. He turned his attention back to the smiling girl.

'Either will do. But I would really prefer you to call me George. If that isn't too informal? I'm afraid that I didn't catch your name, Miss . . . ?'

'Marsden, Caroline Marsden. You may call me Caroline, if you wish.' She laughed. 'Don't look so shocked, George. Times are changing, even in Westport. Though I normally live in London. Nobody stays in London during August, you know.'

George hadn't known. At a loss he took off his cap, and then, to gain a little time to marshal his confused thoughts, held out his hand.

'I really am delighted to meet you, Miss Marsden. Caroline? What a lovely name.'

Looking at her he thought she was the loveliest girl he had ever seen and wondered what she was doing standing talking to him when the lawn must be full of far more suitable young men. But he didn't intend asking her that.

'I'm afraid I didn't know that nobody stayed in London in August. How interesting, but isn't it rather inconvenient?'

'Not really. Anyway, it isn't important. Would you like a cup of tea, Lieutenant? George? They say it is most refreshing in this weather. Shall we find out?'

She turned and led the way towards the marquee while King fell into step beside her, wondering was he suddenly transported into another world where escorting lovely young ladies into tea tents was a normal event.

Fully conscious of the envious looks he was getting from some of the young men in whites, though Caroline seemed to be unaware of the interest they were arousing, they found a small table with two unoccupied chairs and sat down. While they waited for the tea to be served he became more at ease and found himself able to chat quite easily and freely to her. Whatever interest either of them had in cricket disappeared after a short time and they found it far more interesting just talking to each other, learning about their different lifestyles.

They had become almost totally isolated in a little fascinating world of their own when an elderly man dressed as a footman materialised beside the table. For a few moments neither noticed him until he coughed discreetly to attract their attention. Caroline looked around, puzzled, then recognised him.

'Oh, Staunton? What is it?'

'Sorry for disturbing you, Miss Caroline. I have a message from his lordship for Lieutenant King.'

King, surprised, looked from one to the other. How did the footman know Caroline and why on earth should Lord Mulrany be sending messages to him? He didn't have long to wait. Caroline told Staunton to deliver it.

'His lordship's compliments, sir. I am to tell you that there is a gentleman in the library who wants to see you before you leave.' With that he inclined his head slightly and walked away.

They looked at each other, wondering what it was about. Then King remembered his surprise.

'How did the footman, Staunton, know you Caroline, if you are just a visitor here like me?'

She looked puzzled, then laughed. 'I'm sorry, George. Did I give that impression? Staunton has known me since I was a child. I live here.'

It was King's turn to look puzzled. 'I thought you lived in London and just visited Westport in August?'

'Not Westport, Westpark Manor. This is my parents' home. Now let's go and find out who wants you and why. I'll show you where the library is.'

It took him a few seconds to work out the new situation. He stopped walking and looked at her. 'But that means you aren't Miss Marsden at all . . . you must be . . .' He stopped, confused.

'I'm afraid so, George. Lady Caroline, but around here nobody calls me that. And you certainly aren't allowed to call me anything but Caroline. Now let's find out who is in the library.'

With his emotions totally mixed up he followed her into the house. As they entered, the transition from bright sunshine to shade left him blinded, and he had to stop while his vision returned. Then he saw Caroline standing by the open door waiting for him and behind her the dim outline of two men. He crossed the hall and as he reached the door she preceded him into the high ceilinged library.

'Good afternoon. You want to see Lieutenant King?'

George was in the room, standing just behind her watching both men rise to their feet. With a sudden shock he recognised Carrington, whom he had last seen in the harbour captain's office in Queenstown. The other man was a stranger.

'Thank you, miss,' Carrington said as he strode across the room. 'Lieutenant King, how nice to see you again.' Dazed King took the proffered hand and shook it.

Carrington looked at Caroline. 'I must apologise for interrupting your tea party, but it is important that I speak to Lieutenant King this afternoon. Lord Mulrany has given me permission to use the library as we have a confidential naval matter to discuss, but I promise you that I won't take up too much of his time.'

She looked at King in surprise. 'Do you know this man, George?'

'Yes, Caroline, I do. I'm sorry about this.' He glared at Carrington. 'This is unforgiveable, Mr Carrington. What is it that cannot wait until tomorrow morning?'

'As I said Lieutenant, this is a confidential matter. Would you please excuse us, miss?' As he was speaking he moved smoothly to the door and held it open for her. After a brief moment of uncertainty she shrugged and walked out, saying as she passed King, 'I'll wait for you at the top of the steps. Don't be too long.'

'Now what is all this about?' King felt his anger beginning to build up. If Carrington wanted to be taken as a civilian, as he apparently did, then his authority over King was very much in question. He was far out of line with his present conduct and King was in no mood now to make any allowances following the brusque dismissal of Caroline.

But if Carrington recognised his mood, he totally ignored it.

'Please sit down, Lieutenant.' He waited silently watching while King considered what he knew was an order. His companion, in the meantime had quietly seated himself and now produced a notebook which he opened and spread on his knee. King felt the beginning of alarm replacing his anger, and slowly seated himself at one end of the couch positioned at right angles to the desk.

'Thank you. I understand your feelings, Lieutenant, and I assure you that I wouldn't be here unless it was absolutely necessary that we meet today.'

He held up his hand to silence King who was obviously about to launch a series of questions and complaints. King sat back, fuming.

'Before I say anything else I had better introduce myself. My name is, as you know, Carrington, and as you may have guessed I am not a civilian. I am an assistant commissioner from Scotland Yard and in charge of the newly formed Special Irish Branch. Have you heard of us?'

King was shocked. He had, naturally, heard of the Special Irish Branch. Everyone who read the papers knew about it and that it had been assembled to combat the atrocities of the Fenians who had been carrying out attacks on politicians and other eminent people, as well as on what they called 'strategic targets' in both Great Britain and Ireland for some time past.

Thinking rapidly he remembered that the members of the SIB were always armed and before leaving Portsmouth he had taken part in a discussion in the wardroom one evening after dinner, during which the new force was described as a private army. The news that Carrington was one of the top men in this organisation was so unexpected that he was at a loss for words.

'The Special Irish Branch?' His voice was faint. 'Why are you interviewing me? What have I got to do with Fenianism? I assure you that . . .'

Carrington interrupted again.

'Will you please be quiet and listen, Lieutenant. I am ex-RN, an ex-commander and as such, still have access to certain people in the Admiralty. I know perfectly well that you have nothing to do with Fenianism. I also knew, long before you did, that you were being posted to the *Wasp* and have been waiting for you to arrive here. Quite obviously I couldn't do anything to expedite this, but now that you are here it is very important that you be put into the overall picture. Do you understand?'

Numbly King shook his head. 'I'm afraid not.' Then as an afterthought, '. . . sir.'

'Good. Now we know where we stand.' The hard face eased into a tight smile. 'I'll begin at the beginning. For some time, in fact since long before the SIB was formed, certain people have felt that the Fenian movement should be taken a lot more seriously than the anarchistic organisations which preceded it. Its planning and intelligence gathering is far superior, its members appear to be more ruthless and dedicated, and the only way to describe it is that it is very dangerous.

'So far the police have managed to contain it but that can't go on as their resources are limited. In fact they aren't trained to deal with an enemy such as the Fenians, so we've been formed to take on the job.'

'Yes, I understand so far.' King felt he had recovered sufficiently to venture the opinion that he wasn't a totally illiterate idiot. 'But how does all this affect me?'

'I'm about to tell you,' Carrington said coldly. 'Please pay attention . . .' He walked across to the window and studied the activity outside. King remained still. For a few seconds there was silence, then Carrington spoke again as if he was thinking aloud without turning round to face the room.

'From information in our possession it appears that naval and military targets prove attractive to these criminals. Ships especially. Because ships at sea are highly vulnerable.

'There is no such thing as a ship half prepared to be attacked, either it is fully prepared, or not at all. The army, on the other hand, can double the guard while normal routines are being maintained. So a ship at sea, operating under peacetime conditions, is unprotected if there is an enemy poised to strike.

'In some cases the enemy could already be on board. A member of the crew. Just think what a coup it would be for the Fenians if they could sink one of HM ships and what a blow it would be to the prestige of the Royal Navy.'

King jumped to his feet looking aghast. 'Do you think that the *Wasp* is a target?'

'Do you?' Carrington left the window and stood facing him. 'Have you found out anything, anything at all, while you have been on board regarding the problems we have been having with your ship? What about the captain and the crew? Is there something going on that hasn't appeared in the reports which you read? Think, man. The reason you are here is to act as my eyes and ears. Has anything happened which shouldn't have?'

King couldn't think of anything. The voyage so far had been perfectly normal and the captain hadn't expressed any concern. Then suddenly he thought of his conversation on the bridge with the quartermaster, Rattenbury.

'Well . . .' he began hesitantly, 'I had a chat a few days ago while on watch with a petty officer who was on board when the *Wasp* failed to make a rendezvous at sea with a merchantman coming in from Galveston. Do you remember the occasion?'

The two SIB men were suddenly very alert. 'Yes, go on.'

'Perhaps I have forgotten the details of that incident. I had a lot to read in a short time, if you recall, but I don't remember reading about the compass being fixed to give a wrong reading. It was, if I remember rightly, just reported as "compass error". Or am I wrong?'

'What about it?'

Out of the corner of his eye he saw the man at the desk open a document case and take out a file which he rapidly flicked through. Ignoring him, he continued speaking to Carrington. As briefly as he could he recounted the story which Rattenbury had told him, mentioning in detail the washers embedded in the tar which was found when the binnacle was dismantled. As he finished he saw Carrington look at his partner who shrugged and shook his head negatively.

'So what happened then, Lieutenant?'

King recalled how Nicholls had been very angry, according to Rattenbury, and had questioned everyone on board without success. This seemed to him to be an anti-climax, but he explained that a course change had come about just then and an opportunity to continue the conversation with Rattenbury hadn't arisen. His voice tapered off into silence.

'You didn't find out anything further about the problems with the engine?'

'No. As I said the opportunity didn't arise. But . . .' he looked at Carrington in embarrassment.

'But what? What were you about to say?'

'Well, the story as told to me by the petty officer doesn't sound right. I haven't any evidence that it is wrong but I don't believe it altogether.'

Carrington sat forward in his chair to get closer to King. 'What do you mean? You think he was telling you lies?'

'Not deliberately perhaps. But let me put it to you this way. Rattenbury told me that after about ten days at sea the *Wasp* tried to rendezvous with a merchantman coming in from America, because fever on board was suspected. Right?'

'Well. Go on.'

'Since the *Wasp* had put to sea it hadn't been in communication with anybody or any other ship, so the captain must have known about the merchantman before he left Queenstown, ten days earlier. Now that was about the time the merchantman left America. But there isn't any way that a ship would sail with fever on board, which means that the *Wasp* was not looking for a fever ship.'

Carrington and his partner exchanged looks but made no comment.

King continued. 'Of course, as I said I have no evidence to support this theory, but I believe that Nicholls was told, before he put to sea, to stop the merchantman for quite a different reason, and that someone else knew his orders. Someone who arranged for the compass to be interfered with. Don't forget there is a whole lot of people who could have known about the ship, including the civilians who work for the underwater telegraph cable company. But that's another matter.

'The important question really is why he was supposed to search the ship. A wanted Fenian perhaps? Or bombs? Guns? Money? Whatever it was, it got through — because the *Wasp* didn't meet the merchantman — and it arrived safely in England or Ireland or wherever the ship was bound for. Don't you think, Mr Carrington, that if I'm to be your eyes and ears, as you say, you should tell me what is going on, instead of wasting my time and insulting my intelligence, by blaming the captain and crew of the *Wasp* for mistakes made by the SIB? Well . . . sir?'

Despite his air of indignant confidence George was inwardly petrified at his own temerity. The attack he had just made on Carrington and the SIB had been totally unplanned and unprepared, but it seemed to have struck home very hard.

Carrington sat back looking nonplussed at the young officer. Perhaps he was remembering his own Navy days when a mere lieutenant would never have dreamt of criticising a commander, but if he was, that was water under the bridge. Now was now. He stood up and walked around the room, then came to a stop in front of King.

'You surprise me, Mr King, and I must apologise for having underestimated you. You are right, of course. We knew the merchantman, as you call it, was on its way and we were bitterly disappointed that we didn't manage to stop it. I admit we didn't know, until now, that it was the sabotage of the compass which caused the *Wasp* to miss the rendezvous so if you have a saboteur on board you could be in serious trouble if he isn't caught. But, as you suggest, it could have been an outsider and if that is the case we will look into it.

'Now, as to your question. I believe that the ship was carrying guns and money for the Fenians. A message was received from Galveston that this was what the ship was carrying and we badly wanted to stop it. Incidentally, what do you know about the Fenians?'

'Frankly, very little. I gather that they are armed and very dangerous subversives, but that's all.'

Carrington sat down and closed his eyes as if collecting his thoughts.

'I'll try to make this brief and simple because I know your young lady is waiting for you, Lieutenant. But it is neither brief nor simple. You have probably heard of the land war here in 1870. It was a disaster for everyone concerned and this country has been seething ever since; you know the story, the usual elite groups using events for their own purposes, keeping the pot boiling. We call them by a lot of names — nationalists, home rulers, land leaguers — but the whole bloody lot are anarchists. For simplicity we just call them all Fenians, Mr King.

'Then four years ago things got worse, the usual bad harvest and general agricultural mess. The landlords and their tenants have been at each others' throats, it's all about money or the lack of it, and the agitators have been having a field day.

'You may ask where America fits in to this scheme of things, Lieutenant. The American connection goes back to a fanatic called Davitt who went there in '78 and tours around like an Irish messiah pushing the most simplistic drivel about the troubles here, that it's all due to the landlords, that they should be stripped of everything including the clothes they stand up in. You see, Lieutenant, his listeners are children of the famine emigrants, they're not exactly on the side of the landlords.

'Anyway, money has been pouring in from America, fuelling the agitators – a quarter of a million pounds came in last year. We've got to stop all this. We've got to protect these people from themselves. If we don't stop it, it will swamp all of us in time. Sometimes I see no end to it.'

He put his hands up to his temples and gently rubbed them. Then he stood up and said, 'You had better rejoin your young lady, I think.'

In a state of stunned stupefaction, King came to attention, nodded, and left the room.

Caroline was waiting on the steps which led up from the lawn to the huge hall door when he emerged. The cricket match had finished and the players were chatting with cups of tea in their hands, as she sat watching them. Seeing King she jumped to her feet and putting her hand on his arm wanted to know what had happened in the library. This brought him back to earth rather quickly.

'Something pretty serious has been worrying Mr Carrington recently, and it seems that I'm the only person who can help him. He wanted my advice, that's all.'

'Phoo, I don't believe that. Are you in trouble?'

It took a few minutes to reassure her that he wasn't in trouble. In fact, quite the contrary. But explaining what it was all about, without actually saying anything, took all his inventive resourcefulness and he dismally knew that she was disappointed in him.

For the rest of the afternoon they remained together, Caroline inroducing him to the other guests and showing him over the beautifully kept grounds surrounding the house. But no matter how hard they tried to recover the companionable relationship of the early afternoon it was obvious to both that it had been lost.

By 5.30 pm, as the other guests were beginning to board their carriages lined up on the drive, calling farewells and thanks to their friends and members of the host's family, King and Caroline — slightly ill at ease — stood inside the deserted marquee.

'I'm really sorry Caroline, that I allowed Carrington to spoil our day. I didn't know that he would be here, if I had I wouldn't have come, but the meeting was important and I will tell you what it was about, I promise, as soon as I possibly can.'

He took her hand in both of his. 'May I visit you again before you return to London?'

'Of course you may.' She smiled, forgiving him. 'I'll be cross with you if you don't, and so long as you aren't in trouble it doesn't matter what Mr Carrington's problems are. I'm very glad you came to our garden party.'

The next few minutes were spent reassuring each other so it was in a happier frame of mind that King shortly took his leave from the most disturbing young woman he had ever met, and left to rejoin the ship.

4   Eviction on Clare Island

Never for one minute did I think that I could be in two such different conditions at the same time, as I am at present. On the one hand I am depressed at the task which Carrington has set me and find it incredible that I should be expected to spy on fellow officers, while on the other hand I am almost euphoric and floating on air through having met the sweetest, most beautiful and charming girl I have ever known. More important, she seems to like me too, which is equally incredible. Life ashore is becoming too exciting for this simple sailor, I'm afraid. But would I have it otherwise? I really don't know.

I must say that I was very disturbed with the interpretation which Carrington put on the mishaps which have befallen the poor old *Wasp*. Sabotage is an ugly word. I wonder could he be right? For a time I thought it might have been a case of someone wanting to return to port a little earlier than planned and deciding, stupidly, that interfering with the compass would achieve that. But following our talk about the Fenians, which was all new to me, I'm inclined to think that it probably was sabotage. One result of his visit to Westport is that I am now forewarned but why the civilians should think that by attacking the *Wasp* they are furthering whatever cause it is they espouse, is quite beyond me. We are here to help them. Thank goodness I'm not the captain with responsibility for the ship and crew, with this problem on my shoulders. I'm glad Nicholls will be back tomorrow. I must write to my mother very soon.

Early on Tuesday afternoon Nicholls arrived in Westport off the Dublin train and took a jaunting car from the station to the quay where the *Wasp* was lying.

King had been waiting for him since the previous day. The

ship was loaded with supplies provided by the local Quaker brethren, all the ship's company was on board, steam was up and he was ready to put to sea.

So it was with some surprise he received a totally unexpected order from the captain.

'Maintain harbour watch, Mr King, and tell Mr Hudson to bank down the fire. Sailing time has been deferred to 07.00 tomorrow. Please report to my cabin in fifteen minutes.'

When he knocked on the cabin door a quarter of an hour later the ship was secured as instructed. Nicholls had changed into uniform and had been looking through the deck log which he put down on the tiny desk.

'Everything seems normal, George, though I can see you have been busy. It was a pleasure to walk along the quay and see how tidy and efficient the *Wasp* was looking. Quite a change in fact, from the day you joined us in Limerick. I congratulate you.'

King was delighted. Though he did his best not to show it he felt a grin spreading. He had received recognition for a job he knew he had done well and he had been called by his first name by the captain, which was an even bigger accolade.

As he was about to thank Nicholls, the captain continued. 'But the news I've got for you now is not going to please anyone. At 06.30 tomorrow we take on board a party of police and bailiffs to carry out an eviction on Clare Island. That's about a two hour trip under steam, which means we could be back here to off-load them by about 17.00. All being well, we should be on passage for Blacksod Bay and its island by 18.00.'

Although he had heard of the unpleasantness of taking part in evictions, and partly expected it, he was taken aback by the strength of the air of gloom and depression which spread through the ship as soon as news of the following day's work spread. It was so strong that it almost felt as if he was on a different ship with a company of strangers. The prospect of another night ashore didn't seem to make any difference to the crew and in fact most of them didn't go any further than the quayside where they hung around in small groups.

Even his cabinmate, Kerrigan, seemed affected. He just stretched out on his bunk and, when questioned as to why he was so withdrawn, muttered, 'You'll see why tomorrow,' and turned his face towards the bulkhead.

The next morning the ship's company, after an early breakfast, was ready when the eviction party marched onto the quay.

Watching from the wing of the bridge, King was surprised by its size. First came a party of twenty police, marching in formation and led by their sergeant. A carriage followed with four men, whom Kerrigan identified for him as the resident magistrate, the sub sheriff, a justice of the peace, and the district inspector of police. This group immediately made its way to the wardroom where the steward had glasses of gin already poured for them.

Following the carriage came two carts which carried about ten men between them, plus an assortment of tools and ropes. These, King was told, were to smash down the doors of the hovels and then to totally level the buildings when the unfortunate inhabitants were on the roadside with all their belongings. The men chosen to do this job were typical of their class, the dregs of the county town about thirty miles away, who had been accommodated overnight in the local military barracks.

Looking at them King got his first inkling of just how ruthless the forthcoming exercise was going to be and the sorrow which would be left in its wake.

Getting everyone on board, with all the equipment neatly stacked on the deck was the work of only a few minutes. Sub Lieutenant Guppy took up his leaving harbour station at the stern and the lines were cast off. Slowly the *Wasp* went astern from the quay into deep water and turned towards the open sea. Two hours later the whole operation was reversed when the ship came alongside the jetty on Clare Island which is located, like a huge cork, in the mouth of Clew Bay.

Waiting for the ship to arrive was the landlord's agent, a Mr Williams. One of a particular, and despised group of classless officials, he served his absentee landlord with a heartless ambition which permitted no mercy for those of his unfortunate countrymen and their families who had been brought down by the famine some years earlier and poor harvests since.

It was indeed ironic, thought King, that the *Wasp* had on board at the same time relief provided by the English Quakers for some victims of the times, and Irishmen willing to grind down other victims, their own neighbours, and it was pure chance which group was attended to first. All the misery involved was brought about by uncaring English politicians and greedy Irish landlords.

Disembarking took slightly longer than embarking. When the police were lined up the six marines and their corporal took up positions behind them, their red coats and white belts providing a spurious flash of gaiety which their long, single action, rifles belied. The four representatives of authority, their faces now flushed by the gin they had been drinking on the way out, together with the landlord's agent, took their places behind the marines. And finally came the party of bailiffs. While they watched, their equipment was handed down from the deck by the crew. King was about to turn away to write up the deck log when, to his surprise, he saw the sailors move down the gangway and shoulder the bailiff's tools and ropes, then fall in behind, forming a sort of rear guard, and march off.

'Where are those men going?' He swung around to ask Petty Officer Andrews whom he knew was behind him on the bridge. Instead Lieutenant Nicholls was standing there silently watching. He took his pipe from his mouth to answer the indignant and puzzled King.

'Didn't you know?' he asked quietly but bitterly, 'that it is part of our duty to aid and assist the civil powers, which is what we are doing now. But I am sure that their Lordships in the Admiralty didn't foresee that this would involve dispossessing impoverished and helpless fellow British subjects from all that they own, then knocking their wretched hovels to the ground about their ears. Just to satisfy some gombeen land steward trying to ingratiate himself with an equally miserable absentee landlord busy beggaring himself at the gaming tables in London.'

George couldn't belief his ears. Could such remarks from the captain be considered treasonable? Before he had time to consider Nicholls looked at him again.

'What on earth are you doing here? Don't you know that as first officer on this ship you are supposed to be in charge of the shore party? Quickly now, you won't need a side arm, just go as you are and make sure that our people don't do anything stupid or make trouble. You'll have to hurry to catch up.'

King saluted, then took the bridge ladder in two steps, ran across the deck, ignored the gangway and vaulted the rail, and sprinted after the group. Some of the islanders, standing at the shore end of the pier, threw stones at him as he ran past and shouted, but he didn't catch what they said.

Within a hundred yards he had caught up with the others who were slowly making their way up a steep hill, leading to a small group of hovels which surrounded a larger building with a cross on top. He guessed it to be the church.

As the sailors had by far the hardest job, carrying pickaxes, crowbars, ropes and heavy baulks of wood they had gradually dropped further behind the main party. The land steward had noticed this and had come back to chivy them up as King came up from behind. They arrived simultaneously.

'What the devil is wrong with this lot?' he demanded of King. 'A bunch of old women, I declare. If you don't get a move on it will all be over by the time you arrive and that will look well when I send in my report. Now stop dragging your feet, there is work to be done.'

He stood at the side of the path as the angry sailors shuffled past even more slowly. One of them, named Bill Dunn, an able seaman who had a reputation for toughness and had been promoted and demoted so often, between AB and leading hand, for fighting and general misbehaviour, that everyone looked at his sleeve before addressing him to see what his current rank was, grunted ominously as he passed.

King, who knew Dunn's reputation, heard him. 'Pick up the step there, Dunn. The rest of you, close up. We're nearly there.'

Although he had no idea where they were going, he wasn't at all happy about appearing to be on the same side as the steward, but his captain's warning to keep the sailors out of trouble was very fresh in his mind. If trouble did erupt the chances were that it would probably start with Dunn and he wanted to prevent that. He was under no illusions about the burly seaman, he would be the first to agree that Dunn was no angel, but during the past few weeks he had got to know him slightly and realised that Dunn was wasted as an ordinary AB.

Dunn's trouble was that he loved fighting. Not just brawling but professional fighting. He knew almost everything about every professional pugilist on both sides of the Atlantic and liked nothing better than talking about their fights. Before joining the Navy he had ambitions to become one himself and had fought in dozens of amateur fights in London and Portsmouth, mostly successfully, until one day he was overmatched in a supporting bout in Epsom.

That fight changed his life. At the end of twenty rounds the bare knuckles of his opponent had chopped his face into a bloody mess, his chest and ribs had been pummeled to a state of being just raw soreness, his breath came in burning gasps, and only stubbornness kept him on his wavering legs. It was the shouts of the crowd that made the referee stop the fight.

When he was able to think again, after the beating he had taken, he realised that his hopes of ever becoming a professional were over. So he joined the Navy instead. But he was still a fighter, still loved it, and it was second nature to him to use his fists whenever he felt that he, or his mates, or his ship were being slighted either ashore or afloat. And he could never understand why the Navy took a poor view of him for that.

Nicholls had told King about his history, with some amusement and exasperation evident in the telling, and King had since then recommended Dunn for reinstatement to leading hand. He wanted him giving an example to the young sailors and not just being a figure of fun to them. A fight today could set his promotion back for another six months or more.

As the island was not very large the party reached the two small houses from which the inhabitants were to be evicted a few minutes later. King brought the sailors to a halt some distance away and went forward to where the officials had taken up a position from which they could control and supervise the proceedings. They had been joined by a priest who was arguing with the magistrate and sheriff.

The houses, mud built with thatched roofs, were already in a sorry state. Only one had glass in the tiny window, the other had sacking hung over the openings. The doors of both houses were closed and the sound of crying could be heard from inside, indicating that women and children were still there.

In front of the houses, which were about five or six yards apart, stood a group of islanders carrying improvised weapons such as stones, broken oars and rough timbers, and it was clear that they were not going to let their neighbours suffer without putting up resistance. Meanwhile they watched the efforts of their priest to have the proceedings stopped.

The priest's fruitless pleading didn't take too long. The land steward, Williams, hurried over to the three men, flourishing a paper in the face of the priest. This apparently was his legal authority to carry out the work in hand. The RM spoke to Williams who shook his head violently in disagreement. Then the RM turned away from the sheriff and priest, who stood silently looking at each other. It was obvious to all the onlookers that no mercy was to be shown and a groan went up from the islanders.

The inspector of police now ordered the islanders to disperse. Nobody expected them to and his next order, given almost immediately, was to his men to break ranks and move the islanders back. As they obeyed a shower of stones rained down and one or two staggered back, blood streaming from their faces.

Suddenly the mood of the two sides changed.

Sensing victory, the islanders, about sixty or eighty, ran towards the police who had closed ranks and drawn their truncheons and a violent confrontation was imminent when a ragged fusilade of shots rang out. Everyone stopped what they were doing and looked to where the shooting had come from. Even King was taken by surprise.

To one side of the houses there was a small kitchen garden with a few straggling vegetable patches. Standing in the centre of this plot was the party of marines who had just fired in the air over the heads of the locals. The marines had seemingly approached from another direction, and had been waiting behind the houses for just this eventuality to take place, without anyone noticing that they were there. At once the venom of the crowd was directed at the redcoated party, away from Williams, and turned what had up to then been a disturbance into a far more serious incident.

With angry shouts they moved towards the new enemy, stones flying and sticks being waved threateningly. But the police had recovered and now hurled themselves at the crowd from its flank, so that within seconds all was confusion. Under threat from the front while being attacked from the flank, the crowd lost whatever leadership it originally had and broke up into individual scuffles.

King, watching this development with astonishment and dismay, now became aware that the sailors were getting to their feet from the grass on which they had been resting, rolling up their sleeves. It was quite apparent that they were preparing to join in the fray. He could hear 'Bastards. Bloody sodding marines, Landlords, what are we waiting for?' and knew that immediate action was needed to maintain control. He also knew which side of the fight the sailors were about to join and didn't have to be told what the civil powers would make of such 'assistance' by the Navy.

Putting himself in front of them he looked Dunn in the eye. Dunn stood still, watching him. The others continued pushing and shoving forward until King raised his voice.

'Shore party, stand fast.' The pushing stopped. 'This is not our fight. And we are certainly not going to take on the marines and the police at the same time.' There was some jostling at the rear as a couple of sailors who hadn't heard tried to get the group moving again. He raised his voice.

'I said stand fast.' They all heard him this time. When they had stopped muttering and pushing the noise from the battle between the police and the islanders could be clearly heard. There was shouting, cries for assistance and cursing going on everywhere but it could be seen that the police were slowly getting the upper hand. Formed into a wedge, they were relentlessly moving forward, hitting everyone in their path with a brutal effectiveness, so that all one could clearly see was the sight of upraised arms and flailing truncheons. It was impossible to make out individual faces in the melee.

Vainly trying to restore order the middle-aged priest, his soutane partially ripped off, stumbled and almost fell in front of the heaving mob. Nobody paid any attention to what he was trying to say and he looked desperately around for whatever assistance might be given. Dunn was the first of the shore party to recognise the danger.

'Sir, sir . . . the priest,' he shouted, pointing behind King. King swung round, but it took a few seconds to see what was happening. When he did, he reacted quickly.

'Right, Dunn. Take two men and rescue him. Now.'

A couple of minutes later a very shaken priest was sitting on a rock surrounded by the sailors. When his trembling eased a little he tried to express his thanks, but was stopped by King.

'That's not necessary, padre. But what is all this about? Why is there so much trouble here? I can understand people being evicted for not paying their rent, that happens in England too, but surely the use of all this force is unusual and unnecessary, isn't it?'

'Not paying their rent?' The priest's voice was bitter. 'Those two families, between them, owe less than £3. For that mean sum Mr Williams is taking this action so that he can put sheep on their land. The families will be broken up and the younger ones will go to America, if they are lucky. The others will probably be dead within the year and unless someone takes pity on the corpses they will rot away in some ditch. And you are right, sir. The use of all this force is unusual. Six months ago the eviction would have gone off quietly with just a few sympathetic friends here to give comfort, but the Fenians have changed all that, thank God. The likes of Williams will not be able to do this evil work in secret for much longer.' When he paused to draw breath the noise from around the houses became louder and all turned to watch.

The police had quelled the disturbance being made by the islanders and had formed a cordon around the front of the nearer house. Inside the cordon the bailiffs had smashed down the door and were dragging the terrified occupants outside while they cried and screamed in protest. The family consisted of two women – an elderly woman and her daughter – and three children, all aged less than five.

The women, as far as could be seen, were very poorly dressed, the children barefoot and only half clothed. All were weeping with shock and anger as they huddled together, watching their belongings being thrown into the yard in front of the house.

A table, two chairs and cooking pots were thrown out first, followed by bedding and a large wooden home-made bed which was it seemed where they all slept. Following that it was just bits and pieces, extra clothing, a few crudely made toys and a broken mirror, then the house was empty. Looking at the pitiful family possessions King was overwhelmed with anger and suddenly realised why the whole shore party had wanted to join in. It wasn't new to them. They had seen it several times before and each time it must have got worse. This was something nobody could get used to. It was uncivilised, inhuman and worst of all unnecessary.

A thought struck him and he turned to the priest.

'I haven't seen a man around. Is the woman a widow?'

'No. He is on the mainland, working. Somewhere up around Sligo I believe. As a matter of fact I haven't seen him around for several months and he should be here. But he probably doesn't know anything about all this. All the family are illiterate which makes keeping in touch with each other almost impossible. I pity the poor wife who has to shoulder all this by herself.' He looked again at the police cordon which had opened to allow the small family to be led away by neighbours, probably to shelter.

The cordon then reformed around the second house and the bailiffs set to work again.

The same pattern was followed. The door was smashed down, the occupants dragged out and then the belongings hurled into the yard. There was a difference this time. No children were involved. The occupants consisted of two young men and a woman all in their mid twenties as far as King could judge and all were considerably better dressed than the people who had lost the first house. Their clothing wasn't much better in quality but it was cleaner, neater and newer, with holes repaired and seams sewn. They hadn't protested to the same extent as the others had and that puzzled King as he felt they would have been better able to resist. He continued watching with interest, but with no suspicion that anything was wrong.

The heavy baulk of timber which had already battered the first house into rubble was being brought into use a second time. Seeing this the two young men entered into a hurried and urgent conversation, looking more alarmed than they had been. The girl tapped the police sergeant on the arm and spoke to him. He nodded, and she returned to the two men. By this time the area of wall around the front door was breaking and the thatched roof sagging. The battering continued.

Picking up some pieces of clothing and a small parcel from the ground the three went through the cordon joining the watching islanders. After a few seconds they seemed to melt away and King lost sight of them. He continued to watch the total destruction going on in front of the resentful crowd.

Suddenly there was a shout from the bailiff inside the house. The others stopped working and laid down the battering ram, while the one who had called out could be seen bending over, investigating whatever it was that had caught his attention. Seconds later he put his head out of the smashed door and called the police sergeant over. The inspector followed to see what was happening.

By this time everyone was interested, but puzzled, by what was causing the delay. Even the priest was standing, trying to see past the cordon without success and King had to tell his shore party once again to stand fast. He couldn't blame them for being curious though, this was a development which seemingly had never arisen before. There was another call from the doorway as the sergeant attracted the attention of a constable. Following a very brief conversation the constable approached the sailors and came to a stop in front of the puzzled King.

'Excuse me, sir. The inspector would like to see you in the house. Right away,' he added needlessly.

'Very well.' King looked at the group beside him, then made his mind up. 'Dunn, you are in charge until I return. Don't let the shore party wander off or get into trouble.'

'Aye aye, sir. I'll look after them.'

'I'm sure you will,' he thought as he followed the policeman across the yard. The inspector waited in the doorway.

'Lieutenant, please come in here and tell me what you think of this.'

Inside, the scene was one of total devastation. The chimney breast had fallen and the main roof beam had split allowing thatch and joists to sag to within a few feet off the floor. Lying on the floor were some agricultural tools which must have been stored in the thatch, but still half hidden by the debris was a long wooden box. This was partly under the thatch.

Moving closer to examine it he brushed the straw aside and clearly read the painted inscription along the side of the box.

'Galveston Tool and Plough Co. Inc. Galveston, Texas.' he read.

Wondering why the name Galveston suddenly rang a bell in his head he looked closer at the familiar looking box. Then to give himself time to think he straightened up and asked the inspector what he thought a box from Texas would be doing hidden in the thatch of this island hovel.

'That's just it. There isn't any reason why it should be here. I don't suppose anyone on this island has even heard of Texas. But don't you recognise the box, Lieutenant King?'

A glimmer of light dawned. 'It looks very like the boxes we store rifles in. Let's open it and see just what it does contain.'

The sergeant and constable made short work of levering the lid off. Inside, carefully wrapped and packed in grease, were twelve long, paper-covered, metal 'tools' which they instantly recognised.

Tearing the paper off one, King wiped the grease from the brand new rifle to read the name on the side. 'Wilmington Rifle Co. Inc., Wilmington, Delaware.'

Lieutenant Nicholls was not at all pleased at being told that, in addition to the eviction party back on board, he now had a dozen brand new rifles and more than 1,000 rounds of ammunition. This would create a lot of problems which could only throw his programme into total disarray.

It was more serious than might appear at first sight because he could count on only thirteen weeks, or less, to get the relief supplies to all the places where they were needed before the weather deteriorated into autumn gales. From the end of September he wouldn't be able to plan ahead at all, though it would be possible to make a few local shipments, on a spur-of-the-moment basis, when short breaks appeared in the weather.

This would be all right for last minute supplies, but the people on the islands and around the coast needed more than that. Before the *Wasp* had taken up relief work the deliveries had been made by HMS *Valorous*, commanded by the Duke of Edinburgh, which was a much larger vessel. It could safely make deliveries for more than seven months at a time, although it couldn't get into the smaller harbours. Since the *Wasp* could, Nicholls had carefully built up a reputation for being highly conscientious in getting his supplies delivered safely and on time, subject to weather delays only, and he wouldn't take lightly to any interruption, for any other reason, which might adversely affect this. When they needed help the people in the lonely and almost forgotten harbours knew that Nicholls and the *Wasp* wouldn't let them down.

However, the difficulties arising from the interruption to his schedule paled into nothingness as the significance of the find became apparent on the voyage back to Westport.

Although the police hadn't been able to find the three who had been living in the house, despite an extensive search of the island, the fact had to be faced that there was a gun running plot in existence and the island had to be an important part of the network supporting it.

A small council of war was held in the wardroom during the two hours it took to reach Westport, attended by Nicholls and the four men who had led the eviction party. The feeling of all present was that the Fenians were behind it. When King mentioned the priest's remarks, it confirmed this.

At this stage all that could be done was to leave six policemen on the island overnight in an attempt to prevent anyone leaving. It was possible, of course, the three responsible were still on the island but nobody seriously expected them to be caught now. Still the presence of the police would make it very difficult for other weapons to be removed before a full scale search could be carried out the following day.

Pacing the bridge while Guppy practiced conning the ship through the familiar waters of its home port, King went back over his conversation with Carrington. Following the revelations about money and guns which he had been told were coming in from America he had little doubt that the rifles had come from the ship which the *Wasp* had failed to intercept. Carrington seemed certain that the compass had been interfered with by someone on board, but King couldn't accept this. Admittedly he had no evidence one way or the other but his instinct told him that the crew were loyal.

There wasn't any way he could think of to prove this, but there was one thing he could do, without anyone being the wiser, and that was to check the log for the name of the other ship, and since the log was in the chartroom behind the bridge that was easily done. A couple of minutes later he was reading the entries which recorded the ill fated attempt at a rendezvous.

This was the first time he had referred to the log with this objective in mind. Quickly he flicked through the baldly recorded details of courses, weather and other technical matters, none of which added anything to his knowledge. But the name of the ship was there. It was the barque *Liberator*, home port was Limerick, en route from Galveston to Liverpool.

Although this didn't add up to anything, he knew that he had at least found a definite starting point. Where it would lead was another matter.

The *Liberator*, he knew, was the affectionate nickname given to one of the great Irish parliamentarians, Daniel O'Connell, who was long since dead. O'Connell was a man determined to bring about Home Rule by constitutional means, unlike some of the pseudo patriots who called themselves Fenians.

That was an Irish connection. Not much on its own but the ship's home port of Limerick surely indicated that the captain knew these waters well. Finally, a barque was ideal for getting in and out of anchorages like Clare Island. A small three masted vessel with the two forward square rigged and the mizzen rigged fore and aft, it was highly manoeuverable and of shallow draft. Ideal! Even its destination had some significance, if of less validity. Liverpool with its huge Irish population was probably a hot bed of Fenian sympathisers, but following that line of enquiry was a job for someone else.

Arriving at this conclusion took up almost the whole two hours. Making the ship secure and finalising arrangements for the next day's programme, which would involve relieving the police left on the island, and then continuing the search for further weapons, took almost as long. So it was close on 22.00 hours when a weary George King finally stretched out on his bunk to consider his next step.

John Kerrigan came down the corridor a few minutes later, whistling and bearing a mug of tea and two sandwiches, saying that as he hadn't seen George at dinner he thought he might be peckish. To his surprise George discovered that he was ravenous and he sat up on the edge of his bunk to eat the snack. Kerrigan was, naturally, full of the events of the day.

'I say, George, what a stroke of luck it was that you were on hand to discover those fantastic rifles.'

'Steady on, I didn't discover them. The police did. In fact I almost didn't recognise the box when I saw it. But I agree, it was a stroke of luck. Did you hear anything about the three people who lived there? And what was so special about the rifles anyway?'

'Special? They're far ahead of anything we have.' He launched into a technical dissertation covering the rifling in the barrels of the guns, the capacity of the magazines, the rate of fire and accuracy of the sights, which King found totally uninteresting.

Having finished his mug of tea he had lain back thinking about the way Carrington's interpretation of current affairs had suddenly become very real and close to home, so was only half listening to Kerrigan when something the latter said jolted him back to full attention.

'I'm sorry, John. I missed that. What did you say?'

His cabinmate looked quizzically at him. 'I merely said that the resident magistrate — that was the one with the red pockmarked face and swordstick — is all for bringing the new Special Irish Branch into the investigation. The local inspector was a bit upset when he heard, but I think the RM will get his way. Don't you?'

'I suppose so. They always do.'

There was a silence as they considered the implications. Kerrigan was mildly interested in the prospect of seeing the new style police force in action and that was the extent of it. King, on the other hand, had a more direct and personal interest in the arrival of the SIB in Westport. A careless remark, an inadvertent or unguarded comment could reveal to another member of the crew his dual role. From now on he would have to be doubly careful or he would cease to be accepted by his shipmates. Another thought arose.

'I don't suppose you heard how long we are going to remain here, acting as ferrymen to the constabulary?' he asked casually.

'As a matter of fact I did. We return to Clare Island tomorrow and then, since the RM believes that we cannot contribute anything else of use to the investigation, we will be free to resume our summer patrol. A local fishing boat will take over as ferry when we leave. Why?'

'Just curious, that's all.' He let out a silent sigh of relief that his exposure to the needless risk he feared wasn't going to last long. He lay down again, turned down the paraffin lamp over the bunk and minutes later was fast asleep.

During the night the weather deteriorated. With first light an on-shore wind built up, increasing in strength until at 07.30, when the party of police and soldiers arrived, it was blowing almost a full gale. At 08.00 Nicholls decided that the ship's departure should be postponed until the weather improved.

This gave George an opportunity he had been waiting for. The chance to have an uninterrupted talk with Nicholls about Tom Guppy. Although he liked the young officer, he had reservations about him.

During the trip from Limerick he couldn't help but notice how Guppy's moods frequently fluctuated from loutish, bad mannered aggressiveness to friendly, cooperative comradeship, without warning or apparent reason. Apart from the uncertainty of not knowing what he was going to be met with, this aggressiveness was causing problems as the crew resented it. All of them, it seemed, considered it totally wrong that they should have to put up with needled arrogance and scorn from the inexperienced youth, and King agreed with them.

When he knocked on the door of Nicholls' cabin and was told to enter, he expected the captain to be annoyed when told this. But that wasn't the case.

Nicholls listened patiently as King detailed the problem, then sat back to consider it.

'I did know that Tom was becoming a nuisance, George, but don't take it too seriously. His bad behaviour started about a year ago when his twin brother died of typhoid fever. His brother was an army doctor who served in the Russo-Turkish War and picked up the fever on duty in the Ukraine. As you can imagine it was a terrible shock to him because they were very close.

'Of course, of course. I didn't know about his brother, but nevertheless we cannot let him go on abusing the crew. One of the petty officers' — he didn't mention Andrews by name — 'brought it to my attention again last night on rounds, reminding me that I had seen it for myself on the day I joined it. It wasn't very dignified, to say the least.'

'I'm sure that you're right, George. All right, I'll have a word with him before sailing time.'

King had intended mentioning, in confidence, his meeting

with Carrington on Sunday afternoon at Westpark Manor, his intention being to put the captain into the overall picture. This, he felt, was the least he was entitled to and he had no qualms at all in the light of the friendship which was growing between them. But that was before entering the cabin and having his problem treated so casually.

Disquieting doubts had now suddenly arisen. In King's opinion Guppy's behaviour was so serious and irrational that Nicholls should have been alarmed. An officer's treatment of his crew, which resulted in a responsible PO making a complaint, even though it was unofficial, merited more than a casual response. At best such treatment was bad for discipline, at worst mutiny, perhaps. Captain Bligh was still remembered in the Navy.

But Nicholls wasn't taking it seriously, and if the captain's judgement was at fault, though King sincerely hoped that he was wrong about this, then now was not the time to give him more problems.

He didn't consciously reason this out, he just came to the conclusion that it would be better left unsaid and picked up his cap from the table.

By noon the weather had improved and, with the landing party embarked once more, the captain took over from the OOW and ordered King to put to sea.

Clear of the quay, while going astern into deep water, the wind suddenly caught the *Wasp* broadside on and it took all of Nicholls' skill and experience to prevent a grounding. King, on the foredeck, was sure that she touched at one stage and wondered briefly if he had come to the end of his first permanent posting. However Bill Hudson had foreseen problems arising and had more than enough steam available when it was needed. Slowly the *Wasp* pulled clear of the rocks and with a blast on the whistle headed for Clare Island.

Following the disembarkation of the landing party normal routine was resumed. Relief supplies were unloaded on Achill Island but the islanders, unlike the recipients on the mainland whom King had seen, were unfriendly and uncommunicative. They refused even to speak to Otway Browne when he set up his clinic on the pierhead leaving him alone for the whole period that the *Wasp* was alongside. When he came back on board King asked him why no patients had turned up.

'Isn't anyone sick on Achill, surgeon? I noticed that you have had an easy day.'

'It's always the same, George. When we have helped to evict some poor devil, none of the Irish want to know us. We might as well be lepers and the crew feel the shame of what we have to do. You'll recognise it when you have been on board a bit longer.' With that he went into his cabin and King heard the door bolt being shot.

Uncertainly he tried to raise the matter with the others at dinner but very quickly realised that it was a touchy subject which nobody wanted to discuss. Short answers, that said very little, were the best he could raise forcing him to drop the matter for the time being.

During the following few days while the unseasonable weather continued they stayed in Blacksod Bay, visiting the small harbours on its fringes. Each was the same as the one before with only the minimum contact with the natives. Friendly gifts of fresh fish and the occasional turnip ceased, to be replaced by a sullen acceptance, as if under duress, of the supplies being unloaded. This led to a growing resentment which was voiced by Rattenbury the next time he was on watch with King.

'What is wrong with these people, sir? Don't they understand that we don't evict them, our job here is to help them? The way they go on, letting us know that we aren't welcome but still taking the supplies we bring, would make you wonder if they know what we're doing. Do they know that we have to do as we're told? I can tell you, sir, that we are just about fed up with them all and as far as the lower deck is concerned, we'll be happy to see the back of them.'

The indignant outburst took King by surprise. Simply because he hadn't considered the possibility, he hadn't realised that all the crew had been affected. Nor had he directly faced the fact that the efficiency of the ship was suffering because of the part the crew had played in the eviction. A fed-up crew caused trouble which made them dangerous to themselves and to the ship. King had no answer to give.

Fortunately Rattenbury didn't give him time to answer.

Pale faced, he looked appalled at King. 'I'm sorry sir. I didn't mean to speak to you like that. It isn't any of my business. I didn't mean to tell you what your job is. I'm sorry.'

'I'm sure you didn't, Rattenbury,' King reassured him. 'And if it is any comfort to you, you aren't the only one who isn't at all at ease with the present situation. Have you noticed this happen before?'

There was silence as the petty officer considered his answer.

'Not to this extent, sir. But one of the seamen, James Eva, was going on about it two nights ago in the mess and he said something that struck me as very peculiar. He said that, apart from the way the locals treat us, every time we take part in an eviction something always happens the ship. Some bit of bad luck always follows. Mind you, sir, I don't hold with such superstition myself but could it be that we are cursed?'

King was astonished at this admission from a man whom he already respected as a level headed, no nonsense petty officer. He searched the face before him for some sign that he was joking but it was only too apparent that he wasn't. Rattenbury couldn't have been in more deadly earnest.

'Do you really believe that? I know that sailors are reputed to be very superstitious.' He smiled to show Rattenbury that he didn't consider this too serious. 'But this is, after all, a modern ship of the Royal Navy and we don't set any store by such old wives tales. Cursed indeed? I doubt very much if that could be so . . .'

His voice tailed off as a vague memory surfaced reminding him that someone else had said this same thing earlier. He couldn't remember who it was though. He put it from his mind and continued speaking . , .

'Besides, nothing happened to us following the Clare Island eviction.'

'That's true, sir. But something nearly did. And the trip isn't over yet.'

'I don't understand. What nearly did?'

'Don't you remember, sir. As we were leaving Westport with the soldiers and police we all but went aground. You were on the foredeck, you must have noticed it, sir? We were within a hair's breadth of hitting the rocks beam on, then the captain gave the order for full steam ahead when we were going astern at the time, and the stern came round. Just in the nick of time.'

'Now that you mention it, I had forgotten. But that must have been a coincidence. Every ship has good and bad luck at different times. There's never been one that was lucky all the time.'

'I know that, sir. But whether it was a coincidence or not, we could have lost the ship. Since Eva mentioned it I have been thinking about the other times when things have gone wrong for us. You heard about the trouble we had with the engine last year? That was the same sort of coincidence and it happened after an eviction we took part in. In West Galway that was. We would have lost the *Wasp* that time had we been depending on the engine but with the sails we got back to port safely. Then when we went into dock and the ship was inspected nothing was found to be wrong. I tell you, sir, something is causing these coincidences. Or at least Eva says so,' he finished lamely.

'Maybe you're right but I doubt it. Anyway, we have survived so far, let's wait and see if anything further happens. Now, when we put to sea tomorrow I want you to get a party chipping rust off the gun platform and railings. It's a disgrace.'

'Aye aye, sir.'

The rest of the watch was completed in silence but King's mind worked furiously as he considered Rattenbury's extraordinary theory. Of course there couldn't be any substance in such a ridiculous idea, but he had been standing on the foredeck and he too thought that the *Wasp* was going to strike and had that happened nothing could have saved the ship.

Suddenly he remembered where he had heard the suggestion that the *Wasp* was cursed. His friend Hannon, on the *Sea Witch* had mentioned it and nobody could ever describe him as 'an old woman'. Maybe? Just maybe there was something going on he didn't understand. He decided not to dismiss it completely, at least for the moment.

5   On Board the *Alona*

Two weeks had gone by since Joyce and I had started our research into the loss of the *Wasp*. Actually 'research' hardly describes my contribution as I was still hobbling around Rathmullen, discussing the events of the day with the locals and spending an hour or so in the late evenings with the log of Lieutenant George King, RN.

Joyce, on the other hand, was taking the investigation much more seriously.

Armed with photocopies of the original manuscript she had gone back to her university in Galway to research the background. For a couple of days I heard nothing from her, then a card arrived saying that she was making progress and would be back at the weekend.

That pleased me enormously as I had discovered how much I missed her and so on Friday evening I was sitting, like an anxious schoolboy, outside the local hotel waiting for the first sign of her car.

To my relief she seemed pleased to see me, though maybe not quite as much as I was to see her. But she agreed, after making a quick phone call to her home, to have dinner with me in the hotel. It was to be a nice, peaceful dinner at which we could bring each other up to date, in romantic surroundings – or so I thought.

Inside the hotel was packed. A small flotilla of yachts had come across Lough Swilly from Fahan, with an average of six on board each one and everyone determined to enjoy themselves.

The owner of the hotel was in the bar, being assisted by a youth who was, it seemed, totally incapable of either getting an order right or producing the correct change. This led to complete confusion and a lot of shouting and laughing, adding to the din as the customers struggled to make themselves heard. A quick glance into this chaos and we turned towards the dining room.

Here everything was quieter, not peaceful exactly, but certainly quieter although the room was full. Some of the 'yotties' were at tables, waiting to get a meal and passing the time reasonably patiently as they worked their way through the stockpile of drinks they had assembled in front of themselves. There was a certain amount of boisterousness as they conversed with each other in loud voices across the intervening tables but, on the whole, it was an improvement on the bar.

As we watched from the doorway a couple of residents rose from a window table for two and we made a dash to claim it.

'I thought for a few minutes that we hadn't a hope of getting a table,' Joyce remarked as she moved the empty coffee cups to one side. Then she glanced around the room.

'Most of these people seem to be from Derry.'

'Really?' I was surprised. 'While waiting for you I met a couple of them and they said that they were from Fahan. That's in the Republic, isn't it?'

'It is, but quite a number of sailing people from Derry keep their boats there. It is only about twelve miles from the city, and they like to get out of Northern Ireland to relax. They think it is safer here, though sometimes I wonder.'

This conversation was carried out almost at the top of our voices. What with locals, visitors to the area like myself, hotel residents, and the 'yotties' from Fahan there were about sixty people in the dining room being served by three semi-trained local waitresses, so delays were inevitable. Not that this bothered anyone very much. For myself, I was quite happy to be sitting across the table from Joyce, nodding in agreement, or in sympathy, as she tried to tell me about the progress of her research.

I could only hear the occasional word, certainly not enough to make any sense of what she said, but I guessed which nod would be appropriate from her expression and got it right most of the time. During the recounting one of the overworked waitresses came to clear the table and I persuaded her to bring a bottle of wine which we sipped while waiting for our meal to be served.

Suddenly the lights went out.

We were in darkness for just a couple of seconds, then the lights came back on again and some of the Derry people started to cheer. Just like we used to do when the reel in the one-projector cinema broke when I was much younger.

Five seconds or so later the lights went out again and a whistle was blown from, I gathered, the reception desk. The dining room went silent.

'My God, I don't believe this,' said Joyce. As the lights con-

tinued to flick on and off there was a general movement throughout the room. The diners were getting to their feet as she caught
me by the hand and pulled me up.

'Let's get out of here, now! Come on. Through the kitchen, I
know the way.'

Totally bewildered I let her lead me by the hand towards the
kitchen entrance, followed by ten or twelve people from nearby
tables who had heard her.

'What is going on, Joyce? Where are we going?'

By then we were passing through the deserted kitchen where
pots still simmered gently on the stainless steel stoves and plates
with food waited to be collected by the waitresses. The lights had
now steadied, remaining alight, as the hotel quickly emptied onto
the lawn.

Once outside she found time to talk.

'There is a bomb scare on. The flashing lights and the whistle
were the warning for everyone to evacuate the premises. Look
around. Everyone seems to have got out, including the staff. Now
we just wait for the Army to get here from Letterkenny and
knowing them that could take an hour. Or even more.' A thought
struck her. 'I don't suppose that you are a bomb disposal expert,
by any chance?'

'So that's what it is all about. A bomb scare? How do you
know that it isn't a real warning? And no, my dear Joyce, I am
definitely not in the bomb disposal business. Sorry.'

'A pity. Still, one can't have everything I suppose. But that is
the end of our dinner date, I'm afraid. Whether it is just a scare,
or the real thing, our meal won't be worth eating by the time the
Army is finished with the place. Come on, I've got an idea.'

Nothing loath I took her arm and we made our way around
the hotel to the car park. Driving out we had to take our turn in
the queue of cars leaving in case the building blew up with a bang.

Even the 'yotties' were straggling out, heading for the nearest
pub where they might get a couple of sausage rolls as a poor
substitute for their missed dinners. I settled back in silence
waiting to see what Joyce had in mind.

The journey wasn't much more than a hundred yards. Stopping
the car outside a shop, she jumped out and knocked on the door.
A light came on inside and the door opened. She entered, the
door closed again. A few minutes later she reappeared carrying a
parcel.

'How do you fancy a nice big steak with all the trimmings?'

'Great. Are we going back to your house?'

'No. Dad isn't well and I don't want to disturb him. He knows we were going to have dinner in the hotel and if he heard that there was a bomb scare he would be upset. So I've thought of a better idea. Let's eat on the boat.'

This suited me perfectly. On the boat we would be free from interruption and eating a well cooked meal, in good company, on a boat moored on a motionless sea under the moon is perfect bliss. I told her so, then suggested that I buy the wine and got her to pull up at the village off-licence. Minutes later we were rowing silently out the hundred yards or so to where the *Alona* lay.

An hour passed very quickly. Joyce busied herself in the tiny galley as I laid the table in the walnut and pine panelled saloon, lit by the soft glow from the low powered lamps. The blue corduroy upholstered settee creating a cosy, intimate atmosphere which the radio in the background enhanced.

When I had lowered the two bottles of wine carefully over the side in a small net, to cool, I stretched out comfortably on the settee to watch her work.

'This is where we should have come in the first place,' I remarked thoughtfully. 'Isn't it odd how one can be blind to a . . .' I groped for the right word, then came up with . . . 'an amenity like this, right under one's nose?'

I caught the quick glance she threw me as she stirred the onions and mushrooms simmering in the pan. 'Very odd, indeed. Do you often miss, 'er, amenities under your nose then?' she asked innocently.

'Sometimes. Take tonight for example. My intention to wine and dine you in the hotel was totally misguided. I see that now. But you were the person with the answer.' I tried to bow in acknowledgement while still stretched out, and managed a deep nod. 'Actually, I sometimes think I am totally blind in these matters and if someone were to dig a hole in the social environment in which I move, I would without a doubt fall into it. That is, if I could find it,' I added in a deep mournful voice.

She laughed as she took the plates from the grill where they had been warming and dished up the two big steaks smothered in the vegetables. 'Let's see if you can find the bottles of wine. I hope they are still part of the social environment and haven't fallen to the bottom of the sea.'

Fortunately they hadn't. The meal was eaten in leisurely, companionable silence, broken only by comments of appreciation and encouragement to eat more. The wine wasn't anything special but that didn't matter. It was cold, palatable and when I raised my glass to toast her at the end of the meal, it couldn't have served the purpose better had it been the finest champagne.

'Let's have our coffee on deck. It really is a beautiful night.'

I grabbed an armful of cushions and spread them around the small cockpit. As I did I looked across the dark water towards the hotel from which I could hear a dance band playing, or maybe it was a radio. Whatever it was it seemed that the bomb scare was over and the hotel was back in business. The night was still and the moon about to come up.

A few moments later we were sitting sipping from mugs of coffee which had been generously laced with brandy.

'I raided the first-aid box for the brandy,' explained Joyce, 'but I am reasonably confident that we won't need it for medicinal purposes tonight.' She moved slightly closer, as if to get out of a draught. 'Now do you want to hear how my research has been going? I don't think that you got it all when I tried telling you in the hotel.'

Putting down my mug I put my arm around her shoulder and drew her closer.

'I would love to hear all about your research, but I can only concentrate on one thing at a time. And as my eyes have suddenly been opened I want to catch up on some research of my own.'

Next moment she was inside both my arms and I kissed her.

For a few seconds I wondered was I going to get my face slapped. Then she responded, her arms went around my neck, and she moved even closer.

Coming up for air, but being careful not to move far away I told her how I'd missed her while she had been in Galway. I didn't say I loved her, because I wasn't at all sure that I did, but I knew that I was beginning a more important relationship than ever before and liking it. Just then, however, all she wanted to hear was that I had missed her. She leaned back and looked at me as if she had never seen me before, then put her hands on each side of my face.

'I've missed you too. You don't know this but ever since I was a schoolgirl I've been in love with you. For years I didn't think it would come to anything but now that we're here I can tell you that it is everything I dreamed of. Now kiss me again.'

I don't know how long it was before either of us remembered the dishes piled up in the sink, but eventually we realised that the music ashore had stopped, the hotel was in darkness and the moon almost down.

Then it was back to reality with a rush. Water was heated as the saloon was tidied up and made ship-shape again, dishes washed and stowed away, hatches secured and the dinghy loaded with the debris of the meal for disposal ashore. Finally the row back to the pier and the car.

As the tail lights of the mini disappeared along the shore road and I walked the short distance home, it dawned on me that I still hadn't heard the results of her research. But there was always tomorrow . . . tonight I had other things to remember and other thoughts to think.

The next morning dawned warm and sunny and to my mother's astonishment I was out and about shortly after seven o'clock with about four hours sleep behind me. Actually I was a bit astonished too, I hadn't been up so early since attending Britannia College in Dartmouth years earlier.

I made myself breakfast, ate it, glanced through the previous day's newspapers and it was still quite a few minutes short of eight. Bored, I went outside and sat on the garden seat, wondering why time was hanging so heavily. Then deciding to put it to use I went into the sitting room and took the Admiralty chart of the north west coast of Ireland, which I had been using to plot the last voyage of the *Wasp*, from the writing desk drawer.

Going outside I went over it once more, for probably the fiftieth time, and wondered just what had happened on the fateful night of 22 September, 1884.

The log of Lieutenant King finished the day before the ship was lost. That was understandable. But during the two months, or so, that he had been aboard the *Wasp* he must have formed some opinions about his fellow crew members which might provide an answer. Towards the end he had become chummy with the captain and developed total confidence in him, but little about the others which might have helped, appeared in the log. It was all very frustrating.

Leaving the chart and log on the hall table since I wasn't getting anywhere, I decided to find out what had happened the night before, after we had left the hotel. Obviously it hadn't been blown up, we had sat listening to the dance music across the water, and now, as it was almost time to collect the daily papers and mail in from Dublin and the rest of the world, I could kill two birds with one stone. I headed for the village.

The village newsagent is the source of all wisdom amd knowledge. Nothing goes on in the area which he doesn't know about. Perhaps not immediately, but sooner or later he knows it all. So when I arrived at the shop shortly after eight I wasn't at all surprised to find four or five customers already there discussing the happenings of the previous night in the hotel.

Waiting to speak to him I went across the small shop to look at the magazines displayed on the racks. Browsing through one I couldn't help overhearing the conversation behind my back.

'Is that so? Do they know who did it then?'

'I hear they do, but they're not letting on. Anyway it was just done out of badness. Sure half these fellas are too thick to make a wee bomb even if the instructions were pinned up on a wall in front of them. But it is easy enough to pick up a phone and say one is planted. Any fool can do that.'

'Aye indeed. But why? We've had no trouble here up to now. Why would they do it? And which side was it anyway?'

'The fella who made the phone call said that he was with the IRA and that the bomb was planted because the hotel was accommodating British soldiers. It was just as well there was no bomb, because there wasn't any British soldiers there either, just thon crowd from Derry out for a good time and the holidaymakers who've been there all week.'

'Well, I hope they get the bugger. We can do without that sort of nut case, ruining the tourist trade and giving us all a bad name.'

This last opinion brought forth several murmurs of agreement as the customers took their departure. I put the magazine I was looking at back on the rack and moved across to the counter.

'Did I hear someone say that they hadn't found a bomb at all? That it was all a hoax?'

'That's right, sir. Irish Times and Daily Mail, isn't it?'

As he took the money which I was holding out he continued. 'Like most wee villages around here we have our share of lunatics. They aren't all locked up in Letterkenny Asylum, you know. And the one who rang the hotel was definitely one of ours.'

'How can you know that?' Such a positive assertion made me curious and interested.

As there wasn't anybody else in the shop he was prepared to tell me. 'Well, consider all the trouble and upset that was caused to the hotel by making that phone call at that time. Right in the middle of dinner. With a full dining room too. The guests could, and did, go elsewhere for their meal, didn't they? So it was aimed at the hotel and that makes it personal as I see it.'

I nodded and asked him to go on.

'Next, only a local is likely to have a personal grudge against the hotel, which is owned by a local family and gives good employment to the village every summer. If it was the IRA from Derry or Buncrana, or somewhere like that, they have enough targets on their own doorsteps not to have to bother with a wee one here. And, the receptionist who took the call thought she recognised the voice as that of a local chap who got sacked a fortnight ago for drinking. Maybe it was, and maybe it wasn't, I don't know. But it all adds up.'

'Maybe. But wouldn't a local know that there weren't any British soldiers there? I heard one of the customers in here a few minutes ago say that that was the reason for the call.'

'That's what he said all right. And that's curious. Because I haven't heard anything at all about soldiers being there. But then the IRA isn't famous for telling the truth and one excuse is as good as another if it was the IRA.' As he was talking he moved away to deal with customers who had just then entered. Picking up my papers I left the shop.

Walking back home I mulled over what I had heard. Could the newsagent be right and it was just a malicious hoax by a local with a grudge? Or was it more sinister? A warning from a politically twisted supporter of the IRA who believed he was striking a blow for the freedom of the Republic? That lunatic theory might hold a little water if there actually was at least one British soldier there and the newsagent hadn't heard that there was. Well, it wasn't any of my business, besides I had more important matters on my mind, like seeing Joyce again, maybe going sailing too. The day ahead was full of pleasurable possibilities.

However it was more than two hours later before she arrived. By then I had read both papers from front to back and had started over again. When I heard her car pull up I eagerly went to the hall door to meet her with a warmth stemming almost entirely from the boredom I had been suffering from all morning.

'Hey, what's this for?' She laughed as she drew back from the kiss I had just planted on her lips. 'It isn't even lunch time yet, or haven't you noticed?'

'I'm just glad to see you again, that's all.' To tell the truth I was a bit surprised at how glad I was to see her, not having realised that I was missing her the more and more I waited for her. Any-

way, she passed it off with a laugh, instead of making fun of me
as I feared. I think that was when I knew I was in love. But it
was far too early to say anything as soppy as that.

'Well, here I am. Now let's sit here in the sun and discuss the
progress each of us has made concerning the mysterious loss of
Her Majesty's Ship *Wasp*. Go and put the coffee on while I get
my notes organised.

Her research had involved old records in both the university
and public libraries for background material on the three or four
years leading up to September 1884. It also meant going through
copies of century old newspapers which told the stories of the survivors, filling in the findings of the court-martial which enquired
into the tragedy and analysing the details so helpfully provided
by the naval historical branch of the Ministry of Defence in
London. I was most impressed.

My own contribution was decidedly less exciting. I had plotted
the *Wasp*'s route on my chart, drawn wind and current vectors,
estimated probable courses and tracks made good, allowed for
known variation and guesstimated deviation, taken the absence
of a moon that night into consideration, made provision for the
time of night when the accident happened and the fact that most
of the crew would have been asleep down below . . . and hadn't
a clue where it all pointed.

When I made this confession she sat back, staring at the chart
spread out before us, pulled on her lower lip, then said, 'Well,
there isn't anything else for it.'

'For what?' I asked bewilderedly.

'I've been thinking about this for the past week and now that
I've seen all the work you've put into this . . .' I looked sharply
at her to see if she was being funny, but she was deadly serious.
'. . . my mind is made up. We'll leave tomorrow morning about
first light. That's . . . let me see . . . about 04.50. I'll meet you
down on the pier then.'

'Hold on there for one minute. What is all this about meeting
me on the pier at some god forsaken hour tomorrow? Where are
we going? I'm an invalid and need my sleep, you know.'

'Nonsense. If you're an invalid I'm a mermaid. Tomorrow we
head south in the *Alona* as far as Donegal Bay. Once there we
heave-to and wait.'

'Wait for what?'

'Oh didn't I say? Sorry. We wait until it is time to return so
that we arrive at Tory Island at 03.30, same as the *Wasp*. We are

going to retrace the last few hours of that poor ship's life as closely as we can. I know that we won't be able to have everything the same, the weather will be different I suppose, but as far as we can I want to see if following in its track will give us a lead. Your work on this chart will be invaluable. We'll be able to make allowances for the wind that night and we'll be able to figure out courses and so forth from my papers. Maybe, just maybe, we'll be able to solve the mystery once and for all.'

'My darling Joyce, I honestly believe that you are out of your gorgeous mind. Do you seriously think it will work? Mind you I will not say "no" to another trip with you, in your boat which, after last night, I will always look on with affection, but I must tell you that I have the gravest doubts about all this. The very, very gravest doubts.'

'Don't be such a pessimist. I bet we'll find out something that nobody else knows. Just wait and see. Now, what have you been doing since I saw you last?'

'Funny you should ask that. Tell me, did you notice any members of the British Army in the hotel last night?'

'No, why?'

I told her about my conversation with the newsagent earlier, and his theory that one of the locals had made the hoax call because of a grudge with the hotel. She looked doubtfully at me when I finished.

'What exactly did the caller say?'

'Well, I don't know exactly, but the gist of it was that it was the IRA calling to say that a bomb had been planted because the hotel was catering to British soldiers and it would go off in a few minutes. When the bomb disposal team arrived there wasn't any bomb and that was that. Just an ordinary, everyday bomb scare.'

'I don't like this one little bit.' Now she looked worried. 'You said the receptionist recognised the voice and thought it was a local on the phone?'

'That's right. Someone who had got the boot for drinking.'

'You've been home now for, how long?'

'Three weeks, closer to a month. Why?'

'Most of the locals know you by now and know that you are in the British forces though they might not know you are in the Navy. Perhaps it wasn't directed at the hotel at all. Perhaps it was directed at you.'

'My God.' I suddenly had to sit down. 'You aren't serious?'

'I'm perfectly serious, though I hope that I'm wrong. But one way or another, I don't want you going into the hotel again under any circumstances. From now on you adopt a very low profile.'

I couldn't believe what I was hearing. Why should the IRA be bothered with me? I was a local, born and bred, though I had been away for a long time. Away where, though? In the Navy. But the Navy isn't involved in the Irish troubles? Or is it? I couldn't remember for a minute. No, it definitely isn't and neither is the RAF. What's the RAF got to do with this? This is the Republic, not the North and I'm as Irish as anyone in Donegal so to hell with the IRA. I stood up again, looking at Joyce, and was shocked at the worried expression in her eyes. This was definitely not the time to throw down the gauntlet, no matter how steamed up I was at the temerity of some bloody-minded, half-witted, would-be terrorist. Not if doing something foolhardy was going to put both our families into danger, no matter how remote the possibility was.

'Okay. You're the boss. Whatever you say. Maybe it is a good thing that we're going sailing in the morning after all. Now, what would you say to spending the afternoon in Rosapenna having a swim and early dinner? Then home for an early night.'

She put her arms around my neck, leaning back to look into my face. 'I'd say yes please. Darling I'm probably wrong about all of this but it would be silly to take chances, especially now that your leave is almost over and you'll be going back to work soon. I'm glad, though, you see it my way. Now, let's tell your Mum where we are going but don't say anything about the incident at the hotel.'

On that cautionary note we left for Rosapenna where one of the biggest hotels in Donegal is situated right beside the sea.

The following morning, shortly after five o'clock, as planned, I winched the anchor on board while Joyce tightened the mainsail sheet and the graceful *Alona* slipped quietly down Lough Swilly to the sea.

6   The Hulk of the *La Brujula*

During the past few days there has been a steady and welcome improvement in the weather and we have been able
to unload all the relief supplies on board as well as doing
some of our normal work into the bargain. As this involves
carrying out survey work for the harbour commissioners,
who have been building piers and jetties in the most unlikely
places, as a means of providing relief work, the skill of the
captain has been frequently put to the test to keep us from
going aground on unmarked rocks. The more I get to know
him the more respect I have for his ability as a seaman and
the more I approve of him as a person. On the other hand
Tom Guppy is almost unbearable at times and his treatment
of the crew is that of the worst type of bully. I cannot understand why the captain doesn't take action and surprised it
hasn't led to trouble.

As the ship threaded her way out from Broad Haven on the
north west corner of Mayo and turned towards Erris Head and
the run south to Westport, everyone on board was relieved.

Even George King was aware of the change in the crew and
felt himself react to it. It hadn't been a happy trip. First there
was the near accident in Westport, then the hostility of the locals
had bred resentment in the crew, and the bad weather which
made the inshore work very difficult capped it all.

Some of the older company even took a delight in trotting out
old wives' tales about ships with curses on them and King had
no doubt he knew who was behind that. However, being a com-
parative newcomer he felt that he should leave whatever action
the captain felt should be taken, to someone else. Kerrigan, for
instance, could deal with it if necessary.

So this afternoon, following a good lunch, he was content as
he paced the bridge as officer of the watch. The sea was calm,
the wind a gentle Force Three, and the prospect of a few days

alongside the jetty in Westport pleasing to consider.

He still had one or two worries. Not too big but still they were niggly. He was concerned in case he had misjudged the captain and that whatever had been bothering him in Limerick would arise again. If it did he wondered would he have the courage to take over the command or the understanding to give Nicholls his support when it was needed. Fervently he hoped that choice would never have to be made.

Another worry he had was the advantage Tom Guppy was taking of the latitude the captain was allowing him. Since he had mentioned this to Nicholls there hadn't been any improvement in the Sub's behaviour, and now he doubted if the captain had spoken to him at all. Both Rattenbury and Andrews had mentioned it to him but he had no answer for them.

Looking around the peaceful scene and the green hills off to port he decided to put these worries to the back of his mind. Two days earlier he had received a letter from Caroline which she had sent care of the postmaster in Belmullet. Already he had read it so often that he practically knew it by heart.

It couldn't really be described as an affectionate letter, much less a love letter, but as it was the first one she had sent him it had an importance which bore no relationship to the contents. The letter merely said that she hoped he was having a very pleasant voyage and that she was looking forward to seeing him again when the ship returned, on or about 15 August. She added that her father sent his respects also and that George was to dine with the family when it would be convenient. She signed the letter 'with respect' above her name.

But in the tail of the final letter forming her name there was a tiny vertical stroke, forming an almost unnoticeable cross, the symbol surely signifying a kiss.

As he was putting the letter away, having read it for the first time, with a feeling of pleasurable anticipation at seeing her again, he suddenly spotted the cross. Disbelievingly he took the letter out again and studied it. Was it deliberate or accidental? He couldn't make his mind up, it looked deliberate one minute, the next it was just an idle stroke of her pen which meant nothing. The problem had him excited or dejected, depending on how he interpreted the rest of the letter when searching it for a clue, but he couldn't find an answer.

As she hadn't been very far from his thoughts since the first time they had met he was more than pleased at receiving a letter from her. But to expect more than friendship would be, he was sure, presumptuous of him. There must be dozens of young men in London whom she preferred and it was a well known fact in every family with a marriageable daughter, that lieutenants in the Royal Navy were not amongst the most desirable catches. In fact they rated pretty far down the list, somewhere between a small farmer and an apprentice dentist.

Still, 'sufficient unto the day'. Even a little hope, no matter how unrealistic, could keep one's spirits up. With this thought in his mind he noticed Nicholls appear up the bridge ladder, and called out to the helmsman.

'Heading, cox'n?'

'Steady on west, sir.'

The captain went to the front of the bridge and peered over the screen at the sailors, in small groups on deck, apparently enjoying themselves. He turned to King.

'Stand by to break out sail, navigator.'

'Aye aye, sir.' He turned and repeated the order to the bosun who had been waiting for it. Immediately there was a scurry of feet as the men took up their positions in response to the trilling of the bosun's whistle. King moved to the engine room telegraph and put his hand on the brass lever.

'Steady as she goes. Break out sail.' The captain's voice was calm and unhurried. 'Engine room, stand by.'

For a few minutes apparent chaos reigned as the sails tumbled down from the yards and spars, then filled and bellied with a series of cracks and bangs as the sheets snapped taut. The engine room telegraph rang twice, signalling it was standing by and that the engineer was waiting to bank down the fire.

The bosun had been closely watching the activity on deck and turned to King.

'All sail broken out, sir.'

Both Nicholls and King turned to watch the cox'n casually move the huge wheel a few spokes, first to the left, then right, then left again. Then steadying it he called out, with his eyes fixed on the compass in front of him, 'Steady on west, sir.'

'Very good, Mr King. I'll be in my cabin. Call me when the next change of course is due.' He left the bridge and made his way down the ladder.

The whistle on the voice pipe from the engine room blew. The bosun pulled it from the tube, then listened by putting his ear to the opening. King waited.

'Sir, can the engineer bank down the fire now?'

'Very well, but the captain will want it at twenty minutes readiness for the next two hours.'

This was repeated and the whistle replaced in the tube.

'The engineer said he understands, Mr King.'

From the deck below the bridge the ship's bell was struck twice. Hearing it the bosun asked King for permission to pipe the hands to tea, then left to supervise the issue of food from the galley. King and the helmsman remained alone on the bridge.

While the *Wasp*'s performance when steaming was a respectable 9½ knots, under sail it fell sharply to, at best, 6 knots. This could only be achieved under favourable conditions and a Force Three, which would be described on land as a gentle breeze, did not constitute ideal sailing conditions. So progress was made in what might best be called a dignified wallow. The ten miles or so to the point where the course would be changed to head south was, therefore, to King's experienced eye going to take over two hours.

As a result, the atmosphere on the bridge was relaxed. There wasn't any sign of a change in the weather, the coast slipping past five miles away wasn't a hazard and a peaceful run all the way back to Westport could confidently be anticipated.

Had Petty Officer Rattenbury been with him, King would have engaged him in conversation, if only to break the monotony. But as it was someone whom he didn't know very well on the wheel, he contented himself pacing to and fro in silence. At the end of each traverse of the full width of the bridge he stopped, glanced fore and aft along the side of the ship, turned and walked to the opposite wing where he did exactly the same. Occasionally he stopped amidships, glanced over the sails which hadn't been changed since they were set, then resumed his pacing.

Without warning, everything changed.

Although apparently outwardly alert and attending to his duties, King's mind was miles away. He knew that on his return to Westport he would be expected to submit a report to Carrington of the SIB, and since, following a month on board, he had been unable to find anything at all which might be considered suspicious, treasonable, or even detrimental to the efficiency and performance of Her Majesty's Ship *Wasp*, he intended writing one which would exonerate both ship and crew.

Putting it together, however, was quite another matter. He knew that both Captain Whitehouse in Queenstown and Mr Carrington wanted a scapegoat, convinced that something was wrong.

This problem had recurred to him regularly as the date of return to Westport drew closer, until now it was the most compelling consideration in his mind. As he paced to and fro, his mind actively explored every possible circumstance and situation since he had joined the ship, seeking unsuccessfully to find a way to use them to close the files. Concentrating on the problem he at first failed to hear the helmsman call him.

'Sir, sir! The lookout . . .' The urgency in the man's voice penetrated King's problem. Suddenly aware of his whereabouts, he focussed on what was being said.

Seeing that the OOW was listening the helmsman pointed up at the crosstrees on the forrard mast. 'The lookout, sir. He's been calling the bridge.' As he spoke, the bosun raced up the bridge ladder saying, as he reached the top, 'The lookout, sir, he . . .' He stopped when he saw that King had picked up the megaphone and was about to hail the lookout.

'Lookout . . . What's up?' he shouted.

'Bridge. Object in the water, dead ahead,' the man in the crow's nest yelled through cupped hands.

King peered ahead across the spray screen but couldn't see anything. However, he knew that what the lookout could see was much more than he could see from the lower vantage point of the bridge. He called to the bosun, who was anxiously searching ahead, from the other side of the helmsman.

'Bosun, pipe general alarm, and get the captain up here immediately. Helmsman, bear four points to port.' He put the megaphone to his mouth again, pointing towards the lookout.

'Lookout . . .' He waited until the man acknowledged with a wave. 'Lookout, how far ahead?'

'About half a cable or less. It seems to be a vessel floating just below the surface. No sign of life.'

'What's going on, mister?'

Recognising the captain's voice King lowered his megaphone to face the man at his side.

'Object in the water, dead ahead, sir. About half a cable or less. I can't see it from here.' He swung round to watch the helmsman who was looking anxiously ahead while holding the wheel as far round as it would go. What's the heading now?'

'Still steady on west. We haven't enough steerage way to bring her bow around, sir.'

King picked up the voice pipe and blew into the mouth piece. When it blew back he took out the whistle.

'Engineroom, we need steam. Right now. Have you got it?'

As he listened he glanced at the captain and raised his eyes heavenwards. 'Well, what you have. Right now.' He replaced the voice pipe, then reached behind to move the brass engine-room telegraph lever from 'Finished with engine' to 'Full ahead'. The bell rang in answer.

'For what it is worth, sir. There is very little pressure in the boiler now. It will take at least fifteen or twenty minutes to bring it back up and if we use what is remaining now it will take even longer to get full power. I've told him to give us all he has got. In twenty minutes we won't need it.'

The lookout's frantic voice was heard again. 'Bear away, bear away. We're going to strike.'

By now all the crew members were at their action stations wondering what was going on. As they couldn't see any other ship they were confident that they weren't going to be attacked but from the shouted conversation between lookout and bridge it was obvious that this wasn't an exercise either.

Underfoot, those on the bridge felt the vibration of the engine as it slowly turned under the effect of the low pressure steam. Fingers tightly gripping the edge of the screen, King and Nicholls waited for the worst. Behind them, the helmsman in a relieved voice, said 'Turning now, sir.'

As he spoke the *Wasp* and submerged object met.

The impact wasn't at all severe. There was a slow, heavy grinding noise as the two hulls absorbed the shock of collision, the bow of the *Wasp* rose out of the water, riding over the object beneath, then poised, hung on top of it for what seemed an age but couldn't have been for more than twenty seconds or so. Very, very slowly it sank back to its rightful level, and as it did, about twenty feet to starboard, the capsized bow of a ship reared up.

With water streaming from its ports and bow it came up to about fifty degrees from the horizontal and stayed there, pinned in position by the *Wasp*. There was a shocked silence from the crew, watching as if mesmerised.

The bosun recovered first. 'Let go all sheets. Jump to it lads, lively now.'

His voice broke the spell and the sailors raced to the bulwarks, snatching at the belaying pins to pull them clear so that the neatly coiled lines suspended from them could fall free. Released from the constricting ropes the sails billowed out, then hung flapping from the yards.

This took the way off the ship and with the engine now using the last of the steam to go astern, it ponderously, awkwardly and slowly extricated itself. Minutes later the *Wasp* lay motionless alongside the hulk, now lying sideways in the water and visible for its full length.

'Bosun, stand by to lower the gig. Mr King, tell the gunner to take a party aboard the hulk. I want to know what it is and anything else he can find out about it.' He looked at the sky, studying it, and then at the horizon. 'I don't think there will be any change in the weather for the next few hours, but I don't want to hang about here either. By the way, you might let the engineroom know that we have finished with engine and have the carpenter and engineer check the hull for damage.'

Discomfited at having forgotten to let the engineroom know what was happening, he hurriedly made up for it, then made for the bridge ladder to seek out Kerrigan, whom he thought would be at his action station on the forrard gun platform. Kerrigan had already left the deck, on his way below to secure the magazine, since it was obvious that he wouldn't have to engage an enemy by gunfire and he turned back when King caught up with him. Both men made their way to the davits where the gig had already been swung out and was being held, awaiting the boarding party.

Nicholls, watching from the wing of the bridge, called down, 'Mr Kerrigan, rig a line from the hulk to ourselves so that she doesn't drift too far, and take care. It could sink at any moment.'

Kerrigan acknowledged the instruction, then followed his party aboard the gig. A command from the bosun and it was lowered into the sea. A couple of minutes later the party was scrambling up the weed covered side of the hulk seeking a way to enter.

By this time everyone on board the *Wasp* who hadn't been given a specific task, was at the rail watching the five who had boarded the hulk, waiting to see what would happen next.

The evening was calm and they could easily hear, across the narrow space between the ships, everything that was being said. It seemed that the hulk was that of a bigger ship than the *Wasp*, possibly about 170' in length as against the *Wasp*'s 125', and it was wholly made from timber. One of the party had made his way to the bow and was kneeling, scraping the weeds off to reveal the name underneath. He now stood up, very carefully on the treacherous surface and called to Kerrigan.

'Her name was *La Brujula*, sir, as far as I can make out.'

As Kerrigan cupped his hands to his mouth, to relay the information back to the *Wasp*, Nicholls called out, 'I've got that, Mr Kerrigan. How long do you think she has been drifting?'

'From her general condition, I'd say about a year, or more. We're going down the other side now to see if we can find any sign as to why she was abandoned.'

As he moved up the sloping side and across the top, the engineer appeared on the bridge and caught the captain's attention.

'We're taking water forrard, Captain. When we hit some of the rivets sprung and at least two plates have been loosened. We're bolstering them up now and unless the weather deteriorates before we reach Westport, we'll have no problems.'

'Damnation. Thank you, Mr Hudson. How are our coal stocks?'

'I checked that about an hour ago when we shut down. We have enough for about twenty four hours steaming at half speed. Maybe I could stretch another four hours, but no more.'

'We won't need that I hope. Navigator, how far have we to run to Westport?'

'Sixty five miles, sir.' He had known the question was coming and had done his arithmetic. 'About thirteen hours steaming if we're to nurse the plates all the way.'

'I agree. I think that getting home now takes priority over investigating the wreck of the Spaniard. Mr King, please recall the boarding party. Mr Hudson, I would be obliged if you would raise steam.'

'It will be at least half an hour, sir, before we have enough to get under way. However, if you wish to continue under sail I'm sure that it won't affect the bow plates one way or the other. In fact by going slower it will give my gang extra time to make the bow secure.'

The ringing of the ship's bell soon brought the boarding party back into view and within a few minutes they were back on board the *Wasp*.

Kerrigan had managed to see inside some of the deck houses, the sides of which were now slightly above water level, but there was nothing to tell them why the ship had foundered. He had also found the remains of a lifeboat still in its davits and had removed a broken section with the letters 'LA BRU. . .' still faintly visible, but that was all. As Nicholls was examining this he made a suggestion.

'Might I suggest, sir, that we sink the hulk with gunfire? It is a hazard to navigation and should be removed. Besides, it would give the gun crew some practice.'

'Very good idea, gunner. But wait until we are well clear. We have some damage ourselves which I don't want worsened. Let me know when you are ready to open fire.'

This was the first that Kerrigan had heard of the sprung plates. He looked in surprise at King who shrugged, not understanding what it was that was bothering his friend.

Half an hour later the ship lay gently rolling in the swell coming in from the Atlantic, about four cables from the hulk which was barely visible at this distance. Its location, however, was plain to see because Kerrigan had taken the precaution of fixing a flag, made from a broken spar and piece of sailcloth, firmly to it before leaving.

Apart from the work party which could be heard hammering below, making the plates secure before getting under way, everyone else was on deck.

Looking down on the deck from the bridge King wondered what it reminded him of. Then it was clear. It was like being at a race meeting, the same air of excited anticipation prevailed, bets were being surreptitiously made and noted, self proclaimed 'experts' were advising anyone who would listen that the hulk was out of range, that the gunners were so inept that they couldn't hit the target if it was tied alongside, and that each one of them, personally, had more sense than to throw his money away wagering.

It was ridiculous, he decided. Here they were, on a damaged ship, about to open fire on another vessel and the whole company was acting as if on holiday instead of serving on one of Her Majesty's gunboats.

It was all so far outside his experience that he looked around to see what the captain was making of it all. He surely wouldn't condone this irresponsible behaviour? Or would he? He suddenly remembered the captain's own irrational behaviour and became uneasy. He was about to call the bosun to bring the crew back to its senses when he heard the captain call the petty officer who was assistant captain of the forecastle, the senior hand of the watch.

'Andrews.'

Andrews, who was surrounded by crew members, stepped clear and came to attention. 'Sir?' He suddenly looked serious. The rest of the crew, including King, stopped what they were doing to listen.

'What odds will you give me against Mr Kerrigan hitting the

wreck at least twice with five rounds?'

For a second there was an almost shocked silence, then a cheer and voices shouting 'ten to one'; 'evens'; 'three to one'; 'Go on, give the captain twenty to one, chief'. Andrews looked around at the crowd.

'There you are,' he shouted. 'The captain has more faith in the gun crew than you lot have. He knows how good Mr Kerrigan is.' He looked up at the bridge. 'However, because he is the captain I'll make a special price for him. Eight to one, sir. That's the very best I can do.'

'Right. I'll put a shilling on at that price.'

There was another cheer from the crew, most of whom now proffered bets in all the usual shipboard currencies; cash, tots of rum and tobacco. One impoverished sailor even tried to wager a wooden leg which he had acquired on a foreign voyage and kept in his duffle bag against the day he might lose a leg in action, but this was scornfully rejected by Andrews.

When the clamour eased the captain turned to John Kerrigan who had arrived on the bridge to report that he was ready but now stood with a slightly worried look as he realised that everyone on board had a stake in his performance over the next fifteen minutes or so.

'Very well, gunner. Shoot when ready, but just remember that more than your reputation is at stake here. If I lose my money you'll be cut out of my will immediately.'

They grinned at each other. Kerrigan saluted.

'Right, sir. I'd hate to have that happen. But I wish you hadn't squandered all your money on a bet. However I'll see if I can save it for you.'

Slowly the noise died down, the ship's company lining the rails as the gun crew got ready. There wouldn't be any attempt to show how quickly they could reload or open fire. This was now a straightforward test of both Kerrigan's and the gun layer's skill and the accuracy of the equipment they might have to use one day in deadly earnest.

The gun being used was one of the smaller pair which made up the ship's main armament, a 20 pdr B.L. Slowly it traversed to port, then the muzzle elevated.

In the silence everyone heard the gun layer giving instructions to his crew who had suddenly all developed sweaty hands through nervousness at the prospect of the ridicule they knew awaited them if they failed to hit their target.

'Two degrees left. Up fifty yards. Six degrees right.' This last order was to correct the changing heading of the ship relative to the target.

'Steady, ste . . . a . . . dy. SHOOT!'

Instantly there was a crash of gunfire and those watching in line with the gun could see the shell vanish towards the target, leaving smoke and flame behind. A second later there was a splash of water beyond and slightly to the left of the target as the shell overshot the hulk.

A collective groan went up from all the sailors. Only Andrews, who was acting as bookmaker, looked pleased.

Half a minute later the gun fired again. This time the shot was in line but fell well short. Someone at the rail shouted up to the gun platform, 'Don't shoot when the ship is rolling, you daft lot of buggers. Will you never learn?' This advice was given a cheer since the ship was lying totally motionless on the calm sea.

There was a longer delay as the gun crew prepared to fire a third time. King, in a position to see behind the gun shield noted that Kerrigan wasn't looking too pleased, but he still sounded confident as he gave instructions to the layer.

The muzzle of the gun moved very slightly up, then fired.

This time the shell threw up a splash of water so close to the target that some of the crew shouted, 'We've hit it,' while others equally confidently declared it a miss. It was doubtful which was right and faces turned up to Nicholls standing with his telescope raised.

'A miss, I'm afraid, Mr Kerrigan,' he called down. The crew groaned in frustration. 'Better luck next time.'

Kerrigan didn't acknowledge the good wish. Instead he took over the gun layer's position and carefully inspected the target through the gunsight himself. Then he motioned to the layer to take his seat again, and glancing at the blackboard in his hand on which he had been noting the corrections to angles and distances, gave one final change, followed by 'SHOOT!'

There was a huge cheer as the shell landed directly on the hulk and threw up wood, water and other debris. Voices could be heard offering advice to the now grinning gun crew, even to a relieved, but still tense Kerrigan who had one more shot in the locker to fire. Slowly silence descended again as the gun crew prepared to fire for the last time.

Now that he had the range and bearing right, Kerrigan was

in no hurry. Heads at the rail turned to see what the delay was as half a minute stretched to a minute without anything happening. Kerrigan stepped out from behind the gun shield, wet his finger in his mouth, held it up then nodded his head and disappeared behind the shield again. The men below were looking puzzled and impatient as the delay continued.

Kerrigan appeared again, this time looking very serious.

'Captain, sir,' he called.

'What is it, gunner?'

'Permission to go for an early dinner, sir?' he asked with a straight face.

For an instant Nicholls was dumbfounded. Without waiting for an answer Kerrigan disappeared behind the shield.

There was a roar of laughter as the tension suddenly eased. Nicholls turned to the grinning King.

'If he doesn't get on with it I'll hang him from the yardarm, I swear it.'

'Stand by, steady, steady now . . .' Kerrigan's voice was easily heard now, 'Steady . . . SHOOT!'

For the fifth time the gun belched out smoke, flame and shell and all eyes focussed on the flag in the distance.

This time there wasn't any doubt. The shell seemed to hit directly on top of the flag. Large pieces of rotting timber flew into the air and the flag vanished in the cloud of spray. Both ends of the wreck appeared, rising upwards indicating that the strike had been amidships and that her back was broken. The men watched silently. The bow, or what was left of it, came out of the water vertically for about twenty feet, then collapsed. As it hit the water it disintegrated, bits flying in all directions, until finally the little that was left was dragged below the surface by the weight of metalwork and fittings still attached. The stern section just rolled over and sank without fuss, as if relieved to be going and wanting to get it over.

As it disappeared one or two of the younger members of the crew started to cheer but were quickly hushed by the others who were silently drifting away. One, more enthusiastic than the others, was sternly told by an old AB, 'Son, don't ever cheer a sinking ship. Never. Even an enemy one. The men who sailed her were sailors like us, but not so lucky. Now be quiet.'

Even the bridge was silent. All eyes were still looking at the Spaniard's grave. Then with a sigh, Nicholls spoke to King without looking at him.

'Navigator, make a note of the time and log the destruction of *La Brujula* by gunfire. Don't forget to note how many rounds were fired.'

'Aye, aye, sir.' There wasn't anything more to add.

The sound of the whistle on the voice pipe intruded on their thoughts. The bosun listened, then spoke to the captain.

'Engineer reporting sufficient steam to get under way, sir. He requests that speed be kept below five knots if possible.'

'Very well. Navigator ring "Half Ahead" and set course for Westport. Secure for steaming. Call me as we come abeam of Inishkea North.'

This was one of a group of small islands where the next change of course would be made. Then he made his way slowly down the ladder to his cabin.

As the ship made its way down the west coast the glass began to drop. This was accompanied by drizzle and the stars disappeared behind a layer of stratus cloud. Sub Lieutenant Guppy, who was OOW, began to get worried about 02.00 when the lighthouse on Achill Head, towards which he had been holding a course, disappeared.

The disappearance didn't last very long, in fact it was only out of sight for a few minutes, but then it started coming and going as the cloud and rain increased. He decided to waken King.

King's first action when he arrived on the bridge was to check the barometer. While he had been off duty the pressure had dropped and was still going down. Worse, the wind had increased and was coming from the west, putting the ship in danger from the lee shore to port.

There wasn't any real danger, but the signs were there. He called the engine room to reassure himself that the steam pressure was high, in case it was needed, over and above the half-ahead level now being used.

'You were right to call me, Tom,' he reassured the young officer. 'There's no danger, but it is better to be ready. Now I think I'll take a look at the sprung plates and see how they are holding up. I won't be too long.'

The damaged plates were in as inaccessible a place as they could possibly be. Immediately behind the bow and below the main deck was the fo'c'sle which was reached through a heavy door in the bulkhead forrard of the mess deck. This area was designed to act as a shock absorber in the event of a collision or ramming and the only items it contained were drums of paint and other maintenance stores. Through the centre of this compartment, from deckhead to deck, was a metal tube about three feet in diameter. This carried the anchor cable down to the keelson where it lay while the ship was at sea. Access to the keelson was through a hatch and down a steel ladder.

As he left the bridge he wondered should he change into overalls, then decided that if he took care he wouldn't get his uniform dirty and it would be better to get the job done with, before the bow started pitching up and down as the weather got worse.

Going through the mess deck, where about fifteen sleeping men swung gently from side to side in their hammocks, he held the lantern over each hammock until he found the man he wanted.

'Wake up, Bosworthick,' he said quietly, shaking the man's shoulder. 'We've got to check the bow plates.'

The carpenter, who hadn't long gone to sleep was awake and alert immediately. He rolled out of his hammock and reached for his trousers and overalls neatly folded on his box underneath. He recognised King in the light from the latern and kept his voice low.

'Have they given way, sir?' Then becoming aware of the motion of the ship, 'Are we in trouble?'

'Not yet, but I want to look at them now. Are you ready?'

Bosworthick, an elderly man, a few years short of retirement, had been on board the *Wasp* since before she left the builder's yard and knew every inch of her. He led the way through the bulkhead door into the paint store. Opening the hatch clips took only a few seconds since it had been opened earlier, then he stood back to let the officer precede him.

King sat on the deck, lowering his legs into the opening and feeling decidedly nervous. The smell rising from the opening was a mixture of filthy bilgewater, coal dust and decaying animal matter. The bow was rising and falling to the swell outside, and he could hear water below surging in time with the ship's motion.

Turning round he searched with his foot for the next rung, grasped the lantern in his left hand and very cautiously lowered himself onto it. Working his way down, from rung to rung, he made his way through the darkness until the sheen of water was reflected in the lamp light.

'You'll have to step off the ladder, sir,' the carpenter called down, 'so that I can get past. But don't worry, the water is only an inch or two deep.'

'Right.' King stepped into the water which came to his knees,

causing him to gasp at its coldness. He stood to one side as Bosworthick stepped down beside him.

'Bloody Hell, it has risen. Now follow me.'

He moved about six feet along the port side, then crouched
down to put his hand under water. He searched around in the
filthy, greasy liquid until he found what he was seeking.

'Put your hand here, sir. This is where the plates were loosened.
Can you feel where Mr Hudson shored them up with these beams?
The plan is that the pressure of the sea outside will force the
plates into the opening, but the beams will keep them from
coming through. But I can feel water coming in, can you? Just
here, sir.'

King put his hand where the carpenter had indicated and without a doubt there was a steady flow entering the ship. Exploring
further he traced, with his finger, a gap between two plates where
the flow was strongest. As the ship pitched up and down the flow
eased and then increased, but never stopped. Straightening up
he looked ruefully at his sodden trousers and shoes.

'Right, man. We've seen all there is to see. Let's get up on
deck and tell the captain about this.'

When the voice pipe at the head of his bunk whistled, Nicholls
who had only been half asleep, waiting for it, snatched it up.
His first thought on hearing King's voice was that the Sub had
let things get so far out of control that the first officer had to
step in.

'Captain here. What's wrong?'

'We're taking water, sir, through the damaged plates. I've spoken
to the engineer and he is rigging two steam pumps which he
says will control the intake. At present there's almost ten inches
of water under the engine room, increasing by about eight inches
an hour. I've brought the engine revs down to 30 rpm to take
some of the pressure off the bow though it will slow us down.'

Nicholls thought for a moment but couldn't think of anything
else which King should have done. He wanted to go on deck to
see for himself, then decided that to do so could look as if he
was lacking confidence in his first officer, so he settled for 'Very
good, number one. Call me if the situation gets worse. Good
night.'

There wasn't any need to call the captain after that. The
light on Achill Head slipped abeam, King changed course and
three hours later the passing of Clare Island indicated to the
anxious watchers on the bridge that they were nearly home.

At 04.00 Kerrigan had come to relieve Guppy, but King stayed on reluctant to leave the watch to the gunner. Kerrigan was pleased that his cabin mate had done so, since the alternative, that he would be left alone with the captain when he came on duty, wasn't a pleasant prospect. He never felt comfortable in his presence although, had he been asked the reason why he would have found it hard to give a sensible explanation.

Knowing this didn't surprise King. He was only too conscious of his own ambivalence where the captain was concerned and sympathised with Kerrigan. Until now they hadn't really discussed Nicholls to find out why they weren't sure of him, however the events of the day were so fresh that when they recalled, with amusement, the shock the crew received when Nicholls placed his bet with Andrews, King went easily into confessing how near he had been to ruining the day for everyone.

Kerrigan shook his head when he heard. 'You wouldn't have been very popular, old man, if you had stopped it. I'll say one thing for our captain, he eases up on the crew when things get a bit rough, like this trip has been and they love him for it. I don't know what was wrong with him earlier but it was said in the wardroom that he nearly lost his command. That's enough to make any captain very nervous. But that seems to be in the past now and he is more his old self again. What bothers me about him is that he always makes me feel I'm an incompetent idiot when we're on watch together. No matter how hard I try I can't match up to him and it makes me feel insecure, waiting to have to say, "I don't know", when he asks me something. That's a problem you don't have, George.'

'I think I've been lucky, that's all, John. Lucky too that I was posted to the *Wasp*, because now that I've got to know him better I quite like him. Some of the captains I've had, only for a short time mark you, would roast you alive if they caught you placing bets on the main deck, much less do it themselves. Today it was the right thing to do and he did it. We were talking one night, back in Broad Haven, and I asked him did he enjoy doing this type of work and wouldn't he prefer to be on a battleship, for instance. His answer told me a lot about him. He said, "George, you do what you have to do, and you do the best you can. I don't do anything unless I know it is right." I asked him how could he always know if something was right or not and he said, quite simply, "I know that because the back of my head tells me so." Now that is a philosophy I can understand. It's straightforward, honest and it shows a man who will accept full responsibility for his actions. That makes him unusual, a special sort of person, one I wouldn't be ashamed to model myself on. As I said, I'm lucky to be on board the *Wasp*, serving under John Nicholls.'

Kerrigan hadn't known King to show enthusiasm like this before and was slightly embarrassed. To change the subject he asked King had he ever served on a ship of the line when he was doing relief.

'Indeed I did. For two horrible months during the summer manoeuvres of '78. I was a midshipman then and, as you know, "snotties" get every dirty job going on a ship, but life is bad for everyone on the big ones.'

'How is that?'

'Well I can tell you this, the crew of the *Wasp* would have a tale or two to tell if they were ever pressed onto a ship of the line. On the *Wasp*, while we don't go out on blue water very often, at least we eat well. They say "the bigger the ship — the worse the food", and it's true.

'It wasn't too bad for the wardroom, but for the crew it was lobscouse day after day, for weeks at a time. One day it would be made from salt pork, the next from salt beef, but always with hard tack and rotting vegetables to give it strength. It never changed and the crew was always hungry. I wasn't on board in the winter, but I heard it was far worse then. Lobscouse is bad enough hot, when it is dished up cold and greasy and the hardtack is full of weevils the size of maggots, well, it really is a case of "iron men and wooden ships" because normal men couldn't stomach it. You know, since I've been on board here I've never even seen lobscouse served up.

'And another thing. The bigger the ship the less room there is on it. It's a peculiar thing, but we have more room to breathe and live on this ship than they have on a ship five times the size. I saw a wounded sailor once, nearly lost his arm in an accident, and there wasn't enough room on the mess deck to let him stretch out on the floor. The surgeon had to operate and take his arm off, on a table outside in the rain. The sailor died. No, I don't suppose that our captain would have been very happy on a battle ship, even if Nelson himself was in command.'

King's reminiscences were being recounted as they stood watching the helmsman while the ship slowly made its way through the heavy rain, up the channel. The eastern end of Clew Bay is a maze of islands, the locals say there are over 300 there, one for every day of the year, and while King hadn't counted them he was prepared to believe that it was true.

As each marker buoy was passed Kerrigan read off and called out the bearing to the next one, which the helmsman repeated and steered. It wasn't until they were within a mile or so of the quay that King remembered his friend's reaction the previous evening when told about the damage to the bow plates. Kerrigan had been surprised at the news the ship was damaged. King wondered why and decided to ask.

The captain had now arrived on the bridge and the OOW had handed over command to him, so Kerrigan had time to consider his answer.

'I admit I was a bit surprised. It seemed to be too much of a coincidence.' He paused and King looked at him in puzzlement. Then he continued slowly while marshalling his thoughts.

'For over a year we have had a number of unexplained incidents on board. I don't suppose that you have heard about them although you were on board for the last one. Remember the near miss we had leaving Westport Quay when we were caught by the wind? That sort of thing.'

'I remember. But there wasn't any mystery about that. As you said, we were caught by the wind and the captain's seamanship got us back into deep water with no harm done.'

The thought flashed into his head that Kerrigan was trying to find out, in a not too subtle way, if he was aware of the whole crew's nervousness. If that was it, he was not going to help him until he said more.

'I'd say that too, George, if that was the only thing to have happened. But take yesterday, for instance. Who would believe that we could have collided with a wreck five miles off the coast? A wreck that went down over two years ago, as far as I remember, somewhere off the coast of Portugal. But having collided with it, is it reasonable to believe that a water sodden wooden hulk could damage an iron clad to the extent that we've had to keep two pumps working to stay afloat? And if we had much further to go we mightn't have lasted long enough to get home at all. Is that reasonable?'

'It happened, so it is reasonable.'

'Maybe. I prefer to count is as another unexplained incident.'

'Unexplained, yes. But why describe it as a coincidence? Have you collided with other wrecks which I haven't heard about?'

'No, nothing like that.' He looked a bit sheepish as he continued. 'Let's go below to the cabin. I've something there which may interest you.'

Pausing only to collect two mugs of tea from the wardroom, a few minutes later the pair were in the tiny cabin, King seated on the lower bunk while Kerrigan unlocked a portmanteau which he had taken from his locker. Watching curiously King saw him take a notebook from beneath the folded clothing.

'Look at this George, and tell me what you think.'

'What is it?'

'It's a record of the "incidents" I mentioned while we were on the bridge. I know that they have all been recorded in the official log, but it struck me that if I made a list something significant might show up. What I had in mind was linking them to a particular OOW, or something of that nature. What I found was quite different.' He handed the book over for King's inspection.

The page had been divided into four columns. One of them, headed 'Incident' had ten entries which surprised King. Then he ran his eye down the others.

Date	Time	OOW	Incident
Oct 6	04.25	JK	Mooring broken and anchor lost
Oct 9	15.45	TG	Mainsail halyard parted in F7 gale
Nov 2	06.10	WF	Water tank polluted with oil
Feb 7	20.00	TG	Near grounding in Sligo Bay
Feb 11-19			Compass malfunction (Sabotage?)
Apr 3	17.00	WF	Engine blowout and piston failure
Apr 6	02.50	JK	Prop caught in fishing nets
Apr 8	11.05	JK	AB John Wilson lost overboard
Aug 7	12.20	TG	Near grounding at Westport Quay
Aug 16	17.30	GK	Collision with floating hulk

For three or four minutes he studied the page, eventually admitting that it didn't make any sense to him. Kerrigan sighed, then, using a pencil as pointer, indicated the second column.

'Very well. When I started this record I didn't know what I was looking for either. In fact, this column and the next one which shows the OOW, don't seem to have any relevance, so we are left with two columns. The "Date" and "Incident" ones.'

King nodded as if he had followed his friend so far, but one column was as informative as another and that wasn't saying much for any of them. He waited.

'I don't suppose that the dates will mean very much to you. They didn't to me until I got as far as April, and then the penny dropped. The dates can be grouped and the groups are significant. In fact, from here on the whole thing is bizarre and incredible, and to tell the truth, frightening. At least to me.' He stood up, lifted the portmanteau on the bunk beside King and delved into it until he found a bottle of brandy.

'I think we both had better have a drink before I go any further.'

He poured two good measures into the water glasses and handed one to King. Then with two swallows finished his own. King took a small sip and waited, more puzzled than ever.

'Before I go into the significance of the dates I should point out that all the incidents listed were potentially dangerous. In any one of them the ship could have been lost. You were on board for the last two, and while you dismissed the near grounding when we left Westport on 7 August, you must agree that the damage we suffered on 16 August in the collision could have been disastrous had the weather broken earlier, or had we a less experienced engineer than Bill Hudson. In the same way all the other incidents could have triggered a situation resulting in the loss of the ship, had the circumstances been even slightly different. That just one life was lost throughout can only be put down to the fact that we were lucky, more lucky than we deserve.'

He fixed his eyes on King who was wondering was his friend in his right mind. Deciding he had better humour him for the moment, at least, he mumbled 'Right' and nodded his head.

'Now about the dates. As I said, these can be grouped, but before doing that I must tell you something which I am sure you don't know. Since last summer we have taken part in three evictions.'

Noticing King throw his eyes ceilingwards, then take a drink from his almost full glass, he paused, waiting until King put it down.

'Please bear with me, my friend. I did say that this story is incredible, and it frightens me. I can guess what you must be thinking but I'll be finished in a minute and then you can make up your own mind. Please?'

Affected by the genuine and sincere plea, King felt ashamed and apologised. Mollified, Kerrigan continued.

'As I said, apart from the eviction on Clare Island we took

part in three other evictions. The first on 3 October, the second on 4 February and the third on 31 March. Actually, what I have down as a compass malfunction wasn't a single incident at all since it lasted more than a week, but again it was serious enough to have brought about the loss of the ship had the circumstances been different. We could easily have been trying to make a landfall at night and, with a dud compass, who knows?' There wasn't any need for him to say more.

'Now, what I am saying is that there is a connection between the evictions and the incidents. I don't know how, or what it is, but I'm sure it is there. If only I could find it.' He looked at King with vexation in his eyes, then put down his notebook and poured another drink for himself.

'I'm sorry I bothered you, George, but I have to share this with someone. If you think I'm daft, I won't mind. Just forget what I've been saying and thanks for not laughing.'

King stood up and looked through the scuttle. His mind was in a turmoil. Was there a collective madness on the *Wasp*? He dismissed that thought instantly, but bizarre was as good a word to describe his friend's theory as anything else.

He was quite right about the incidents on his list. All could have been very serious, but on the other hand all had a rational explanation. Looking at the list again he realised that it must have been the captain's seamanship that extricated them from more serious consequences on each occasion and wondered had Nicholls seen a connection also. Could that have been the reason for his behaviour and appearance that first day in Limerick? He now was sure that Nicholls had been behaving totally out of character then, and had he been worried or afraid of the unknown it might explain it. Then there was the lower deck gossip, which Hannon had also mentioned, about a possible cursing. Obviously Kerrigan knew nothing about that. He made his mind up and turned away from the porthole, putting his hand on his friend's shoulder.

'I'm not laughing, John, because it isn't funny. Now let me ask you a question. What would you say if I told you that someone has the power to curse the *Wasp* every time it is involved in an eviction and that every eviction is followed by three of your incidents? This is a hypothetical question, of course, but I'm sure Otway Browne has come across similar curses in the Far East and can verify that they frequently are effective.'

'What would I say?' He was astounded. 'I'd say you're the

crazy one. Then I'd say that while it is possible, I suppose, it is highly improbable. And finally I'd say what reason have you for thinking someone is cursing the ship? That's what I'd say. Of course Otway could tell us that in Africa and the West Indies people die when a witch doctor puts a curse on them, I've heard those yarns myself. But I don't believe there is a witch doctor around these parts doing that to us.'

'But you did say' King pressed him, 'that you know there is a connection between the evictions and the incidents on your list? Very well then, why can't it be a cursing? After all some of these people, especially the ones who live on the islands, are just as superstitious and primitive as the natives of Jamaica or Papua, isn't that so?'

'My God.' Kerrigan sat down beside him on the bunk. For a few seconds he considered what he had heard, looking unseeingly at the notebook in his hand. Suddenly he came alert, focussing on the open page, then gripped King by his arm.

'You know what you are saying? You know what this means, if you're right?'

King nodded slowly and heavily. 'Yes, John. I do. It isn't my theory, but if it is right it means that we are due another incident. So far we have had two following the last eviction on Clare Island, leaving one to come. The question now is what do we do about it? Do we tell Nicholls and have him think we are a pair of gullible idiots, or do we wait, and watch, and hope that we are wrong? Is that good enough? I just don't know.'

'I see what you mean. Is there any hope that we might be able to prove this one way or another? Better still, is there any way we could find out who is doing the cursing, if the theory is right, and put a stop to it? By the way, where did you hear about this theory? For someone who isn't a wet week on board you seem to have a remarkable grasp of events.' He stood up with suspicion in his eyes as he stared at his cabinmate.

'Hold on, John. I know even less than you do.'

It was a minute's work to explain the conversation he had had with Rattenbury while on watch and to tell his friend where the theory had come from. This was news to Kerrigan who hadn't known about the unease in the crew's quarters, but fully accepted it once he had been told. He had one remaining doubt.

'But why did you hear about it, and I didn't? I've been on board a lot longer than you have, they must know me better than they do you.'

'Perhaps that is the reason, John. Perhaps there is a gap between the lower deck and the wardroom, bigger than you realise. Besides, didn't I hear something to the effect that our young Sub has been throwing his weight around, making himself very unpopular with the crew? Could some of that have rubbed off on the rest of you?'

'Maybe. Anyway, that isn't important now. What is, is what do we do next?'

For the following fifteen minutes or so, until called to take up berthing stations, they discussed the situation without coming to any conclusion. As they left to return to work Kerrigan lightly thumped King's shoulder, 'I'm glad we spoke about this, George. I was worried but didn't know who to mention it to. Let's keep our eyes and ears open, with our mouths shut for the time being. If we do catch someone we can make our minds up then what action to take. Right?'

'Right,' agreed King.

7 The Cursing Stones of Tory Island

For the first hour our progress down Lough Swilly was slow. The wind was light and even with the genoa and full mainsail we barely made five knots on the ebb tide. I took the helm and before long the welcome smells of frying bacon and coffee wafted up from the galley where Joyce was organising breakfast.

While eating I asked a question which had been intriguing me. 'Why do you call your boat *Alona*? It sounds as if it might be Polynesian? Don't tell me you have single-handed across the Pacific too.'

She laughed. 'No, I won't do that. Actually it isn't Polynesian at all. It's an old Celtic word which I came across on a research project I was doing and it stuck in my memory. The project gave me an unexpected windfall which I decided to spend on buying a boat. I saw this one at the Boat Show and fell in love with it. I thought she was beautiful. Hence the name. *Alona* means "of exquisite beauty". Could anything be more appropriate?'

Beautiful boat — beautiful owner, I thought.

'No, I think it is a very suitable name for a boat. I'll have no difficulty remembering it.'

'Speaking of remembering things, I came across an interesting little tit-bit when I was digging into the names of the crew. It doesn't add anything to the relevant facts but is interesting nevertheless. About Captain John Nicholls. In 1884 his brother was a captain in the RMA and adjutant at Eastney which is the headquarters of the Marines. He later became General Sir William Nicholls KCB, and was the adjutant general of the Royal Marines during the first half of World War I. With that sort of ability and potential in the family who knows where our man could have finished up. Makes you wonder, doesn't it?'

For the rest of the meal we chatted about that and how harsh the tricks were which fate played on us poor humans, then, the plates washed, we settled down for the 100 mile haul down to Donegal Bay from where we planned retracing the last voyage of the *Wasp*. This meant that Joyce climbed into her bunk to get a few more hours sleep, while I took care of the shop.

Approaching the mouth of the lough the tide turned and the motion of the boat changed. The bows rose and gently dipped and the sails filled as the breeze developed. I unpacked the bag I had brought and put the small transistor radio beside me tuned to pick up the 05.55 weather reports and forecasts.

Before reaching the open sea one passes under the guns of Fort Dunree which has guarded the entrance to the lough since the days of Napoleon. On our earlier trip we had passed by without comment and I had idly wondered if the fort was manned. Now I mischievously decided to find out. Waiting until I was almost abreast of the massive building perched on the cliff high above the water, I lowered the ensign and watched. For maybe half a minute nothing happened, then to my enormous delight, the garrison flag was lowered, returning my salute. When it was slowly raised I brought up my ensign also and waved a greeting to the alert soldier somewhere up there watching my departure.

Settling down I realised that the radio, which had been softly playing music up to then was now in the middle of the forecast. I leaned over and turned up the volume to hear, 'Cold front later coming in from the north west. The news will follow in a moment.' Cursing quietly to myself I switched the set off.

A cold front can be vicious, with heavy rain, and 'later' meant somewhere between twelve and twenty four hours ahead. But long before then we would have squalls, strong gusty winds rapidly changing direction, and drizzle. Not a pleasant prospect, though nothing to worry about either. In fact, I suspected that Joyce would welcome it when I told her because it would be closer to the weather which the *Wasp* had experienced. To a good researcher like her, that would make it welcome. For myself, I prefer sunshine and bikini weather for the crew, but one can't have everything.

Looking aloft I could clearly see the cirrus cloud forming, and pulled out the chart from the chart table just inside the open hatch.

Joyce had already pencilled in our track down to the Bay and I followed it with my finger, very slowly, as I mentally noted where we might have to run for shelter if caught out. The coast of west Donegal is very broken and indented with small bays and some fiord type inlets. Unfortunately, most of them are poorly marked, littered with rocks and likely to be hazardous to anyone approaching on a lee shore. On the other hand, the trip now promised to be considerably more interesting than we had thought.

By 10.30 the change in the weather was established. The swell had increased indicating heavy seas far out in the Atlantic and as we approached Tory Island from the east the wind direction was constantly changing and gusting. I decided to call Joyce and tell her I was shortening sail.

She was already dressed when I put my head into her cabin, having woken up to the changed motion. Tousle-headed, she was brewing up, swaying in tune with the boat, and had unpacked her foul weather gear in readiness.

'I thought you might be along soon. Ready for soup and a sandwich?'

I suddenly realised how hungry I was and told her that it was just what I needed. 'With you in a minute,' she promised.

When she came up to the cockpit her first question was about the weather. I told her about the front and that I planned to take in a reef. She agreed. That taken care of, the *Alona* steadied up and we had a leisurely and comfortable meal while we waited for the next forecast.

Tory Island was now about six miles ahead, looking black and dangerous as the seas broke into spray over its rocks. Like a wall it lay at an angle across our path, as if between the one o'clock and seven o'clock positions on a clock face. At the right hand side, the one o'clock position, the lighthouse was visible through our binoculars. Joyce stared at it for some time then put down her glasses.

'That's where it all happened.'

'I know. Even I can recognise Tory.'

'No, it all happened just below the lighthouse. That's where the *Wasp* went aground, on the other side of the island. In fact some of the survivors were seen by the light keepers and brought inside until daylight. When we're nearer we may see the actual spot.'

I altered course to bring us closer but then the first rain squall hit and as we passed the drizzle prevented us from seeing very much. When the rain had passed over we were too far away and soon the island dropped out of sight astern.

That was that. Joyce took over the helm and thankfully I went below to get my head down and catch up on sleep. For the next four hours I knew and felt nothing.

I wakened shortly after three o'clock, feeling a lot better. The movement of the boat was steady but there was some pitching and I could hear an occasional wave break over the bow and rush along both sides of the cabin roof. Sometime, while I slept, Joyce had put the washboards in position across the companion-way and slid the hatch closed. I now stood on the bottom step, slid the hatch open and poked my head out.

The sky was clouded over and off to starboard I could see a line squall, with rain, approaching. Joyce had replaced the head-sail with a smaller jib and the boat was fairly racing along on a broad reach. As she saw me watching her she gave a cheerful wave.

'Lovely, isn't it? How about putting the kettle on?'

'Right. Where are we?'

'Passed Aranmore about forty five minutes ago. Now hurry up with the grub, I'm starving.'

Investigating the small galley I found a bell-mouth flask filled with stew, just waiting to be served. While the kettle boiled I buttered some bread and within minutes had two cups of hot sweet tea and the hot meal ready. Carefully balancing, I returned to the cockpit and sat down beside her.

Finishing the meal didn't take long and as we packed the remains into a disposable bag I asked her what she planned doing.

'The front coming through has made me rethink the situation. The weather is going to deteriorate over the next twelve hours, so we can either get out to sea, heave to and ride it out, or we can cut short the return to Tory by turning back within the next couple of hours. By then I reckon that we'll have about forty miles to cover getting back, and with nine hours or so to do it we should manage without too much trouble. Naturally I'd prefer to go all the way down to the Bay, but better be sure than sorry. I don't fancy wasting twenty four hours needlessly. Agreed?'

'Whatever you say, skipper.'

'That's that then. We're on a heading of 230. When you see the lighthouse on Rathlin O'Beirne Island go about and steer the reciprocal. If you don't see it because of poor visibility go about at 17.30 hours anyway and make good a track of 050. Give me a call at 19.00. Got that?'

I'll say one thing for her, when Joyce was on her own boat there was never any doubt who was in charge.

'Heading 230. Make good the reciprocal at 17.30 or when the light shows, whichever comes first. Call you at 19.00. I think I've got it.'

She grinned, leaned over and kissed me on the cheek, then clambered over the washboards and slid the hatch closed over her head. I tightened the towel wrapped around my neck inside the foul weather jacket and settled down lower on the seat.

Although it was still afternoon it had got quite dull and the general conditions worsened. The drizzle had become steady rain, with brief intermittent breaks of short duration, and continuous changes of course had to be made to compensate for the changing wind speed and direction. Off to port I could see a headland which I identified as Dawros Head from the chart, but there wasn't another sign of human habitation to be seen, either ashore or afloat.

Before 17.30 I caught my first glimpse of the beam from the lighthouse ahead. It wasn't a direct sighting, just the reflection on the bottom of the scudding clouds, about fifteen degrees over the port bow. But it was a welcome sight although I was mildly surprised to see it at that particular angle. I had been expecting to see it dead ahead. Still, that was the skipper's heading and who was I to question it? I relaxed, waiting for it to get brighter and eventually come into sight.

Thirty minutes later it was in full view and I prepared to come about. Tiller hard over, and as we turned to starboard the port jib sheet flew loose. Smoothly the bow continued turning. I winched the starboard sheet tight as the boom snapped over my head, then tightened the main sheet and eased the tiller back to the weather side. Within seconds the fuss was over, the boat settled on the port tack and we were heading north east towards Tory. I made a note on the plastic cover of the deck log, of the time and new heading.

By 18.00 I had changed course three times trying to make good Joyce's track of 050. Because the front was so much closer now, the effect of the depression behind was greater, and the wind was coming at us from every direction. It was going to be a matter of tacking to and fro across the desired track to cope with, and take advantage of the rapidly changing air currents. I could see a long and busy night ahead if we were going to make a landfall off Tory by 03.00.

Half an hour later the wind had settled down into a near gale and I decided to heave to and take in two more reefs in the mainsail.

Usually this can be done quite safely from the cockpit, using the winch to lower the sail sufficiently to secure the excess material around the boom. This time I ran into trouble.

Having brought the *Alona* to a stop by turning into wind, I backed the jib and secured the tiller hard a lee. Slackening off the main sheet to take the pressure off the mainsail, I wound the halyard around the winch and started lowering it. Two turns, then the winch jammed.

The boat was reasonably steady at this time, slowly drifting down wind. This would eventually put us onto the lee shore unless I did something about it. But what? That was the problem. I checked the winch by the remaining fitful daylight and couldn't see anything to account for its failure. It seemed to be working fine for about three turns in one direction, then jamming, doing the same for one and a half turns in the other direction and jamming again. It looked all right, but without doubt something was wrong and I had neither the experience, skills nor tools to do anything about it.

Which left brute force. Hoping that my almost better leg wouldn't break again, I secured my harness to the lifeline and carefully slithered and crawled along the wet pitching deck until I reached the mast. Thankfully I got both arms around it and then transferred the harness to secure me to its aluminium solidity. Then I rested while considering what to do next.

The occasional wave was still coming inboard, breaking into spray, almost blinding me in the process. I felt totally inadequate and wondered what on earth possessed single-handers to put themselves into situations like this, as they made their way around the world. Or even to the Azores and back. There wasn't anyone there who could answer me.

Leaning out as far as I could from the mast, I looked up. First on the port side, then, having moved carefully around, on the starboard side. Everything seemed to be in order. Nervously I freed the halyard from the cleat at the foot of the mast and eased my weight off it, waiting for the sail to come down with a rush. Nothing happened. The sail flapped and hung there with no visible means of support.

'Dammit to hell,' I thought. I was still looking stupidly up along the mast when a bright beam of light lit it above my head, then travelled slowly upwards. I looked back to see Joyce in the cockpit holding a big lamp plugged into the boat's electrical system.

'There's the trouble,' she called, holding the beam as steady as the action of the boat allowed. 'The sail is caught in the slide.'

There is a slot, called the slide, which runs from the top to the bottom of the mast. In this slot the front edge of the sail is held by a rope grommet, sewn into the fabric, and which is wider than the opening of the slide. Raising or lowering the sail therefore, does not, in theory cause the leading edge of the sail to part company with the mast. The smooth movement of the grommet is supposed to hold it in place.

In this case there wasn't a smooth movement. The grommet had snagged somehow in the slide, and no matter how I pulled down on the sail, or up on the halyard, nothing I could do would budge it.

'I'll have to go up there to clear it,' I yelled. 'Pass me a marlin spike, or even a screwdriver, and I'll try to reach it.'

'Just a minute,' she shouted back, then disappeared down into the cabin. I felt very alone when the light had gone below with her.

Two or three minutes later, as I was leaning back in my harness to look up the mast and wondering which was the best way to clamber up its smooth slippery surface, I felt a hand on my shoulder. Joyce was beside me with a canvas satchel, containing most of the boat's tool kit.

'Take this while I hook on.' She handed me the lamp with its trailing lead paid out behind her. I took it, wondering how I was going to climb holding it.

'This won't take long.' She grabbed the useless halyard swinging freely in the wind, as it passed. 'Now give me some slack and let's have the light on the slide again.'

Puzzled, I watched her pull down the slackened halyard until she had about ten feet of it looped in her hand. Her movements were sure and economical as she made a small bight and wrapped it twice around the main halyard, finally passing it through itself. As she transferred the karabiner of her harness from the lifeline to the bight on the halyard, I suddenly realised that she had made a Prusik knot, the one used by mountaineers to hold a climber to the main climbing rope. At the same time I knew she wasn't making it for me.

'What the hell are you up to?' I shouted. 'Get back to the cock-pit and keep the light on the slide for me. I'm going up.'

'You'd never make it. And if you go overboard I certainly won't be able to pull you back. This is faster and safer. You pull me up, I'll free the grommet, you lower me again and that's all there is to it. Now, are you ready?'

Since the deck of a pitching yacht in near darkness is no place to conduct an argument I just nodded. Then, doubtfully, I heaved on the free end of the halyard, watching her harness tighten around her chest and under her arms. She nodeed at me to go ahead and on the next pull her feet swung clear.

Perhaps it was the adrenalin coursing through my system, but whatever it was, she felt surprisingly light. I was able to hold her in position with my left hand as I looped the end of the halyard around a cleat. That made it a lot easier. I now had a three to one advantage thanks to the effect of the pullies. Two further heaves and she was swinging safely alongside the jammed slide, the halyard securely anchored around the cleat.

Directing the beam of light up I watched her work a spike into the tangled grommet. It took less than two minutes to clear, then the sail dropped a foot or so, being brought up by the same halyard to which Joyce was secured. A minute later both sail and girl were at deck level.

Five minutes later the sail was fully reefed and as I carefully fed the grommet back into the slide Joyce winched the sail back up, then secured it firmly. Gratefully and ungainly, I half crawled half slid back along the cabin roof to the comfort and safety of the cockpit.

'I wouldn't want to do that too often,' I gasped. 'But you were bloody marvellous. Where did you learn to make that knot?'

Wiping spray from her face she laughed. 'A year ago I was sick for about a month and someone gave me a book on knots and splices and a piece of rope about six feet long. Before I left the hospital I had learned the ones I thought might come in useful some day. That was one of them. Now before we get under way again I think a tot of rum might come in handy, then I'll make some soup. How does that grab you?'

'Perfect.' My leg was beginning to ache and I knew, without a doubt, that I'd never have managed the mast. I sat down.

While waiting for the soup I managed to get two fairly good bearings with the hand compass and had them plotted on the chart before Joyce reappeared. As we sipped the hot, thick, nourishing drink I showed the result to her.

'That's not so good,' she said thoughtfully. 'I had hoped that by turning back early we would have had time to reach Tory by 03.00, but now I'm not so sure. I got a weather forecast before the 18.00 time signal and we can expect a deterioration over the next few hours. If we average four knots on track we'll be lucky and that means it will be after 04.00 by the time we get there.'

'How about taking a chance on the forecast?' I suggested, adding, 'I've been trying to maintain a track made good of 050 as you said. But why not head closer to north, say on 030 or even 020, until we are abeam Tory, then turn and run east. In that way we'll have a close reach followed by a broad reach, without any time wasting tacking. The distance will be a bit longer, but the saving in time should make up for it.'

She tapped her teeth with her finger nail as she considered, glanced up at the low, black tumbling clouds overhead, and shivered.

'Okay, we'll compromise and try to maintain 025. We've got about thirty miles still to run, so if we can pick up two knots we'll have time in hand.' She stood up and clipped her harness onto the cockpit strongpoint. 'Let's get the show on the road, then you can take a couple of hours to rest that leg.'

A minute later we were under way, on the new heading, riding more easily with the well reefed mainsail and storm jib working with the boat instead of against it. Thankfully I went below and tried to dry myself before stretching out on my bunk.

Lying there I looked around, comparing our present situation with the previous night. Now it was all action, wind and rain, bouncing around as we hammered through an incoming cold front, while last night it had been soft music and low lights on a stretch of moonlit, still water. Wondering what insanity had led us to give one up for the other, I drifted off to sleep.

I don't know what wakened me but I suddenly started up, alert and anxious, knowing something was wrong. Quickly I pulled on my oilies and slid back the hatch. Outside was total darkness and driving rain. I clambered over the washboards and slid the hatch closed behind me.

To the right of the companionway there is a small low-powered light on the bulkhead. I pressed the switch and turned to apologise to Joyce for destroying her night vision. To my shocked disbelief she wasn't there.

It was incredible. The *Alona* was sailing steadily despite the gusting wind and rising sea with nobody at the helm. From where I was standing to the helmsman's seat was about four feet, which I crossed in one long step. Automatically I went to clip my harness to the strongpoint, to be brought up short when I saw Joyce's karabiner still hooked on. The line from it was tautly stretched back over the transom.

I tried to pull it inboard and could make no impression. Whatever was holding it was either jammed, or was too heavy for me to raise, and there was only one way to find out which.

Using the ends of the mainsail sheets I secured the tiller centrally, making it unlikely that the bow would veer off the wind, at least for the following few minutes. Then, lying along the top of the stern locker, holding on as tightly as I could to Joyce's safety line, I pushed my head out under the rail which surrounds the after end of the cockpit.

For a few seconds I couldn't see a thing. Then as the bow pitched down and the stern rose, Joyce appeared out of the water. She was still secured to the boat but was in a bad way.

She was slumped unconscious in her harness, with her hair and face streaked with blood. As the water poured over her she swung from side to side on the end of the line, banging heavily off the stern. She was totally incapable of helping herself and in immediate danger of drowning.

From then on I seem to have gone onto auto-pilot. There wasn't time to plan anything, what needed to be done had to be done right away. All I could hope was that I was making the right decisions, in time, and that I could carry them out.

On the cockpit bulkhead there was a cleat with a thirty foot rope permanently looped to it. This was the all-purpose line, available for all the odd jobs when such a rope might be needed unexpectedly, such as to stop the boat in a hurry beside a jetty, or to lower bottles of wine into the sea to cool. It was just a useful piece of equipment with no particular function, a semi-retired halyard.

Praying now that it would stand up to the hard use it was about to be put during the next few minutes, I snatched it from its cleat and fashioned a bowline at one end. Then looping it three or four times around a winch, I brought both ends back to the stern.

As I did so I realised that my own harness was dangling free. If I went over the side now we would both die. Shocked, I secured myself to the track carrying the main sheet traveller, then crawled back under the rail, directly over Joyce's safety line.

Stretched out to the end of my lifeline I could just reach her shoulder when she surged up as a wave swept under the stern. Then, a second later, she would sink back down out of reach. Five or six times, or maybe more, I touched her, only to have her drop away until, at last, I managed to grab her harness and hold on.

As the stern rose I thought that my arm would be pulled from its socket, such was the weight of water soaked clothing which was dragging her down, then as the stern went down again I was able to gain an inch or two. Two, three, four times the procedure was repeated until, at the point of exhaustion I managed to slip the bowline under the shoulder strap of her harness and pull it up. From then I was able to speed up the rescue. I looped the bowline over a stern mooring cleat and hauled on the free end of the rope. The winch took up the strain and a couple of seconds later I was lifting her over the railing and into the cockpit.

All I wanted to do then was collapse, but commonsense told me that there was still work to do if Joyce was to live. First I had to get her breathing before anything else was done. Not knowing how long she had been in the water could mean that I was already too late, but I refused to consider this prospect. Where she was lying on the exposed cockpit floor there was enough space to start giving the kiss of life, and that would have to do. I undid her harness and got started.

She couldn't have been in the water very long because, to my enormous relief, she responded in less than a minute with a cough. The water in her throat and breathing system poured out, and she coughed again. Colour came back into her cheeks, slight but perceptible, and a second or two later her eyes opened. I almost wept with relief.

Ignoring the spray coming on board I opened the hatch and threw the washboards from the companionway. Then, picking her up I staggered and lurched into the cabin and laid her down on the bunk.

The boat seemed to be doing all right by itself for the time being so I concentrated on my patient. A close inspection of her face and head showed a small cut under her hair which was the source of the blood, but wasn't serious. Leaving it, I got her out of her wet clothes and quickly dried with a big bath towel. Then wrapped in a blanket I zipped her up in her sleeping bag.

Up to this she had only been semi-conscious, although her eyes were open. As I put the pillow under her head the blankness cleared from her eyes and she focussed on my face, then looked around the cabin.

'What happened? What am I doing here? Who is on the helm?'

She tried to struggle up and I gently pushed her back down.

'Steady on, my dear. You banged your head, but you are all right now. I'll have cocoa for you in a minute. The boat is perfectly all right for the time being. Now, how do you feel?'

'I'm a bit cold. How did I bang my head?'

As this conversation was going on I was at the cooker heating up a saucepan of milk. I opened the small oven and lit it to get the cabin warmed up and almost immediately felt the heat pour out. By the time I had spooned the sugar and cocoa into a mug the milk was hot enough. Then I supported her with my arm under her shoulder as she sipped the hot, sweet, life restoring drink.

'That's good, but it is awfully hot. Now, how did I bang my head?'

'What do you remember?' I asked.

She concentrated for a few seconds. 'Not much I'm afraid. I saw a light dead ahead and stood up to get a better view of it. Then my hat blew off, I grabbed for it, and next thing I'm here.' Realisation suddenly dawned on her and her face went pink. 'Did you put me into my sleeping bag?'

'Of course. Nothing new to me. I do it all the time in the Navy. Now finish off this drink and get some sleep. Are you feeling any warmer?'

I could see that her shivering had stopped and she seemed to be recovering quickly, but with the danger of shock ever present I knew I had to get her to medical help as soon as possible. So making sure that she was comfortable I gave her a couple of Panadols, turned off the oven, and left her to sleep. Outside the sky seemed to be clearing to the west but it was still raining.

The boat had turned into wind while I had been busy and had come to a stop, wallowing in the heavy sea. It was the work of only a minute to back the jib bringing the bow around, loosen the sheets holding the tiller, and get under way. A few minor adjustments, then we were back on the earlier heading of 025.

That taken care of I then had a number of problems. The first being my present position. I remembered her remark about seeing a light dead ahead and braced myself to stand up. Sure enough, there it was, about five degrees off the starboard bow.

I watched it flashing while I tried to time it, but the rain made reading my watch difficult, and the pitching of the boat made counting the flashes impossible. I gave up and sat down again to consider the situation.

The flashes indicated that it was a fixed light, not another vessel, but until I could identify it that information wasn't likely to be of use. The fact that I could see it in this weather meant that I was within ten miles of it, much too close. Finally, though it was the most likely light, Tory should be between fifteen and twenty degrees off the starboard bow, not five degrees as this one was.

With an injured companion on board my first priority, as I was only too well aware, was to get help. But where from? The big VHF transmitter wasn't much use since I couldn't tell any rescuer who might be listening where I was. I spread the plastic covered chart out on my knees and, totally dismissing the realisation that I was temporarily destroying my night vision, turned the torch on.

A few anxious minutes' consideration, then I decided that the light must be that of Tory. By a process of elimination it couldn't be anywhere else. But why it was fine off the starboard bow was a mystery. I was still on my heading of 025 and, if anything, the light should be coming up abeam. The good thing about it though was that I was a lot closer to it than I should have been, if it really was Tory. I was nearer to the help needed.

During the next two hours we slowly crept closer to the flashing light ahead. As we closed in I was able to get an accurate count of the flashes, so had no doubt at all where we were. At the same time the weather eased and I was able to shake out one reef which slightly increased our speed. But I was getting very worried about Joyce.

I was now going below every ten minutes or so to monitor her condition. Her face was yellow, she was sweating to the point where I had to dry her face each time. Her breathing too, sounded laboured to my unskilled ear, but whether she was in shock or not, I didn't know. Eventually, with the light about a mile ahead I took the decision I had been putting off, not to go to the island but to head for the small harbour on the mainland from which the island ferry operated. This would take slightly longer, but as it would give access to a doctor and ambulance service I felt it worth the delay.

It almost turned out to be not one of my better decisions. In fact, we were in trouble almost from the time I changed course towards the mainland. The wind had increased and we were running downwind onto an unlighted shore, and, if that wasn't enough to be going on with, there was an island, Inishbofin, somewhere ahead.

The only redeeming feature was that the darkness wasn't quite so intense. I could actually see the spray coming on board before it bore down on me, but the noise was as bad as ever and I knew that I wouldn't hear the surf as we came up too quickly to the rocks surrounding Inishbofin.

Using the handlamp, turned up to full beam, I stood up holding the tiller over with my thigh, while I searched ahead. Occasionally, as the boat wallowed over the top of a wave, the light lit up the sails as I struggled to maintain my balance. Someone on the island saw this, because suddenly a bright light was flashing in our direction. It came from a point well above the water level and after a minute or so the flashing changed to a steady pattern of dih – dih – dah, the letter 'U' in Morse.

This letter, in the international code is the signal which means, 'You are standing into danger'. As soon as I saw it I slammed the tiller hard over and bore away to starboard, putting the light almost behind me, while I thanked God for having put my signalling friend in the right spot at the right time.

Once clear of the island I could see, through the rain, lights from cottages along the shore of the mainland, and as I closed in at a new angle, the lights on the small fishing pier were switched on, giving me even more help. Fifteen minutes later I had the mainsail down, coming alongside on jib alone, to where three local fishermen were waiting curiously to see who was foolish enough to be at sea under such conditions.

As I tossed up the bow mooring line I called out that I had an injured person on board needing help, and one of the men ran off towards a nearby building shouting that he would phone the local doctor for me. That taken care of it was with a less anxious mind that I finished securing the boat and checked Joyce again.

She seemed to be a bit better, sleeping soundly and her colour had improved, so I left her and climbed onto the jetty to speak to my new helpers who were still standing there.

Their first question was, naturally, where had we come from. I didn't want to go into details and merely said Rathmullen which they accepted. Then the conversation turned to the weather conditions which had brought us into their tiny harbour. Not knowing the village of Magheroarty I was curious why there should be men on the pier at four o'clock in the morning, and assuming that they were waiting for fishing boats to return I asked how many boats were at sea.

'At sea?' They looked at me in surprise. 'There's no boats from here at sea. What made you think that?'

'Oh, I just assumed it when I saw you here,' I answered sheepishly. 'Or do you always hang around here during the night?'

They looked at each other, then they laughed.

'We're beachcombers. Or at least part-time beachcombers and heavy seas like tonight can be profitable to us. With all the unemployment that's around we can't afford to miss out on the flotsam that comes ashore here. We were waiting for first light to start patrolling the shore when we spotted you rounding Inishbofin.'

I was astonished. For some reason I had always assumed that beachcombers were only to be found on Pacific islands and here they were, almost on my own doorstep. Chatting with them I remembered my Good Samaritan on the island who warned me of the rocks and mentioned him.

'That must have been John Earls. He's an Englishman who has lived on the island since the war, an old Navy man I believe, and he's out nearly every night beachcombing, himself and a bloody great big dog. He makes a good living out of it, from what I hear, and he would know the right signals to flash.' The others agreed that he was probably right and I asked them to convey my thanks to him when next they saw him.

While chatting the time had passed quickly and I was pleasantly surprised when the lights of a car appeared on the road which runs above and behind the pier, across the hill which shelters it. One of the men announced that it was the doctor's car.

A couple of minutes later I led him down the steps and into the boat.

When I switched on the cabin light Joyce wakened and looked at the stranger standing beside her bunk, in surprise. Then she relaxed as she noticed me standing behind him. I introduced them, then totally ignoring her protests that she was fine and perfectly all right, the doctor calmly slipped a thermometer under her tongue and proceeded to take her pulse.

As he was shaking down the mercury he nodded to me to indicate that Joyce wasn't seriously hurt and I left him to continue his examination alone. Outside my new friends were still waiting.

'How's the young lady, then, captain?' one of them enquired diffidently.

'The doc thinks she'll be okay but he hasn't finished his examination. By the way, thanks for getting him here so quickly. I'd have been in trouble had you chaps not been here. I'm very grateful.'

This embarrassed them considerably. 'It was nothing at all,' said the one who had run to the phone. 'We were glad to be of help,' mumbled another, while the third nodded agreement with both.

A thought struck me and I opened the stern locker to find the bag which I knew Joyce had packed away there. Pulling it out I opened it, hoping that my guess was right, and sure enough, on top of her dry, shore going clothes, lay a full bottle of Jameson whiskey.

'How about a drink then?' I asked. Smiles appeared all round as I handed out paper cups and poured good healthy measures into each. 'Sorry I haven't got any water to go with it,' I apologised to be quickly reassured that its absence wouldn't be a great loss. As we sipped in silence the doctor reappeared, closing the hatch behind him. I motioned towards the bottle and he nodded silently.

'Just what I needed,' he said, taking a sip. 'I'm glad I'm not a sailor on a night like this.'

Some small talk followed, then as the beachcombers finished their drinks they drifted off towards the end of the pier leaving the doctor and myself alone.

'How is she, doctor?'

'I'd like to get her into hospital for a day or two, for observation, but she won't hear of it. She is badly bruised where the harness held her, but thank God it did. Had she gone overboard and it broke we'd be looking for her body now. Can you handle the boat alone, long enough to get back to Rathmullen?'

When I told him that I could, he continued. 'In that case keep her in her bunk until you get there and then have her own doctor see her. I'm almost sure that she'll be all right but no harm in having her seen to there. I'd prefer to send her home by car from here, but she won't hear of that either. Are all sailors crazy? Anyway it is only about thirty miles from here and I'll phone ahead and have her parents meet you on arrival.'

Following a further discussion as to the time we were likely to leave Magheroarty and arrive in Rathmullen, and all the details carefully noted, he absentmindedly leaned over, picked up the bottle and poured himself another drink. Then, raising the paper cup he toasted the boat, 'Slainte.' I repeated it.

'This trip hasn't gone very well for you. Has it?'

'What do you mean, doctor?' I asked in surprise.

'First the weather, then Miss Campbell's accident, and now the research you were supposed to be undertaking has to be abandoned. You surely wouldn't describe all that as a major success, would you?'

'Well, put like that . . . I can't argue. But it could have been a lot worse.'

'Indeed it could,' he agreed. 'Miss Campbell tells me that you are in the Royal Navy, is that right?'

Surprised at the way the conversation had changed course, I agreed that I was. As I tried explaining that I wasn't a sea-going officer he interrupted me.

'I'm not very superstitious, and times have changed, even around here . . .', he balanced himself against the boom now safely secured in its crutch, as the boat rose to a wave which suddenly swept around the end of the quay. Then continued . . . 'but if we had been standing here, holding this conversation, just about one hundred years ago, I'd have said that you brought it all on yourself, all this bad luck.'

Astonished and intrigued I asked how he could have thought that. Again he changed the course of the conversation.

'Have you ever heard of the Cursing Stones on Tory?'

When I said that I hadn't he finished his drink, poured another for himself, and added some to my cup. Finally he took out a pipe and slowly filled it. He was obviously in no hurry to leave. I waited until he was ready.

'About a hundred years ago the people on Tory were in a very vulnerable situation. Evictions were taking place all around the coast as small farmers, who hadn't recovered from the famine, were being thrown off their farms for rent arrears and the people on islands like Tory, Aranmore, and even Inishbofin out there, were losing their homes. Not just in dozens, but in hundreds.

'Some of the islands have remained empty. Tory, however, escaped the worst of it. And people around here will tell you, to this very day, that it is thanks to the Cursing Stones. Are you sure you've never heard of them?'

'Never,' I said, nodding vehemently. 'What did the Cursing Stones do?'

'Well, I suppose you could describe them as a sort of secret weapon. When the people on the island heard that the authorities were about to visit, a group of them would take the stones down to the east end of the island and, having arranged them in a secret pattern, would pray over them asking the Devil to thwart the officials who were on their way. I don't guarantee it always worked, I'm just telling you the way I heard it.' He looked closely at me to see if I was laughing and then, apparently reassured, took another sip and continued with his tale.

'The stones were kept secret, you understand. They wouldn't be used unless the matter was very important and nobody knew where they were kept. In fact, it was supposed to be a secret who had the power to use them, but on an island like Tory it would have been extraordinary if all the adults didn't know which person was responsible for their safety and use.

'Now you, being in the Royal Navy, on a boat heading for the island to carry out some research, would immediately cause the islanders to become very suspicious indeed. I'm speaking of a hundred years ago, you understand. And if they had cause to think that you meant harm to them, out would come the stones, the curse would be cast, and you would be in trouble. What happened after that would depend, I suppose, on a number of things.' He paused for another long sip from the cup.

'What sort of things?'

'Oh, I don't really know. Maybe if you didn't intend the people any harm then you might be all right. Or if you were in a state of grace, as they say, nothing bad would happen.' He laughed mirthlessly. 'I don't know. But the fact remains that the stones did occasionally work. Which is why Tory still has a population to this day.'

'You mean to say they still use them?' I asked in disbelief.

'I didn't say that. I'm talking now about how it was a hundred years ago, remember? When they were last used the curate on the island made the guardians of the stones hand them over to him and he buried them somewhere. They have never been found, or so they say. But I have been holding clinics on the island now for over twenty years and I think I'd have heard about it if they were being used. Secrets like that are hard to keep.'

'I suppose so. What happened the last time they were used?'

'I thought you knew. When I mentioned your connection with the Royal Navy I was referring to that time in particular. It was one of your ships and the islanders thought it was coming to evict them, so they used the stones. The ship went aground and nearly everyone was drowned.'

I felt the hairs on the back of my neck prickle as I knew, with horrible certaintly, what he was about to say. Faintly I asked him did he happen to know the name of the ship.

'It's well known in these parts. Her name was HMS *Wasp*.'

8   Beaching at Westport

A month ashore in Westport has left its mark on all the crew.
The repairs took longer than anyone thought possible, due
to the difficulties which arose when the ship was beached.
But engineer Hudson performed his duties in an exemplary
manner and I am confident that we will not take a drop of
water through the plates since he repaired them. While the
work was being done all the officers with the exception of
Hudson, Otway Browne and myself took leave. The two
mentioned have now taken their leave and will rejoin us in
about three weeks when we return from Moville. I, of course,
am not long enough on board to be due any leave.

There is to be another eviction on an island off Malin
Head. Although the crew has not been told about it there
is a general feeling of unease as if they suspect something
is up. John told me last night that he feared another 'incident' and while I tried to reassure him I too feel unhappy
about the outcome.

As soon as the ship was secured alongside the pier in Westport
the captain called a meeting of all officers in the wardroom. He
had given careful consideration during the night to the options
which he had and had already decided on his course of action.
However, he would value the view of the others.

It was a formal meeting with everyone seated around the
dining table, Nicholls at one end and Hudson at the other. He
started by asking Hudson to report on the damage to the bow
and asked how he proposed to deal with it.

Although Hudson was chief engineer he had no naval rank,
and like the surgeon was addressed as 'mister'. This didn't however lead to any want of confidence on his part. On the contrary
he felt it gave him considerably more freedom in his relations
with the captain than the regular officers enjoyed. Having been
on board since even before the *Wasp* was commissioned he had

an authority which none of the other officers had and Nicholls recognised this. His report, therefore, was succinct, precise and left no room for misunderstanding.

'I'm sorry to have to tell you, captain, that the ship will not be going to sea again for some time. She will have to be beached before we can inspect the damage, much less repair it and until that's done I can't say how long we'll be out of action.'

'Could you even guess, Mr Hudson?'

'I could, sir, but I won't. When I have seen the damage I'll let you know.'

Nicholls looked around the table. 'That's it, gentlemen. Thank you, Mr Hudson.'

Hudson nodded in acknowledgement. The captain continued, 'I intend seeing the harbour master as soon as he gets here, that will be about 08.30, and I shall requisition the large shed at the end of the pier. When that is arranged we will lighten ship as much as possible by removing all the stores, ammunition, coal, yards and spars, and everything else that is movable. These we will store in the shed. Weapons and small arms' ammunition will be removed to the Castlebar military barracks for security by the militia.

'There will of course be a guard put on the shed from now until the materials inside have been brought safely back on board. Mr Kerrigan, you will arrange that with the marine corporal.'

Kerrigan made a note and answered, 'Yes, sir.'

'When the ship has been lightened we will beach her to the west of the quay on the south side of the bay, in two days' time at morning high water. That gives you ample time to locate and prepare the most suitable place, number one. Mr Guppy will assist you with this.'

King and Guppy answered, 'Yes, sir' as in one voice.

'Mr Kerrigan, you will be responsible for the safe transfer of all remaining materials and stores into the shed. Mr Browne, I intend to let the crew have shore leave while the repairs are being carried out and I would be obliged if you would arrange with the bosun to have the crew divided into two watches, for this purpose, one to maintain the ship while the other is absent.'

Browne nodded silently.

'Please let me know by noon today what progress you have made. Any questions?' He looked around the table but nobody spoke.

'Good. That's it then. Meeting adjourned.' He rose and left

the wardroom. For a few moments there was silence as each considered what had to be done. Kerrigan groaned theatrically and looked at King.

'You've done it again, George, old boy. Going off to laze on the beaches while I sweat around here, humping sacks of this and barrels of that, between here and that damned shed. There just isn't any justice, is there chief?'

'I wouldn't say that altogether, gunner,' Hudson grinned. 'Look at it this way. While you are working off that excess fat from around your waist, poor George will be putting it on as he sits there drinking beer provided by the lovely young Irish maidens who frequent the beaches.'

Knowing that lovely young maidens were as plentiful on the beaches around Westport as penguins, George slung a cushion at the engineer as he rose to leave.

'Come along, young Guppy. There's work to be done.'

For the following two days the work never stopped. Everything that could be taken off the ship was transferred into the shed and stored under guard. Some was easy to remove but other material was secured by nuts and bolts which had been painted over many times since the ship had first entered service and chipping the bolts free was a time consuming task. Eventually though everything, including the unused coal, was off and the ship was ready to be brought to the beach which King and Guppy had earmarked for the repair work.

Dinner that night was a spartan affair and when it was finished Kerrigan threw himself on his bunk complaining loudly that he hadn't joined the Navy to be overworked, underfed, and treated as a coolie. 'Next thing you know' he said, 'the captain will give us handfuls of rice and expect us to do a day's work on that.'

When there wasn't any reply from King he propped himself up on his elbow to say, 'Don't you agree, George?'

'Eh, what did you say? I'm sorry, I didn't hear you.'

'Never mind, I was just letting off steam. What time do we move out in the morning?'

'Oh . . . about five. That means that all spare hands, including you, have to be fed and ashore before then. It will take about an hour to march to the beach so you'll be there long before high water which will be at . . .' he produced a notebook and flicked over the pages until he found the information he was seeking, . . . 'will be at 08.27.'

He got up and looked out through the small scuttle. 'I hope

the weather holds. By the way, how many hands are you taking around to help?'

For the next half hour or so, until George blew out the lamp and they settled down for an early night's sleep, the discussion centred around the activities planned for the following day. It wasn't until he lay in the darkness waiting for sleep that Kerrigan suddenly wondered what it was that had George so preoccupied earlier that he didn't hear his cabinmate speak to him.

Had he but known, King was also awake, wondering if the next day would bring the third incident and what it could possibly be.

The following morning the weather had deteriorated again and a stiff breeze laced with rain blew straight in from the Atlantic. For the short journey Nicholls had decided that only three members of the crew would be needed together with himself, King, an experienced man at the wheel, and Hudson in the engineroom. The trip was expected to take about a half-hour, then the ship would be beached on the sand almost directly below the steep slope of Croagh Patrick, where the national saint had fasted and prayed fourteen centuries earlier.

Shortly after six Bill Hudson helped shovel the last few sacks of coal on board into the firebox and watched the pressure gauge creep round into the green sector. Then, checking that both pumps were busily working, he called the bridge to tell the captain he was ready to put to sea.

Nicholls had been pacing the bridge waiting for this, outwardly calm but inwardly growing increasingly worried as the wind veered and backed in no particular pattern. Beaching a ship presented problems at any time, doing it under adverse weather conditions would be described by the Lords of the Admiralty as plain foolhardy should anything go wrong. If the worst came to the worst Nicholls knew that his career would be over, but the die was cast. To stop at this stage would be equally foolish as the *Wasp* was slowly sinking under him.

He took a deep breath, turned to his number one and said, 'Mr King, I would be obliged if you would cast off the bowline, then await my order at the stern.'

King acknowledged the order and moved away to carry it out. The captain picked up his telescope, swept it around the bay for the last time, then rang 'Stand by' on the engineroom telegraph.

Slowly the little gunboat moved astern of the quay. The three men on the bridge were now joined by the engineer who could do nothing more for the time being.

To take the pressure off the bow plates Nicholls had decided to cross the stretch of water to the beach by going astern. This, in a single screw vessel, is extremely difficult, requiring seamanship of a high order to keep the ship travelling in a straight line. The gusting wind, now veering to the north, was putting pressure on her side forcing her to crab along at a most difficult angle.

Progress was further impeded by the fact that the funnel's position behind the bridge meant that the captain's vision astern was severely limited, so he had to rely on King and Hudson who had stationed themselves on the wings, one to each side, and from there called out every time a hazard appeared, or corrective action had to be taken.

As a result it was very close to high water when Nicholls turned the ship and lined it up on the beach where the ship's company was already waiting on the sand to take the mooring lines as it ran aground.

He hesitated for the merest second with his hand on the brass telegraph lever, then firmly pushed it forward into the 'Full ahead' position. Hudson back in the engineroom, signalled receipt of the order, and fully opened the valves to drive the ship forward.

The *Wasp*, by now bow heavy from the sea water which had entered since leaving the quay, moved at first sluggishly then picked up speed. This forced more water through the opened plates and it became a race to beach as high as possible before the angle of the bow became so low that it might not reach shallow water.

The wind eased as if to help and the three braced themselves for the impact as the beach came closer. Just before the bow raced up out of the surf, Hudson pulled the siren lanyard and held it to blow off the remaining steam. With spray flying in every direction and a loud rumbling noise the ship slid ashore exactly between the two lines of waiting men and came to a stop half out of the water.

There was silence on the bridge, broken by the cheers of the men ashore. King turned to the captain and engineer who were smiling in relief.

'Congratulations, gentlemen. I couldn't have done it better myself.'

That broke the tension. Hudson went back to his engine to close everything down when the steam had finally blown off and King threw the already prepared lines over the side for the men to secure the ship. By 09.00, long baulks of wood borrowed from the harbour master were already in position as props and the ship was as secure as it could be.

Five hours later the full extent of the damage was easy to see. With her bow high and dry the four loosened plates, each held in position by a couple of rivets, hung uselessly over the large opening in the hull. The captain and engineer had completed their inspection of the damage and were in agreement that a full day would be all that was needed to make the ship seaworthy. Already preparations for the work had been completed and an anvil was in position on the sand between the hull and a roaring bonfire in which iron rods were beginning to glow red.

For the rest of the day the beach was a scene of furious activity. As each plate needed almost one hundred rivets to secure it, the blacksmith was busy cutting the rods and hammering out new rivets on the anvil. As he was shaping the last ones the incoming tide was lapping around his bare feet and the fire couldn't have survived another ten minutes. But the job was completed and three buckets, filled to the brim with new rivets, were hauled up the ship's side to the safety of the deck.

While the blacksmith was working the water in the ship had been manually pumped out using an apparatus like a fire engine's. As it took a dozen men to operate and because it was hard work King stopped every fifteen minutes to change over the men pumping before they collapsed from exhaustion. The only break in the activity was thirty minutes at midday when the cook produced a basket full of sandwiches and two huge cauldrons of tea. This respite was gratefully received by officers and men alike. The carpenter in the meantime fitted a temporary patch over the opening designed to keep out the sea at high tide.

With the tide on the flood work had to stop but Nicholls was satisfied at the progress which had been made. Straightening the plates and repositioning them shouldn't take too long when the tide ebbed again and the captain was confident that his ship would be afloat on the next high tide.

Now all would get some sleep as soon as the cook dished up the stew which had been simmering throughout the afternoon on a fire at the end of the lane leading down to the beach.

That was the plan. Unfortunately it didn't work out.

Like everyone else King had fallen asleep as soon as his head hit the pillow. Kerrigan, who had been in charge of the party scraping the hull below the waterline, and applying fresh tar to it was similarly prostrate, so it was with some exasperation they wakened long before daylight to the sound of their cabin door being urgently knocked on.

King was the first to waken. 'Go away,' he shouted. 'We're both asleep in here.'

The knocking stopped and a nervous voice outside the door replaced it.

'I'm sorry, sir. Is Lieutenant King there?'

King rolled over on his back and reached out for a box of matches on the small shelf over his bunk.

'I'm here. What's wrong?' As he was speaking he lit a match and applied it to the lamp. 'Come in, man.'

The door opened and a cabin boy put his head around the corner. Both officers were awake, looking curiously at him.

'Well, what is it? What do you want?'

'The bosun told me to tell you, sir, that he wants you on deck. If you please, sir. As soon as possible.' With that he backed out of the cabin, closing the door behind him.

'Damn it. Now what's wrong?' As he was speaking he threw back the blanket and put his feet on the floor. Kerrigan turned his back to the light saying that it was probably someone returning from the town with too much drink and the bosun was being just an old woman about it. Anyway, he was going back to sleep.

Feeling that there was probably more to it than that, King pulled on a sweater, picked up his hat, and stepped across the tiny floor to the door. As he reached for the doorhandle he realised something was wrong. He couldn't reach it. He had taken the two paces between his bunk and the door so often, without any trouble, that for a few seconds he couldn't reason out the problem. He stopped and considered why he couldn't reach the handle. Then it dawned on him. The floor was tilted and because he was upright the door was out of reach. Further realisation followed instantly.

'My God, John, the ship is going over. Get up at once, very carefully and follow me on deck.'

Kerrigan's shocked face reappeared from under the blanket and he looked around the cabin. King was already disappearing into the passageway outside as he called after him. 'Are you sure?'

Walking along the passageway, balancing himself with a hand on the handrail, King found the tilt of the ship even more apparent. Reaching the door leading out onto the deck he paused for a second, reluctant to proceed further downhill, from an acute feeling that to do so might lead to being trapped under the ship should it fall completely over on its side.

Dismissing the feeling he went outside and turned right towards the ladder hanging over the side where he guessed he would find the bosun.

At the top of the rope ladder the bosun was talking quietly to the marine on guard duty. The cabin boy was standing a few feet away watching what was going on, with interest and worry on his face in roughly equal amounts. Hearing King approach the older men turned to wait for his arrival.

'This isn't good, bosun. When did she begin to move?'

The bosun glanced at the marine, then looked back at King.

'Private Broomhead called me about twenty minutes ago. He has been on ladder duty since midnight. The ship was all right when he took over the watch, he thinks, and he didn't notice anything wrong until about twenty minutes ago when he noticed the tilt. That's when he called me. I have been measuring it since. If you would be good enough to follow me, sir.'

Without waiting for an answer he led the way to the opening in the rail where the ladder was attached and swung over the side. As he dropped swiftly down from rung to rung King followed until both men were standing, in three feet of water on the hard sand.

'When I saw what was happening I rigged this plumb line.' The bosun stood beside a thin rope suspended from the rail above, which King hadn't noticed. Only about twice the thickness of a fishing line it had a sackful of new rivets tied to the end and hung, almost motionless, about six inches above the sand. The ebbing tide caused it to sway slightly as it dangled in the water. Below the sack, parallel to the ship's side, two lines had been scored in the sand about three inches apart. The inner one was more than two feet out from the hull.

'My God, man. It's already nearly half a fathom from the vertical. How long did it take from one mark to the other?'

King was shocked. As he waited for the answer he was bent down close to the water, peering at the marks. The bosun took a slate from his pocket and looked at it.

'By the chronometer on the bridge, it took sixteen minutes to move out three inches. I can't be rightly accurate because of the water acting on the sack, but I'd say she's moving a foot an hour.' He put away the slate. 'Shall I call the captain, sir?'

'Yes, send the cabin boy.'

'No need, George, I'll do it.' They looked up to where the voice had come from to see Kerrigan peering down from the deck. 'It this it?'

'Is it what, John?' answered King, knowing perfectly well what Kerrigan was asking, but needing time to think.

'Is it the third?'

'I don't know. Now call the captain while we go around the ship and try to see what's wrong.'

With every passing minute the sky got brighter so it wasn't long before they saw what was causing the trouble. Wading alongside the hull, checking each timber baulk supporting the ship as they went, they quickly found three in succession, about midships, starting to sink into the sand. The others were still resting securely on the planks beneath them, but deprived of the support from the three, a tilt had developed. As they were inspecting the situation a voice called from the deck above.

'Lieutenant King, are you there?'

Recognising the voice King stepped out from beneath the overhang and looked up at the captain.

'Yes, sir. The bosun and I are looking at the support baulks.' Quickly he explained the problem and Nicholls joined them to see for himself. After a close and careful inspection he straightened up, looking from one to the other.

'If the other baulks don't sink too we should be all right. But in case they do we'll have to get more supports. I don't want her to fall over on her side, if that happens we'll have to abandon her, but we have a long way to go before we cross that bridge.' He stopped speaking and looked up at the false dawn sky, turning slowly through a full circle as he scanned the horizon.

'It will be full daylight in a couple of hours. Since there isn't very much we can do until then, and the tide is out, we might as well get some sleep. Have someone call me at four bells bosun.' He steadied the rope ladder, then climbed it as nimbly as a midshipman with water pouring from his saturated trousers and shoes, swung through the opening in the rail, and disappeared.

King and the bosun, who watched him in silence, looked at each other in stupefaction. The bosun spoke first.

'He's a cool one and no mistake, sir. Here we are, struck all of a heap like, in case the old *Wasp* falls over while the captain, with most cause to worry, goes back to bed like a little baby.'

'That's why he's the captain and we're not. Any case, it looks as if we'll have a busy day tomorrow and I'm going to follow his example. I suggest that you do the same, but make sure we all get called at six o'clock. Good night, or rather, good morning.'

The light was on in the cabin when he returned to it shortly after two o'clock, and Kerrigan was sitting up in bed waiting to hear what had transpired. As King explained about the supports sinking he took pains to emphasise the fact that the captain didn't seem to be too alarmed, so it wasn't likely that this was another serious incident. Kerrigan wasn't altogether reassured.

'Maybe, maybe not. Anyway that's his style, my friend. But don't be under any illusions. You'll see just how seriously he's taking it in the morning when he'll have us all swinging from the yardarm if the ship isn't back on an even keel by breakfast. Now I suggest that you get to sleep too. Good night.'

With a muttered response King blew out the lamp and a minute later was snoring softly.

Getting the *Wasp* back on an even keel was a lot easier said than done. By seven o'clock, the crew sleeping in tents ashore had been roused, mustered, checked and fed and were busy securing ropes between the ship and the shore.

The sea was within two hours now off high tide again, which would bring the water level high above the temporary patch covering the opening, and although there wasn't any apparent improvement in the situation King was confident that by then the ship would be afloat.

He was relying on its natural buoyancy for this, plus the help which would be given by the crew hauling on the ropes, to break out the keel from the sand. The fact that the captain and engineer seemed to be equally confident reinforced his opinion, so, although there was some tension as the water level rose, the atmosphere on the bridge was relaxed.

The beach was a small semi-circular stretch of sand with a headland protecting it on each side. The *Wasp* had grounded almost in the centre, leaving it about fifty or sixty yards clear of the high ground on each side. It was now tilted at an angle of about fifteen degrees to starboard and a network of hawsers linked it to heavy boulders and rocks on the headland to port.

A series of pulleys were fitted into the network with the crew standing by with four horses hurriedly brought into service for the final fifteen minutes before high tide.

Slowly the water level rose around the lifeless ship. Nicholls stopped his pacing across the deck and called to Hudson to get the proceedings started. King waited to help out.

During the past hour, however, he had grown more and more uneasy and now apprehension had totally replaced his earlier confidence. This was due entirely to a decision which Nicholls had taken to attempt to float the ship with the patch still in position instead of waiting until the plates had been permanently replaced.

This decision was taken because the carpenter and blacksmith had been unable to get the plates straightened out in time. At first Hudson had agreed with the captain that floating the ship, in any condition, was better than leaving her to bed down into the sand. He was influenced by the carpenter who assured him that the patch would hold out for at least one tide and when it had passed the plates would be ready to fit.

George didn't agree but nobody had asked his opinion. All he could do now was wait.

Picking up the megaphone Hudson called to the shore party to stand-by. A petty officer responded with a wave and the men took up the slack on the ropes while the horses were led into positions giving a clear area into which they could pull. Everything was ready.

Again Hudson raised the megaphone to his lips.

'All together now, HEAVE!'

As the petty officer waved again the marine drummer gave a ten second roll while the men and horses strained. Nothing happened. Again the drum sounded and again the strain was taken. Four more times the strain was taken by men and horses to the sound of the drum beats before those on board felt a slight movement. It wasn't much but it was encouraging.

'She's moving, men. Another couple of pulls and she'll float off,' Hudson cried excitedly. 'Put your backs into it.'

Each time the drum rolled the ship inched closer to the vertical. This had the effect of putting the patch deeper under water. Guppy had been stationed in one of the ship's boats close to the bow to keep an eye on the patch as best he could but nobody other than George had any qualms about it. It was more a matter of keeping him out of the way while the real work was being done. So it was a surprise to everyone when he suddenly stood up in the boat shouting and waving his arms.

'Stop. Stop pulling. The patch, the patch,' he called.

Not taken totally by surprise, King was the first to react.

'Belay the pull,' he yelled to the shore party. As the order was acknowledged he leaned over the side to call down.

'What's the matter down there? What about the patch?'

'I think I saw it move during the last pull,' he answered nervously with the knowledge that everyone was looking at him.

By now the captain and engineer had joined King and all three looked worriedly at the junior below who was pointing at the water. From their position on deck, however, they couldn't see either the patch or what Guppy was pointing to.

'Number one, I think that you had better take a look,' Nicholls said and Hudson nodded in agreement. 'Mr Guppy, bring your boat to the ladder so that Mr King can join you,' he called.

By now the shore party was relaxing on the ground but still taking a keen interest in what was happening. They were of course too far away to hear what was being said but being sailors they could guess.

As he lowered himself down a rope, King glanced at the surface of the water underneath and was dismayed to see a stream of bubbles rising to the surface. Once in the boat he told the oarsman to take a position beside the bubbles.

The bubbles were rising in such a broad stream that it was impossible to see their source. There was only one thing for it, he would have to go down. Telling Guppy what he was doing, he quickly stripped to his underwear and stood up, making ready to dive.

This brought forth a loud ironic cheer from the shore, causing the captain to call down since he couldn't see the cause.

'What the devil is going on down there? How is the patch?'

'When I'm in the water back off and tell the captain what is happening. I won't be long,' he told Guppy.

'Right, Mr King. Good luck.'

Being a good swimmer King had no difficulty reaching the patch and quickly seeing the problem. The water was crystal clear which helped also and was warm enough to be enjoyable if the occasion wasn't so serious.

The patch, which was made of timber with canvas stretched tightly over it to make it waterproof, was held in position over the opening with long nails driven into planks inside the hull. As it had been intended to last for only one tide, under calm conditions, it wasn't particularly strong and relied on the pressure of the sea to hold it in place.

Running his hands around the edge, concentrating on where the bubbles were rising, he soon found a gap between the edge of the opening and the side of the frame. A look along the hull reassured him that there was just the one gap, then he surfaced for breath and swam clear to look up at Nicholls and Hudson leaning anxiously over the rail.

Quickly he explained what was wrong, adding that if he had tools he might be able to secure the frame, but, to make sure, he was going down again. Warning him to be careful, Nicholls called out 'good luck' as he dived.

This time he was able to inspect the whole patch. He was puzzled by the opening because he knew the carpenter to be a good tradesman, unlikely to leave a botched up job, like this, so he took extra care and spotted scratches he hadn't noticed before.

The scratches were on the hull, some inches away from the opening, and he only had a glimpse of them before having to surface again for a breath. But a few moments and a quick breath later he was running his fingers along what were obviously fresh marks. Then he eased his fingers into the gap between the patch and the edge of the opening, and gently pulled at the wooden frame. To his surprise it moved without resistance. Then he had to surface again.

As he came up for air he saw the tool bag being lowered into the boat and swam the three or four yards across to see what was in it. This took him clear of the overhanging hull and again into view of Nicholls and Hudson. Seeing him, Hudson called down.

'You should have everything you need now, George. How does it look?'

'Bad, I'm afraid. The patch must have been loosened by the tide. Have you checked down below?'

'Not yet. I'll do it now.' With that he disappeared.

Taking another breath King dived again. This time he pushed at the patch to position it over the opening, but to his consternation it suddenly broke free and, in a rush of huge bubbles, floated to the surface.

It was obvious now that the ship was flooded with about ten feet of water or more at the bow, with possibly fifteen feet at the stern which was lower. He surfaced and swam back to the boat.

Hanging onto the side it took him a few seconds to get his breath. On the rail, ten feet or more above him, the captain was leaning, with some impatience, waiting for his report. Suddenly there were raised voices on deck, the captain swung round, his back to King, and Hudson joined him. Both men peered over at King.

Before they could say anything King pointed to the remains of the patch floating clear of the hull.

'I know, I saw it. There must be two fathoms inside her and there isn't a thing we can do until the tide drops again. I'm coming back on board now.'

Guppy's boat towed him back to the line which hung down and a minute later King was standing, with a towel, on deck. As he dried himself Nicholls was making furious notes in the deck-log while Hudson waited in silence. At last, without looking up, Nicholls asked of no one in particular, 'When was the bilge last sounded?

Hudson looked at King who just shrugged. After a second Hudson spoke.

'I took three soundings after the patch went on, at about two hourly intervals. By then the patch was holding firm. There was a slight trickle, more a seepage than a trickle, I suppose, but certainly nothing at all to worry about. The last time I checked it was about ten o'clock and the situation was the same. I don't understand it, sir.' The 'sir' was almost an afterthought.

'Excuse me, sir.' They looked at King who had spoken.

'I think the damage was done during the last few minutes. If you remember, the Sub was stationed at the bows for well over an hour while the pulling was taking place and there wasn't any sign of bubbles then. He certainly would have seen them if there had been. Yet the patch was so loose that it broke free when I touched it, so it would have come adrift earlier had it been disturbed then.'

He turned to Hudson. 'How long do you think it would take to fill with water, chief, with free entry through an opening six feet by four feet which is what is down there?'

Hudson thought for a moment. 'I can't be sure, but I would expect it would reach its present depth in under five minutes.'

'And the flow through the opening?' prompted King.

'The flow? Oh I see. The flow would be a torrent which would certainly be noticed.'

'That's it then, sir. The bubbles Guppy saw was the last of the water pouring in and pushing out the last of the air. There wasn't any torrent when I was down, or I wouldn't be here now. And had it occurred earlier the Sub would have seen it. Remember, Guppy was facing that way while the pull was going on,' he finished with conviction.

The captain studied King thoughtfully while he considered

the explanation. 'Maybe you are right. I'll accept it for the time being, but I'm not fully convinced. If, later on, I find that someone's negligence is to blame it will be a very different story. Now, what are we going to do about it?'

It didn't take long to appreciate that until the water subsided outside, allowing the level inside to drop as it drained, so that a full inspection could be made, there wasn't anything to be done.

In the meantime however, King was to prepare a telegram and, when it had been approved by Nicholls, take it to the local telegraph office and have it sent to headquarters in Cork. With that done he could have the rest of the day to himself as the engineer and gunner, between them, could do whatever chores had to be done.

Hardly able to believe his luck King composed the telegram in less than a minute and five minutes later presented himself with it to the captain who was on the bridge gazing moodily up at Croagh Patrick, the holy mountain. Lost in thought he didn't at first notice King's arrival.

'The telegram, sir,' ventured King.

'Telegram?' He seemed to wake up, then taking the slip of paper read it aloud to himself.

'Wasp beached to repair leak and storm damage in Westport. Expect to complete repairs in seventy two hours. Nicholls, Commander,' he read.

'Brief and to the point. And reasonably accurate I suppose. Very well, Mr King, enter it in the deck-log and then despatch it.'

'Aye aye, sir.' King threw up a hurried salute, then made for the bridge ladder as fast as he could without actually running to get away before Nicholls could change his mind. Pausing only long enough to copy it into the deck-log, he whistled to Guppy to bring the boat alongside to ferry him ashore.

Since the ship had been beached he had been working or sleeping continuously, with breaks only for snatched meals mostly taken standing up. But that hadn't prevented him from thinking about Caroline, wondering where she was and who she might be with.

Now, strolling along the road leading to the town all traces of fatigue dropped from him as he thought, pleasurably, of the possible prospect of meeting her again. For the time being he had far more personal things to think about than the state of Her Majesty's Gunboat *Wasp*.

Approaching the back gate of Westpark Manor his pace got

even slower with the hope of catching a glimpse of her, but this was foiled by the thick stand of trees shielding the house from casual eyes. Fifteen minutes later he entered the telegraph office and handed over the message for despatch.

As he was leaving the operator called him back.

'You wouldn't be from the *Wasp*, would you?'

On being told that King was indeed from the ship, his next question surprised George.

'Do you know a Lieutenant King? I have a message here for him and would be obliged if you would take it to him.'

'I'm King. What's the message?'

'I beg your pardon, sir. I didn't recognise you.' He took an envelope from a row of pigeon holes and handed it across the counter. 'This came in last night, but I have nobody to deliver it.'

Curiously King opened it and spread out the flimsy form it contained, looking first at the name at the end of the message. Without too much surprise he saw 'Carrington' and went back to the beginning.

The message was terse. 'Report not received. Imperative we meet. Westpark Manor 2.30 Thursday.'

Wondering what would have happened had he not come in at that time, and so missed the meeting, he went out into the sunshine to consider the change in his planned afternoon.

A bench in the centre of the market square attracted him and having bought a newspaper he sat down, leaned back, and let the sunshine wash comfortably over him while he thought about what he was going to say to the Special Irish Branch.

The time of the meeting meant that Carrington would be arriving on the train which got in at two o'clock. He glanced up at the town clock mounted on a pedestal, called the Octagon, in the centre of the square. It was already twenty minutes to two.

The day felt colder although the sun still shone brightly. Unaccountably he felt nervous. He stood up, putting his newspaper under his arm, and walked down the street to where the river ran along the Mall. Standing under an elm he stared, unseeingly, into the brown, peaty water.

Since he had arrived in Westport he had been too busy to even think of the Special Irish Branch, much less prepare the report which he had planned. The one which would clear the captain and crew of suspicion. Now, within minutes, he was going to have to convince the sceptical policeman who had recruited him that his suspicions were unfounded. It just couldn't be done.

He started walking towards Westpark Manor. As he strolled along the sunlit street his mind vacillated between delight at having been given the opportunity to visit the house where Caroline was, and disquiet at the thought of the forthcoming interview, until rounding a corner the gate came in sight and his pace became even slower.

All thoughts of Caroline vanished and his mind suddenly concentrated on Carrington waiting for him.

As he climbed the steps to the front door Carrington appeared at the top, having been watching his arrival through a window.

'There you are, at last, Mr King. How have you been keeping?'

With an artificial smile he held out his hand as he approached so that an onlooker would have thought it was merely two friends meeting. But as he came close, without losing his smile, his words changed.

'What the devil have you been doing, King? I've been waiting to hear from you for the last three days. Now come inside at once, I have no more time to waste.' He turned his back and re-entered the house, King following with a feeling of foreboding.

Once more the meeting was held in the library but this time Carrington was alone. Pointing to a leather armchair he muttered 'sit', as if to a dog. Then he took up a position standing with his back to the window.

Coming inside from the strong sunlight George could only make out Carrington's profile against the window. He sat down, waiting for the policeman to speak first. He didn't have to wait long.

'Well. What have you to report? Have you found the person responsible for the sabotage? And what about the gunfire? Wasn't that worth reporting?'

The questions were delivered in such an intimidating manner that King was thrown off balance. It was as if he was being tried for a crime. Bewilderment gave way to shock, then, finally, shock turned to anger.

He pushed himself up from the chair and moved out of the direct sunlight so that he could get a better look at the man in front of him. His voice shook with fury.

'I have nothing to report to you, Carrington. There wasn't any sabotage. And I will not be your spy any longer. Good day, sir.'

He turned to make for the door but Carrington was there ahead of him, standing back to the door, so that the way out was barred.

'Just a minute, King.' The sneering voice was a further goad to the naval officer, but this time he kept his temper. He waited.

'I think you misunderstand the situation. You are not my spy, remember? You were asked to take on this job by your seniors before you left Queenstown. You agreed. All that happens is that you report to me.' The voice subtly changed. 'Now sit down again, like a good man, and let me have your report.'

For a full minute there was silence as they stared at each other, then King returned to the chair and sat down. 'What do you want to know?'

'That's better.' Carrington took the chair opposite so that King could clearly see him. Then taking a notebook from an inside pocket he opened it and laid it on the arm of his chair. 'I'll have to make a few notes as we go along. You understand?'

Unused to the tactics employed by detectives King was taken in by the apparent reasonableness of the question, and nodded. He was still unsure, but decided to take the remark as a tacit apology.

'Now then I have seen your telegraph message to Queenstown but . . .'

He was interrupted. 'How could you have seen my message, it was only sent about an hour ago?' asked King in surprise.

Carrington smirked. 'Mr King will you please get it into your head that I am not without some authority. As a matter of routine and for reasons not altogether unconnected with the affairs of the *Wasp*, I made it my business to visit the telegraph office when I arrived and go through all the telegraphs which have been sent to and from Westport within the past few weeks. Since I was last here, in fact. Your message was the first one I read.'

In his ignorance King had assumed that telegraph messages, like letters, were confidential. To be told now that they weren't was a shock and he immediately revised his opinion of Carrington again. From now on, he decided, Carrington was definitely not to be trusted.

'However, as I was saying' the policeman continued smoothly, 'your telegraph message to Queenstown leaves too much out. How did you suffer storm damage when there hasn't been any storms recently, and the coastguard in Belmullet reported gunfire which could only have come from the *Wasp*? There was nothing about that in your message either. Now what is going on?'

It took King about fifteen minutes to give Carrington, who continually interrupted with demands for greater details, the full story of the voyage from Broad Haven until the ship was beached a mile or so outside Westport. When he had finished the SIB man sat back and looked thoughtfully at him.

'I see. There hasn't been anything at all suspicious? The damage can easily be repaired, and you expect to be afloat tomorrow?'

'That's right.'

'And you are satisfied that you haven't got a saboteur on board?'

Again King agreed.

'So who interfered with the compass? Even Nicholls seemed to think it was interfered with by someone on board when you told us about it before. Why did a minor leak, which was expertly patched by an experienced tradesman, give way, flooding the ship? And would it surprise you to know that the Fenians have a sympathiser on board your ship? You remember the Fenians?' he asked sarcastically.

The voice had hardened and Carrington sat leaning forward so that he could get a clear view of King's shocked face. 'Did you know that, Mr King?'

'A sympathiser. What does that mean? And who is it?'

'I'm hoping that you can tell me that. Some locals were overheard in a tavern recently, talking about the *Wasp*. It was hard to make out what they were saying because of the noise, but they were definitely talking about your ship. Our informant heard one of them say "We'll ask him when she docks, he'll know", or words to that effect. How many other ships dock here, Mr King?'

'I don't know. Not many.' He was stunned at what he had been told. The thought of a traitor on board was incredible. Dimly he realised that Carrington was still talking.

'I'll tell you how many. None. The *Wasp* is the only ship here, or expected here, for the next month.' He paused, then added, 'Are you certain you haven't a saboteur on board?'

King rallied in defence of the crew.

'Is that all you have to go on, Carrington? For a minute I thought that you had proof positive. A conversation half heard in a noisy ale-house isn't good enough. The men could have wanted information about fishing grounds, or how to join the Navy, or the colour of his wife's hair, or a hundred other things.

Just idle curiosity. But you have to make something of it, or try to. Even if they were Fenians it doesn't follow that the man they were going to make enquiries from was a sympathiser. Maybe he was just a sailor from the ship they knew casually. You'll have to do better than that. It's no wonder the Special Irish Branch has such a poor reputation.' A thought struck him. 'If you know them as Fenians why don't you arrest them, eh?'

'Never mind why I don't arrest them, that's none of your business. All right we'll leave it for now. If your ship is afloat tomorrow, when will you be going to sea again?'

'We're in for at least three days but I think we'll be here longer, maybe five days or even a week. The engine will have to be thoroughly cleaned and greased again, having been submerged in sea water, and I'm not sure how long that will take.'

'Five days? We'll see. All right, King, you may go now but keep your eyes and ears open. I still think something is amiss, and I want to know what. Understand?'

Outside the room King leaned up against the wall for a few moments, feeling absolutely drained. He hated Carrington for his suspicions, but at the same time was worried in case there was something in what he said. The Fenian threat was very real and to ignore it could put the lives of all on board in danger if there was a saboteur amongst them. One thing he was glad of was that he hadn't mentioned the possibility that the ship was cursed. That would really have given the policeman something to laugh at, and sneer at the gullibility of sailors in general — and King in particular.

Straightening up he was about to make his way towards the hall door through which the sun was streaming and the green lawn could be seen, when he heard a voice he recognised behind him.

'Well, I do declare. If it isn't Mr King of the Royal Navy, home from sea.'

He swung round, his heart lifting as Carrington and all his ugly suspicions vanished from his mind in a flash. Standing watching him, with a smile, was Caroline.

9   *Huntsman*

Without any thought or regard for the proprieties King stepped forward and took the girl into his arms with such enthusiasm that she was swept off her feet. She threw back her head so that she could see his face as he held her, both taken by surprise at his impetuosity, but both laughing with delight. Reluctantly he lowered her until her feet were back on the floor, then released her with embarrassment.

'I'm sorry, Caroline. I don't know what came over me. What must you think of me?'

'That's a silly question, George. I'd have been very disappointed if you had just held out your hand and said, "Hello, Caroline." I didn't expect such enthusiasm, I must admit, but you have my full permission to greet me like this every time we meet. When we are alone, of course,' she added, laughing.

The rest of the day was everything he had looked forward to. They sat and talked in the sunshine, then walked in the woods stopping frequently to embrace and kiss, had lunch alone together and made plans for the future with a total disregard for the cold hard realities of life, until it was time for him to return to the ship.

By then he had told her about the ship's problems and his involvement with Carrington. She listened intently as he poured out his worries and doubts, anxious to help but not knowing what she could do. For his part, just telling it helped, and as he talked it out for the first time he realised how obsessed Carrington had become with the Fenian movement.

'It has just now occurred to me, Caroline, that I'm getting caught up in something which is really none of my business. I'm being turned into a policeman, asked to spy on people I like and respect, answerable to a man I believe to be either crazy or frightened, and I'm going to put a stop to it from this moment. Damn Carrington, I'm an officer in the Navy, and one job is enough for me.'

As he was speaking he had risen to his feet and was pacing to and fro on the wide steps leading from the hall door to the gravel driveway. Caroline watched gravely, aware that he had a crisis and concerned that he might, unthinkingly, get into more serious trouble unless he was very careful.

'My dear, sit down for a moment.' She patted the step on which she was sitting, and sheepishly he came and sat beside her.

'I'm sorry for blowing off like that. I shouldn't bother you with my problems.'

'Why not? I want to share them. Now please listen to me a moment. I don't know what is behind all this but since it is very important to you, and therefore affects me too, we'll face it together. But we must have a plan. You cannot go up to Carrington and say, "Damn you, sir. I'm finished working for you" and hope that will be the end of it. That will get you into further trouble, yes?'

He grinned shamefacedly. 'Yes. You're quite right. I'm not thinking clearly. What do you suggest?'

'I suggest that we both go and think about this for a day or two. There is no immediate urgency, is there?' When he shook his head, she continued, 'Good. You'll be at sea next week and if he isn't in touch with you before then, we'll have time to decide what to do. Incidentally, do you have even the tiniest suspicion that there might be a saboteur on board? The interference with the compass worries me.'

'It worried me too when I heard about it. I wasn't with the ship then, so I can't be sure, but no sailor in his right mind will put his ship into danger while he is on board. I think the compass was interfered with before the *Wasp* left Queenstown, and if I'm right, anyone could have been responsible. On that trip they were out of sight of land within a few hours of leaving, so they wouldn't have had any occasion to take bearings on points ashore. Nicholls would have navigated by eye, since he is such a good seaman, while close to shore. Then, out at sea he wouldn't have known that the compass was in error.'

'Perhaps.' Her voice was doubtful. 'I don't suppose that we'll ever know now. Very well. Let us assume that there is no one on board with designs on the ship, but I still want you to be very, very careful.'

As they were taking an extended farewell of each other there was the sound of a pony and trap approaching along the drive. They hurriedly stepped apart and turned to await the arrival of the unexpected visitor. As the vehicle approached they recognised Kerrigan who waved his whip when he saw them.

'There you are,' he greeted them. 'I am the bearer of tidings, both good and bad.' He was obviously in high good spirits and the couple's solemnity disappeared instantly. They went down the steps as he came to a stop.

'Our revered master, Lieutenant Nicholls, commander of Her Majesty's Ship *Wasp*, despatched me with a message which I am now pleased to deliver. Unfortunately, it is in two parts. Do you want to hear the good part first, or last?'

Laughing, King told him to deliver the good part first.

'Very well. The good part is that we sleep ashore tonight and, unless the repairs are completed tomorrow, perhaps tomorrow night as well. The Railway Hotel is preparing rooms for us at this very moment.'

'And the bad news?'

'The bad news, my friend, is that as you have had the day off, you are officer of the watch tonight, and have to stay on board with the guard.'

Caroline's face fell, then brightened. 'That means that you'll be off tomorrow night, doesn't it?' She didn't wait for an answer. 'I insist that you stay here instead of in the hotel. My parents want to meet you again, though why I cannot imagine, and I think you'll be more comfortable here than in an hotel. You will stay, won't you?' Her words came out with a rush.

Kerrigan looked silently at King, his face absolutely expressionless, though his friend knew exactly what he was thinking.

'I'd very much like to, Caroline, but honestly I can't answer now. I'll have to get permission from the captain. But I'll try,' he added as he saw the pleading look in her eyes. 'Now I'm afraid that I must go. John didn't come here to tell us his news, the real reason was to collect me and make sure I get back on board.' Kerrigan grinned.

'I wanted it to be a surprise. However, now that I'm here you might as well return with me.'

Conscious of Kerrigan's eye on them, George and Caroline's leave taking was formal and brief. But the glance they exchanged as he climbed in beside Kerrigan told each other what they wanted to know.

On the way back Kerrigan brought King up to date on the progress being made. It wasn't very good. The plates had been straightened and replaced over the opening, and most of the water had been pumped out. Hudson was sure that by ten o'clock, or thereabouts the bilges would be dry. However the engine was in a sorry state and stripping it down and greasing it was going to be a long job.

George had expected this and wasn't surprised. His main interest was in getting the ship afloat, and he asked what the prospect of that was.

'Not good, I'm afraid. When the tide was fully out we inspected her position very closely and I'd swear she has sunk even further into the sand. We've now got a good arrangement of hawsers and blocks rigged and they'll be in use tomorrow. We'll also have fourteen horses which the captain has hired, but I don't hold out much hope. Maybe I'm wrong. We'll see.'

'I hope we soon get off the sand. The men must be fed up sleeping ashore under canvas.'

The rest of the journey was spent discussing the alternatives should the activities the following day prove fruitless.

Conditions the next day couldn't be bettered. The sun shone, the sea was calm and the crew was eager and willing. By noon everything, and everyone, was in readiness, waiting for Hudson to complete his checks and give the signal to start the operation.

Despite having been on duty all night King was as eager as anyone. He had had a few hours rest and was reasonably alert, fit to take on any job provided that it didn't require a long sustained physical effort. What he was doing now as everyone waited was well within his capabilities.

According to his tide-tables high water would occur at 13.35, more than an hour away. In the meantime he was assisting the engineer to make his final checks. All the work ashore had been carried out to their satisfaction and Kerrigan was ready to go into action as soon as the word was given. All that remained now were the last checks on board.

Once more he lowered himself down the ladder leading from the paint locker to the keelson, this time accompanied by the carpenter and Hudson. Each of them had storm lanterns which, although smoky, gave off sufficient light to show that the bilge was dry. This was a relief. He had changed into work clothes this time, but even so he hadn't relished the thought of wading through two feet or more of bilge water to reach the patched-up opening.

That was his first surprise. The second one was that there wasn't any patch. Leading the way he was several feet past the spot when Hudson called him back.

'Where are you going, George? Come back here.'

He looked back to see the other two grinning at him.

'We're not just pretty faces, you know. While you were on holiday yesterday, some of us were working. Look here.'

Following the direction in which Hudson was pointing King couldn't see anything unusual, and said so.

'That's it. That's where it was, fixed now as good as new. Isn't that so, chippy?'

The carpenter nodded in agreement. 'Probably better than new, Mr Hudson.'

The repair was indeed probably better than new and King was suitably impressed. Peering closely he could see the new rivets holding the plates in position, but that was the only sign of two days hard work by the crew under Bill Hudson. There wasn't the smallest trickle of water seeping past the edges of the plates.

'If we don't float off now we don't deserve to, Bill. We couldn't have had a better job done in Portsmouth. I hope the old man ordered at least an extra tot for the men who did the job.'

Hudson and the carpenter grinned with pleasure at King's enthusiasm. As they made their way out through the deserted crew quarters onto the deck King led the way across to look over the rail at the water level.

'Another quarter of an hour and we'll have high water, but the repair must be at least a fathom down already. I think we should make a start pulling her level, Mr Hudson. Do you agree?'

The engineer looked at the cat's cradle of ropes leading to the shore where men and horses were already waiting.

'Might as well. Will you please tell the captain we are ready, Mr King?'

As he reached the top of the bridge ladder the captain got up from his chair. 'Well, Mr King. Everything in order?'

'Yes, sir. The engineer has advised me that he is ready to start the pull whenever you say.'

'Good, good. Give him the order, Mr King.'

George turned at the top of the ladder and called to the deck below where Hudson and the carpenter were still waiting.

'Engineer. Start the pull when ready.'

King joined the captain on the wing of the bridge from where they could see the activity ashore. At Hudson's shout the crew took up station on the ropes and the horses were led forward until they were leaning easily into their harnesses. Kerrigan quickly got everyone into order and when the slack had been taken up waved towards the ship. Cupping his hands around his mouth Hudson yelled 'HEAVE' at the waiting men.

To the roll of the marine drummer's kettle-drum every one heaved, the horses strained, their owners cracking whips and shouting, and almost imperceptibly the ship slowly moved upright. Very slowly the needle on the inclinometer moved back towards zero while Nicholls and King anxiously tried to watch it and the activity ashore at the same time.

At last the needle stopped. Not on zero but within three degrees of it and Nicholls decided that it would suffice.

'Belay the pull, Mr King.'

King leaned over the rail and repeated the order at the top of his voice. The drum roll stopped. Slowly the strain on the ropes eased as the men slumped on the ground and the horses backed off. Nicholls' eyes were now fixed firmly on the inclinometer which trembled slightly, then slid back to the five degree mark and stopped.

'Five degrees, Mr King. Not perfect, but it will do. Advise Mr Hudson to make ready for phase two.'

Not knowing what phase two meant, King rejoined Hudson on deck and, having passed on the captain's instruction, asked what came next.

'You'll have to wait and see, Lieutenant King, but I assure you that all will be made clear in a few minutes.' With a grin at King's discomfort, he cupped his hands to call to Kerrigan who was waiting near the headland.

'Make ready for phase two, Mr Kerrigan.'

Kerrigan responded with a wave and turned to give orders to the crew. Once again, all appeared chaotic for a short while, then order returned though things were not the same.

Watching closely King saw that eight of the horses had been unhitched and were being led away by their handlers. The men and the other six horses were lined up and being positioned along a stout hawser by the bosun and marine sergeant. As he watched, the horses' harnesses were secured to the hawser. Still not knowing what was being done King looked back along the hawser and saw it disappear under the rising tide. Mystified, he looked further out to discern, in line with the stranded *Wasp* and about sixty yards out a buoy with a small orange flag hanging limply in the still air.

'Of course' he chuckled to himself, 'they're going to kedge us off.' He leaned over the rail to see what the eight horses were doing and saw them being led down the beach to where a similar hawser appeared from the water on the other side of the ship. While he watched, the horses were led into position and had their harnesses hooked on. His musings were cut short by the voice of the captain.

'How long before high water, number one?'

'About thirty minutes sir,' he answered, having checked the time with the clock in the wheelhouse.

There was the sound of footsteps on the ladder and Hudson's head appeared. 'Everything ready, sir. Permission to start phase two.'

'Go ahead. And good luck, Mr Hudson.'

Three minutes later, to the sound of the drum roll, the slack was taken up on the two hawsers and they rose, dripping, from the sea. Everyone waited for a moment while Hudson raised a white flag above his head, then suddenly he brought it down.

Immediately there was shouting and action on the shore. The horses strained on both hawsers and the men leaned into their ropes as if their lives depended on it. To King's eye it was obvious that everyone knew exactly what had to be done and was determined to do it. The drum roll got faster as the men heaved, now in silence, while Kerrigan shouted encouragingly. But to no avail. For three, four, five minutes men and horses struggled but the *Wasp* remained rock steady. Four more times the operation was repeated. Then the captain sighed and told King to belay the pull.

As he passed the order to the shore Hudson and the captain looked silently at each other. Then Nicholls shrugged and said, 'Never mind, Bill. Maybe she'll break free next tide.'

'Maybe,' Hudson agreed, but it was obvious that he was very disappointed.

On shore the horses were being released from the hawsers and the crew were tidying the area. Ropes were coiled and placed on handcarts which had appeared and several men had slumped to the ground in exhaustion. King couldn't believe it was all over.

'What happens now, sir?'

'We wait until the next high tide, George, and try again. If it doesn't work then, we wait for the next tide, and the one after that until we do break free. Unless we can think of a quicker way of doing it.'

For the next week the struggle was resumed at each high tide, to no avail. The half of the crew who had gone on leave returned, and took the place of the others who were only too happy to catch the train and head for home.

After four days, following another telegraph to Cork, an Engineer Commander appeared, having come on horseback from Queenstown. Nicholls visibly brightened up as he waited for the senior officer to provide a solution to the problem.

It was about an hour before slack water when the Commander took over. His first action was to check the anchor which had been laid astern of the ship, and having found that securely bedded into the sand, added another hawser to the two already placed through the anchor's block. This new hawser was then led back to the poop deck and taken up on a winch.

'This will do the trick,' he announced confidently.

Even with ten men on the windlass when the next high tide came, the effect was exactly the same as before. Extra horses had been brought into service, local men took their places on the hawser to support the crew and on Hudson's signal, men and beasts did their best. Ten minutes later it was all over once more.

When the next high tide had come and gone the visitor announced that he had to return urgently to Queenstown. With mixed feelings the crew watched him depart, wondering if they were going to spend the winter on the beach. Nicholls called a conference in the wardroom.

At the conference, in addition to Nicholls, there was only George and Bill Hudson. Kerrigan had asked for leave and been granted it, and the Sub, Tom Guppy, was in the local hospital with one of the crew, both suffering from strained backs.

'Gentlemen,' Nicholls began, 'I think it must be obvious that we are not going to get off this blasted beach by our own efforts. Commander Wade agrees with me. So I am putting the ship on a care and maintenance basis for the next week or two. By then Commander Wade will have arranged for a steam tug to be here and, hopefully, that will get us off. There isn't anything else to be done. Any questions?'

Hudson broke the silence which followed. 'I think you have made the right decision, sir.'

Knowing that nothing further was going to occur until the tug arrived the two officers quickly settled into a comfortable routine. The billetting arrangements for the men became more organised than the earlier day to day system, with tents set up on lines and sentries posted to keep the curious locals at a distance. The reservation in the Railway Hotel for the officers was cancelled and, with the exception of Nicholls and Guppy, the others moved back on board and harbour routines were adopted.

Taking OOW duty on alternate days meant that George and Bill had alternate days off. George, of course, spent his time off with Caroline and their affection for each other grew steadily, while Hudson spent his time off walking and exploring the countryside to the south of Clew Bay.

The captain moved into the mess in Castlebar barracks to be close to the military telegraph and contented himself with visits to the ship, usually every morning.

For ten days this idyllic existence continued. During it the ship was scraped, cleaned and painted down to where the hull was embedded. Every piece of rigging was checked and, where necessary, replaced, every bit of brasswork polished until it shone.

The engine wasn't missed. Its immersion in the sea water hadn't been of long enough duration to cause damage but, with ample time in hand, Bill Hudson stripped it down to the block, checked and greased every moving part, then slowly and lovingly assembled it again until it was in as pristine a condition as the day it was installed in the ship. Now it sat gleaming and silent in the engine room waiting to be fed the steam it needed from the temporarily dead firebox.

Standing on the bridge one morning, watching the crew slosh buckets of water over the freshly holystoned deck, King wondered how he was going to keep the crew occupied until the tug arrived since he already had the smartest, cleanest, neatest and best painted ship in the Navy. The fact that it was solidly aground was a pity, of course, but then one couldn't have everything in life. It struck him that with Kerrigan due to return on the afternoon train another problem would arise. Would the captain permit a further splitting of the OOW duties so that the officers need only work one day in three?

Idly he enjoyed the thought of the picnics Caroline and he would take with so much time off. The trips to Galway and Dublin they could go on, even a quick visit to Belfast might be possible. Head in the clouds he was suddenly jolted back to earth by a shout from the foredeck where a marine sentry had been posted to maintain an air of authority and capability.

'Bridge, sir.'

'Yes, sentry, what is it?'

'Vessel approaching sir. From astern, about three mile . . .'

He didn't wait for the end of the sentry's message but grabbing his telescope dashed to the back of the bridge, across the roof of the deckhouse, past the funnel until he reached the mizzen mast. Holding on to the shrouds he swung up to stand on the rail from where he had a clear view.

Expecting to see an Admiralty tug he was nonplussed at the sight of the vessel coming nearer.

It was about half the size of the *Wasp*, painted a gleaming sparkling white apart from the funnel which was a dark blue. The crew was lined up on deck as if for inspection, the sails furled neatly, and a wisp of smoke drifting upwards showed the vessel was under power. As he watched, a puff of white steam issued from the siren and the whistle sound reached his ears a second or two later.

Below him he could hear the excited chatter of the crew who were already lining the rail, also expecting to see the tug.

Slowly the vessel approached, then passed astern and continued on towards the quay. As it passed George closely examined it through his telescope and wasn't surprised at seeing ladies with parasols and gentlemen in top hats promenading on the poop deck under a snow white canopy stretched overhead. Nobody on board made any signal to him, nobody waved or called a greeting. In fact the gunboat was totally ignored and he wondered had the whistle been blown as a salute or merely to warn the harbour master of its approach.

'A fine ship, sir,' a voice said, and looking down from his perch King recognised Dunn.

'A beauty,' he agreed, 'do you know her?'

'Aye, sir. She's well known around here. *Huntsman* is her name, owned by Lord Carrigart up there in Sheep Haven in Donegal. I'd say that she is here visiting the folk in the Manor. She usually visits here every summer.'

They watched in silence as the steam yacht edged closer to the quay. Suddenly the crew broke ranks and ran to take up berthing stations, then the vessel passed out of sight behind the headland with a final blast from its whistle. King sighed enviously.

'How does one get a job on a vessel like that, Dunn?'

Dunn grinned as he turned away from the rail. 'I don't know, sir. But you wouldn't want a berth on that one. She's not a very happy ship from what I've heard.'

During the heat of the afternoon it was George's practice to get a few hours sleep when he was on duty overnight. It wasn't always easy as the tiny cabin became very warm unless the ship was underway. Being motionless, even with the door and scuttle wide open there wasn't any current of air and he lay on the bunk, stark naked, while the sweat poured off. He knew he wasn't going to sleep but even dozing would help, so he lay with his eyes closed and a damp towel spread across his midriff.

But he did sleep, so it was a shock to be awakened by a stream of cold water pouring across his chest.

He sat up with a roar, looking searchingly around for the culprit, then saw Kerrigan outside the door with an empty glass in his hand, his face open in a wide smile.

'Did I waken you, George? I'm sorry.'

'If I wasn't so glad to see your ugly face, gunner, I'd have you courtmartialed for interfering with an officer on duty. You could kill a man giving him a shock like that.'

While he got dressed and Kerrigan unpacked they exchanged gossip. Kerrigan had spent the week in Portsmouth, so had lots to tell his friend and the next hour passed quickly as they brought each other up to date.

At one point Kerrigan asked King had he seen the yacht which was lying at the quay in Westport. On his way from the train he had passed the end of the quay and being struck by the sight of such an unusual vessel, had walked down to inspect it.

'What did you think of it, John?'

'I don't think much of her owner, but she is a fine ship.'

This cryptic answer surprised King and he pressed for an explanation.

There was silence for a time while Kerrigan considered his answer. Then, leaning back against the bulkhead which formed one end of his berth, he held up his hands, palms outward, as if to say that he didn't know. This didn't satisfy King who might have accepted one adverse comment about the *Huntsman* without question, but certainly wasn't going to accept two.

'Come on John. Did you meet the owner?'

'Well, no. I didn't. But I've been around ships for a long time now and I think I can tell when something is wrong. And there is something definitely wrong with that yacht. It looks all right from a distance, you saw that yourself. But up close it's different. The crew is not what you would expect, for instance how many yachts do you know, owned by an Englishman, that have a French speaking crew?'

'French speaking? Now that is very odd. You're right, I don't know any. But there could be a simple explanation even for that.'

'Maybe,' Kerrigan said doubtfully. 'All right. But have you ever seen an armed sentry on gangway duty on a private yacht?'

'Are you serious? An armed sentry?' He was shocked. 'Isn't that illegal?'

'As far as I know it is. But apart from the sentry, one of the officers never took his eyes off me while I strolled along the quay. I really believe he thought that I was trying to do the ship a mischief. And another thing, one would expect a vessel like that to have a full complement of passengers, enjoying themselves and taking the sun. But apart from one elderly man whom I noticed on the after deck as I approached, and who disappeared when I got close, the yacht was deserted. Not a sound to be heard.'

'It couldn't be,' King exclaimed. 'As it passed us I saw a number of ladies and gentlemen on board. Now that you mention it, they didn't seem to be having much fun, but I assure you they were on board.'

'Well, they aren't on it now. The yacht was silent and deserted. And furthermore, I didn't meet a group of ladies and gentlemen as I came from town, so where are they?'

King was silent as he considered the problem. Then he had an idea.

'I certainly don't know, but Dunn thinks that the yacht put in here to visit Westpark Manor. If he is right, Caroline will know where the people are and I'll see her in the morning, first thing. We'll know then.'

'I think we ought find out now, George. Why wait until tomorrow if something is amiss? By the way, you don't happen to know who the owner is?'

The name of Lord Carrigart didn't mean anything to John, any more than it did to George, but when he offered to take over the OOW duty so that George could visit Caroline to make enquiries, King enthusiastically fell in with the suggestion. Twenty minutes later he walked across the sand and up the lane leading to the road.

As he walked along his thoughts were mixed. While he agreed that there was something wrong aboard the *Huntsman*, he was reluctant to accept that it constituted such an emergency that an explanation had to be found immediately. But, on the other hand, if visiting Caroline was the way to find the explanation, he would cheerfully agree that the puzzle had to be solved without delay. Whether it was serious or not, was quite another matter.

Approaching the quay he slowed his pace to get a closer look at the mystery yacht as he passed. It looked even more impressive than when he first saw it from a distance. Snow white canvas furled along varnished booms, the dark blue funnel and shining brasswork all made a picture any seaman would appreciate and King was no exception. His pace slowed further as his eyes roamed over the *Huntsman*'s lines.

'What do you think you're looking at? This is a private vessel. Away about your business.'

Hardly able to believe his ears at the truculent voice obviously directed at him, he stopped and looked for the speaker. He turned around.

Standing behind him were two men in sailors' uniforms who must have been hiding behind the store at the end of the quay, as he hadn't seen them as he walked past.

They were both big men, coarse looking and out of place in their peaceful surroundings as they armed themselves with pick-axe handles which they were swinging casually as they stared at him. They were looking for trouble and not likely to listen to reason.

'I'm talking to you. What do you want?' The speaker was the one on the left, who now took a step closer so that he could poke George on the chest with the pickaxe handle. George stepped back, holding up his arm to ward off the blow. Suddenly he felt the situation was getting serious.

'I don't want anything. I was just admiring the yacht.'

It wasn't the answer he had wanted to give but under the circumstances it might be foolish entering into a discussion with this pair. Had he been in uniform it would have given him an authority, which he certainly didn't have in his shore-going clothes. He was only too well aware that he hadn't impressed the men.

As he faced the speaker the other man had moved behind him, out of his line of sight. Suddenly he felt a heavy blow in the small of his back which drove him onto his knees in the dust. As he supported himself while he recovered his breath, with his hands on the ground, he managed to gasp that he was a naval officer and that he could have them arrested for this attack. They seemed totally indifferent and stood to one side, about six feet away, watching him in silence.

It took him about a minute, or so, to recover sufficiently to stand up. The second man now addressed him in French which he didn't understand. He knew he was being asked a question but, by then, had no intention of answering even if he had understood what it was. As the question was being repeated he looked at the other man.

'Did you understand me? I said that I am a naval officer, and that an assault on me can lead to life imprisonment for you both, and for your master. Now, move to one side.'

Whether it could lead to life imprisonment or not King had no idea, but the time for half measures was past. He took a step forward, expecting to pass to one side of the men, and to his surprise was gripped fiercely by the arms and swung around facing the yacht. Moments later he was hustled on board and thrust across the deck, past another sailor holding a rifle who was standing in shadow under the awning, and shoved into a luxuriously appointed saloon. One of the pair followed him inside and took up a position beside the door, where he stood swinging his pickaxe handle, making the point that King was now a prisoner.

Totally confused by the unexpectedness of it all, whatever trepidation he had now disappeared and he felt his anger begin to boil. He turned to face the saloon window so that his anger wouldn't show, staring unseeingly through it while he tried to marshal his thoughts.

This wasn't easy as he had no idea what was going on, or what he was supposed to have done which would justify his being imprisoned in such a manner. He waited in silence for the situation to develop.

The waiting wasn't long. A door in the panelled bulkhead opened silently and someone stepped into the saloon. As he did so the sentry at the door straightened himself, as if trying to come to attention. Hearing the rustle of clothing, King turned to face the new arrival who proved to be a tall, middle aged man of about forty, with arrogant features.

For an instant the two stared at each other, then the man, whom King guessed to be Carrigart, turned away and sat down behind a desk from where he could examine his captive. King decided to remain silent, forcing the other to make the first move.

It wasn't long in coming.

'Why is the Navy interested in my yacht?' The voice was harsh and rough, as if the man normally shouted, educated perhaps but with an unmistakable Donegal accent. As he spoke his eyes never moved from King's face and it was apparent that he considered himself far superior to the dusty, dishevelled and angry young man before him.

'What makes you think it is?'

'I ask the questions on this vessel,' was the withering reply. 'But if you are a naval officer, as you claim to be, you are the second one today who has been showing an interest in the *Huntsman*. I want to know why. I also want to know why you have chosen to spy on me while wearing mufti. Now answer me.'

King was speechless at the audacity of the man for a few seconds, then recovered his composure.

'How dare you accuse me of spying,' he said indignantly. 'Since when has it been forbidden to walk along Westport Quay? For whatever reason. And I must protest in the strongest possible terms at the treatment I have received from your . . . your thugs. You realise that I can have this vessel impounded and you and your crew courtmartialed for carrying out an unprovoked assault on a naval officer? A cowardly, sneaking, contemptible attack.' His ire was in full spate now. 'And I certainly have no intention of answering your questions regarding the Navy, or my actions. I'm now leaving this vessel and I warn you not to try to stop me, you are already in considerable trouble and unless you are a complete fool, you won't want to get in deeper.'

With that he turned and made his way to the door, suddenly wondering what he would do if the sentry refused to let him pass.

There was silence behind him as he came face to face with his erstwhile attacker, and stopped. He waited. Then the harsh voice growled, 'You may go this time. But if you come spying around me or my ship again, you will only have yourself to blame if you don't like the consequences. I'll remember you. Now, get out.'

The sentry moved to one side, permitting him to pass and shaking with relief and frustration he made his way down the gangway to the quay, wondering what had brought about the humiliating and deplorable affair.

He didn't look around until he reached the road, then he stopped and tried to tidy his clothing and remove the dust with his handkerchief. He was only partially successful, and wondered should he continue to Westpark Manor and try to meet Caroline, or return to the ship. Then deciding that the puzzle of the yacht and its owner had now become an emergency, as Kerrigan had guessed it might, it was more important than ever that he try to learn what was going on.

Making his way up the drive he saw Caroline strolling across the lawn with her father. They were deep in conversation and for some time didn't notice him as he made his way over the grass. As he got close, moving silently, he clearly heard Lord Mulrany say, 'He is mad. I don't want you having anything to do with him, my dear. Now please . . .'

Suddenly they realised someone was beside them and they stopped talking, making King wonder had he been the subject of their remarks, but the warmth of their greeting quickly dispelled his fears.

'What a lovely surprise,' Caroline exclaimed, leaving her father and slipping her arm through King's. 'I thought you were to be on duty until tomorrow morning.' Then realising that something was amiss she took another look at him and her face fell when she saw the state of his clothing.

'What on earth has happened to you George? Have you had an accident?'

Feeling slightly foolish he tried to make little of it, apologising for joining their company while in a dishevelled state. Neither Caroline nor her father would accept this and pressed him for an explanation, until eventually he gave them a brief and carefully edited account of his misadventure. As he did so he noticed the changing expressions on their faces. When he finished Mulrany spoke directly to his daughter.

'There you are. That bears out what I was saying. He is mad.' He looked at King. 'We were, just a moment ago, speaking of the person whom you met on the yacht. I will not dignify him with the epithet of gentleman. He is, of course, Lord Carrigart and he has indicated to me on a number of occasions his wish to marry Caroline. I am happy to say that that possibility seems to have receded somewhat recently.' He smiled at Caroline who squeezed King's arm and said, 'Whatever do you mean, father?' in such a tone of shock and wonder that both men burst out laughing.

'Well, never mind. But to be serious, Carrigart has behaved so outrageously to his tenants in Donegal that, from what I hear, he lives in constant fear of being murdered. Several threats have been made on his life and at least one attack has been carried out, though it was unsuccessful. Anyway, the result of it all is that he is now a madman, suspecting everyone of trying to kill him, and never going anywhere without a regiment of guards to protect him. Did you notice the excessive number of sailors on the yacht?'

'No, I can't say I did. But there was one puzzling thing.' He went on to tell them about the ladies and gentlemen he had seen on board, but when John saw the yacht a short time after it had tied up, they were gone. In fact, he himself had seen nobody either, but his two attackers and the owner.

'I heard about that,' Mulrany remarked, 'but I didn't believe it.' Then seeing their puzzlement, explained. 'There were no ladies and gentlemen on board. What you saw were his guards dressed up to look like guests. Had the yacht come under attack, with crew and disguised guards he could call on, perhaps, twenty or more men to repel it. He is afraid to leave the yacht, even in Westport, and is suspicious of everyone who goes near it. But he has already sent word to me of his arrival, asking that I visit him immediately with Caroline.'

'But that's ridiculous. I can't believe that peasants, no matter how badly they have been treated, would follow the yacht here and then launch an attack on it. They aren't savages.'

'Of course they aren't savages. In the main they are decent, God fearing, cruelly done by hard working folk who, through no fault of their own, have fallen on hard times. They aren't the people Carrigart is afraid of. The people who want to kill him are the Fenians.'

As soon as the doctor left I stretched out on my bunk where I could monitor Joyce's condition while getting some rest. I thought about the Cursing Stones of Tory. I would have dismissed them as superstitious nonsense but for the fact that the doctor had been totally serious when speaking of them, and I felt it only fair to at least give some consideration to the tale he told. But, nevertheless, it was only superstition — or was it? One couldn't forget that the *Wasp* had sunk with a great loss of life. As my ponderings became more and more confused I slipped off into a deep sleep.

Some hours later I came to with a start. By then the saloon had grown cold so I quietly relit the open oven and put a kettle on for a hot drink. As I waited for it to boil I inspected the scene outside through the cabin window and was pleasantly surprised.

The storm of the previous night was breaking up. It was still cloudy but the wind had dropped and the sea was easing, though it was raining. The glass was rising and I felt sure that within an hour or two the weather would have settled enough for us to set out for Rathmullen without causing too much distress to Joyce.

With this in mind I turned to look at her and was very pleased to see her eyes open, following me as I moved around the small cabin.

She was so wrapped up in her blanket, inside the sleeping bag, that all one could see of her was a pale face and two big black eyes resulting from the blow on her head. Her eyes were focussing normally and she looked a lot better than she had the night before. But her voice, when she spoke, told me that she was a long way from being her old self.

'Where are we? And who was the man who was here earlier?'

'Man?' For a second I was puzzled, then realised that she hadn't been fully conscious. 'That was no man, that was a doctor. And we are safely tied up in Magheroarty waiting for the weather to clear before heading for Rathmullen. Now, how about a cup of tea and a slice of toast? Or would you prefer something else?'

During breakfast I saw Joyce's condition improve and when she told me to leave the cabin while she combed her hair and did the things a lady feels must be done before she can face the world, I knew that the worst was over. However, I wasn't going to let her get out of her bunk until her parents came on board to collect her.

Which meant that she was immobilised for the time being, and while I was waiting for the weather to improve I decided to recount to her the story of the Cursing Stones and the loss of the *Wasp*, as told to me by the good doctor. She listened to me with close attention and when I finished she lay back on her pillow, eyes closed, as she thought about it. I waited.

'What an interesting story,' she said at last. 'I have heard about the Stones many times, of course. In fact everyone around this part of Donegal has heard of them, but I had forgotten that they were linked to the *Wasp*. Could it be true? Could they have brought the ship to destruction?'

'How could they? A ship of the Royal Navy would be most unlikely to fall victim to what is nothing more than a magic spell. Black magic at that. Even a hundred years ago RN ships were high technology, sophisticated vessels, far outside the scope or range of a basic superstitious and, let's face it, primitive people. No, I can't accept that,' I declared with full conviction.

'Maybe.' She fell silent, but I knew she was sorting something out in her mind and waited. Suddenly she looked at me, her eyes closely watching my reaction.

'Let me ask you something, Stephen, and I want an honest answer,' she began. 'You have been around sophisticated, high

technology much longer than you have been in the Navy. First
there were cars, then ships and aircraft, and lots of other things
that I've heard of but could never understand, like missiles and
so on. Right?'

'Right,' I agreed, wondering what was coming.

'Now isn't it true that all these . . . these . . . machines, for
want of a better word, are assembled in such a way that when
the operator, or driver, does something, a pre-planned chain of
events follows? For instance, putting it simply, when a car driver
turns a key the engine starts, or when a pilot operates a switch
the automatic pilot takes control of the aircraft. He knows what
will follow when he performs a particular action. Isn't that so?'

'Perfectly correct. What are you leading up to?'

'Fine. Now my question is have you ever experienced, with
your high technology machines, an occasion when the machine
did not carry out its pre-planned function? When turning the
key did not start the engine? Or when a machine performed far
in excess of what it was designed to do, against all the odds,
thereby even saving lives which normally would have been lost?'

'Everyone has experienced flat batteries in cars. What does
that prove?'

'It proves that your sophisticated high technology machines
are capable of giving other than their pre-planned performance.
Sometimes less, sometimes more. They are, to a certain extent,
like people in the unpredictable way they behave. I'm sure you've
heard engineers refer to their engines on board ships as if they
were living beings with a life and mind of their own, and I know
that lorry drivers, on long distance routes, sometimes love their
vehicles even more than they love their wives. Their lorries provide them with warmth, shelter, a livelihood, and are good listeners when the driver wants to let off steam about other road
users and the boss. An affection develops between man and
machine, each understanding the other.'

'This is getting into the realms of fantasy . . .' I began, 'and is
ridiculous non . . .' She cut me short.

'Nonsense? Is it? Don't you know anyone who loves his car?
Who lavishes attention and money on it? Who treats it better
than he does his girl friend? Answer me honestly now.'

'Of course I do. The Navy is full of young men who love their
cars, or their boats, or whatever their hobby is. But that's perfectly normal.'

'Is it? Could you for instance, feel affection for, say, an anchor?'

'I doubt it. Though to be truthful I haven't given the matter much thought. Is that of any particular significance?'

'As a matter of fact, I think it is. The difference between an anchor, and a ship's engine, is that one is alive. In other words, machines live, have personalities and foibles of their own. They respond to their owner's moods and behave sometimes in his favour, sometimes against, without any rational reason for it. What I'm saying is that a piece of metal with moving parts and cog wheels, instruments and lubricating oil, is sometimes far more than the sum of its parts. And maybe it could be susceptible to what you call black magic, just as easily as it would respond to affection from its owner or driver.'

I was dumbfounded. I was about to say that I had never heard such unmitigated rubbish in all my life when I suddenly remembered a friend of mine, a hard-nosed practical and unsentimental seaman who, every time his ship came into port, but particularly when the trip had been difficult or hazardous, never left the bridge without running his hand along the rail and whispering, 'Thanks old girl.' Maybe Joyce had something? I nodded thoughtfully.

'All right. But what are you saying? That the doc was right? That the *Wasp* was cursed? You can't be serious.'

'I'm being perfectly serious. Unfortunately I can't prove this one way or the other, but let's not close our minds to it. I'm a researcher, remember? That's my profession and if I've learned anything during my career, it is not to dismiss any rationale or principle until it has been fully proven, one way or the other. So I suggest that we keep an open mind regarding the Stones and their effect for the time being. Agreed?'

'Agreed. Now I suggest that you settle down and have a sleep. While we have been discussing lorries and anchors you may not have noticed that the weather has eased and the glass is on its way up. Now is a good time for me to get back to work and get this tolerant and understanding, not to say affectionate, boat back to Rathmullen with us on board.'

As soon as I said it I regretted the cheap sarcasm and Joyce looked at me as if I had slapped her. Turning her head away from me she pulled the sleeping bag around her ears and I heard her say coldly, 'As you wish'. I stood up and left the cabin.

The voyage back to base took almost six hours and it was late in the afternoon when we tied up. It wasn't the happiest six hours I have ever spent, but at least we were talking again.

That was due in large measure to the thinking I had done en route. Her sincerity gave me much cause for bewilderment at first. I just couldn't believe that she would credit machines with human reactions, nobody was that daft, but that was what she seemed to be saying. On the other hand I could remember myself railing against inanimate objects, such as computers, which behaved in a totally stupid manner despite my absolute conviction that everything the human operator had done was perfectly correct. Then there was my friend who 'spoke' to his ship, plus the lorry drivers that Joyce had mentioned. By the time we entered Lough Swilly I was wondering had I got it all wrong, maybe machines did have feelings? And if they did, perhaps an outside influence might affect them, such as a curse?

When Joyce came up into the cockpit for the last five miles or so before we berthed, I apologised and told her how my thoughts had been running. Initially she wasn't too happy about even discussing her theory with me, but then she thawed and, although we didn't explore the matter further, at least she accepted that my feelings had changed from total disagreement to cautious acceptance and that, I was glad to see, made us friends.

Her parents had seen us arrive and were waiting on the pier, worried in case her condition was worse than the doctor had told them on the phone, so little time was lost in getting her home where the family doctor could give her a check up. I put the *Alona* back on her mooring, tidied up, then rowed ashore in the dinghy and made my way home.

I didn't see Joyce again until three days later. Her family doctor diagnosed a mild concussion and insisted that she stay in bed, without visitors, so I was left to my own devices.

These took on a certain urgency on the second day as a letter arrived from Portsmouth enquiring about my health, mildly suggesting that if I was going to need more than another seven days to get back to full operational fitness, I should report to a service doctor in Derry. If he agreed he would, no doubt, let me have a certificate confirming my delicate state of health. But if he didn't, the Navy would be very pleased to see me, on duty, the following week.

I didn't need any medical training to foresee that an army doctor would be unlikely to let me have such a certificate, so one way or another, our investigation was coming to an end.

In Joyce's absence I decided to start tying up the loose ends. When she was back on her feet, I reasoned, she would have some line of enquiry to follow and now was as good a time as any for me to get a couple of minor points clarified. The first of these was why the lighthouse on Tory should have been almost dead ahead, as we approached on a bearing chosen to keep it well clear on our starboard beam.

An hour later I was back on board the *Alona*, seated at the navigator's table with a plotting chart spread out before me. It didn't take long to transfer the various legs we had covered from the deck log to the chart. Then using the tidal atlas, I plotted the currents we had experienced, and finally pencilled in the winds during our trip.

That was easy enough. The hard part was to make sense of it. I did the calculations, put in the correct position lines, plotted the track made good, then sat back and looked at the result. The line reached up towards Tory, heading to the west of the island, quite different from the reality which I remembered. I checked all the figures, then re-checked the plot, and they came out the same as before.

Muttering a few nautical imprecations I screwed up the chart and tossed it into the litter bin, to begin again. I was in no hurry, this time I was determined to get it right and see why we had finished where we did. Every calculation was checked and re-checked before a line was drawn, every windshift transferred onto the paper, not a factor was missed, I was sure. And as I drew the last, carefully determined line, I watched in total disbelief as it headed, once more, clear of Tory's west side.

I stood up, stretching to ease the ache in the back of my neck and looked out at the weather. While I had been working the sun had broken through and the patches of blue in the sky were joining together to make a perfect late summer afternoon. On the other side of the lough a white yacht was being prepared for a sail and I was tempted to follow suit. Then I put temptation from my mind and decided on a swim instead. Minutes later I was slowly circling the boat, watching the golden sand twenty feet below, in the crystal clear water.

As I swam I wondered about the plotting chart resting on the naviagor's table on board and despite the evidence of my own drawing I was still prepared to swear that all the arithmetic and calculations were correct. There wasn't any way that everything should have led to that final line on the chart. But it had.

While I was towelling myself dry I heard a car horn being sounded on the pier and looked across to see what the noise was about. I recognised Joyce's mini immediately, but couldn't tell who was standing beside it, waving to attract my attention. However I waved the towel in acknowledgement and ducked back down into the cabin to get dressed. Minutes later I rowed ashore and tossed the dinghy's painter up to Joyce's father who was waiting for me.

As he secured it around a bollard he told me that the doctor had given her a clean bill of health and that she wanted to see me first thing in the morning. She had something very important to tell me, he added. I said that I'd be at his house first thing.

Next morning I presented myself at Joyce's front door a few minutes before nine o'clock. She opened the door before the chimes from the doorbell had died away.

'There you are. Come in at once. I've something to show you.' She swung round, skirt flying, and led the way into the sitting room.

'How are you feeling?'

'Oh.' She stopped and turned back towards me. 'I'm fine, thank you very much.' She leaned forward and kissed me on the cheek. 'Now wait until you see what I've discovered.'

I could see that she was bubbling with excitement as she sat down in front of the coffee table on which four or five large books lay open. Glancing at the one on top I saw that it was very old with tiny print that newspapers sometimes used in the nineteenth century.

'Okay, what's all the excitement about?'

'I think I know why the *Wasp* was lost, but first I want to show you a letter I've had from the Ministry of Defence in London.'

Mentally noting the word 'why', and not 'how', I sat up and showed her that I was giving her my full attention.

'Go ahead.'

'Some time ago I wrote to the Ministry asking for the verdict of the court of enquiry which dealt with the loss. This is it.' She took a letter from the official envelope and read from it, 'The loss must be attributed to the want of care and attention in the navigation of the gunboat.' She put it down and said in tones of outraged indignation, 'Did you ever hear a cop-out worse than that? Want of care and attention, indeed? That's like saying an air crash was due to pilot error.'

'But pilots are blamed sometimes,' I protested.

'I know they are. And that's usually a cop-out too. An easy

way of apportioning blame when they don't know what the cause was. Fortunately, however, as I said, we now know how and why the *Wasp* was lost.'

' "How" is pretty obvious isn't it? It went onto the rocks at Tory Island one night about a hundred years ago. But "why", that's another matter if you don't accept the official version.'

'I don't. Now listen. About a week ago it suddenly occurred to me that I hadn't checked on what other shipping was around when the *Wasp* was lost, so I wrote to the harbour masters in Derry and Galway, asking them to check their records. I heard from Galway yesterday.' She picked up another envelope and took out a letter which she skimmed down to find a particular reference, then read aloud,

'According to the coast-guard station at Achill Island the steam yacht *Huntsman*, owned by Lord Carrigart, departed Clew Bay bound for Lough Swilly, at 08.25 hours on 20 September 1884.' She looked triumphantly at me. 'What do you think of that?'

I was at a loss. 'What about it?'

'For a naval officer you can be most provocative at times. Do you really not understand?' Without waiting for my answer, she went on as if addressing a backward child.

'This was the routine report made by the coast-guard to the harbour master in Galway advising him of a ship's movements. The *Huntsman* left Westport the day before the *Wasp* did, to proceed along the same route as the *Wasp* planned to take. This book . . .', she placed her hand on the open book with the tiny print which had caught my attention as I entered the room, '. . . contains copies of one of the Derry newspapers for the whole of 1884. I borrowed it from the editor who is a friend of mine, to check on the arrival of the *Huntsman* in the Swilly, or even in Derry, and what do you think I found?'

'I don't know. What did you find?'

'I found that the *Huntsman* was reported as having arrived in Sheep Haven, that's about ten miles west of the Swilly, the day after the *Wasp* was lost. She left before the *Wasp*, but arrived a day later.'

'So?' I was still at a loss.

'So.' She dragged out the word. 'So, I think that for some reason she was delayed en route. The Tory Islanders were expecting her, and when the *Wasp* arrived in darkness they mistook her for the *Huntsman* which was now behind somewhere. They used the Cursing Stones and the wrong ship was lost.

'Everything points to it. It was just a tragic accident. The islanders had nothing to fear from the *Wasp*, on the contrary they knew the ship well since it had brought relief supplies to them on two separate occasions earlier in the year, and three or four times before that.'

'I didn't know that.' My feeble comment was brushed aside.

'Of course you didn't. Neither did I until yesterday when it all came together.' She relaxed and sat back on the couch. 'Doesn't it make sense to you too?'

'It only makes sense if one believes in the power of the Stones. Which I don't. And if these Stones were as efficient as you seem to think, surely they wouldn't harm the wrong ship? Particularly a ship which spent much of its time doing good,' I added as a clincher.

'That was a puzzle, I must admit. But let us consider the facts known to the islanders. They knew that the *Huntsman* was at Westport. They had probably seen it pass on its way there and then been told of its arrival by agents watching the ship. They knew when it departed for home, thanks to the same agents, and they could calculate its approximate time of arrival in the vicinity of Tory. All the islanders are experienced sailors so that would have been child's play. They must have known that the Fenians wanted Lord Carrigart dead and had already threatened him. So isn't it natural that they would take a hand in helping, when they could? Possibly half the islanders were Fenians themselves, who knows? And the invulnerability of the aristocracy to assassins received a rude and conclusive ending when the previous Lord Leitrim was murdered one night a few years earlier in 1878. Finally, the curse may not have been put on a named ship. They may have just said something to the effect that, "We curse this ship approaching", and no one realised that it was the *Wasp*.'

'How do you know all this? About Lord Carrigart and the Fenians, I mean?'

I had a feeling that I was fighting a losing battle but nevertheless I wasn't going to let her off lightly. I had, however, changed my mind about telling her of my problems with the plotting charts the previous day. I had a suspicion that she would have used that in further support of her case.

'You forget that I'm a researcher. I dig and dig, then I add two and two, and finally I draw conclusions from facts which have presented themselves. That usually gives me the whole picture, but when it doesn't I can quite often fill in the blanks without too much trouble. In this case it was just a matter of putting all the information together.' She fell silent, waiting for my comment, and when I said nothing she continued.

'I know what you're going to say. You're still not happy about the Cursing Stones, are you?'

'That's right, I'm not. I think that's all superstition and your whole theory rests on it.'

'I thought that we had dealt with this in Magheroarty. Maybe I dreamt it. Didn't we agree that certain machines, hi-tech machines, frequently behave as if they were possessed of a life of their own?'

'Didn't we?' she demanded again as I remained silent.

'Sort of,' I conceded reluctantly.

'Sort of?' Her scorn washed over me. 'We agreed. Both of us could cite examples of it. Machines, such as ships, behave on occasions as if they are personally responsible for the safety of their crew and cargo. During the last war ships stayed afloat with mortal damage done to them, until their crews were plucked to safety. That's a matter of record. Other ships, of course, just gave up the ghost when hit far less seriously, thereby proving their individuality. Nowadays the people who build computers have a word for it. They say a machine is "user-friendly". Have you heard the expression?'

'Yes, of course.'

'Good. Now I believe the curse took effect on the *Wasp* because it had given up the ghost. Her crew were good people, and she was an almost new ship. Four years old, which is nothing in the life of a ship. She seemed to have everything going for her. But when the curse was laid . . . she died.

'And the reason she died was that she was sick at heart of the work she was being made to do. She wasn't doing noble deeds in defence of her country, she wasn't engaged in protecting these shores, she wasn't even a particularly efficient ship though that wasn't all her fault. No, it was the work that was the last straw, the work that broke her heart.

'Assisting in carrying out evictions, bringing men to places where they could throw victims of greed and corruption onto the street, destroying homes, leaving widows and orphans to die of starvation, breaking up families and creating hate and bitterness that took a long time to ease. Did you know that she was actually on her way to Moville to pick up a party of bailiffs to evict

everyone from the small island of Inishtrahull? The people on
the island had virtually no possessions they were so poor, but
they were being evicted, thrown out of their hovels, for a total
of eighteen pounds which was owed to the landlord.

'Finally the *Wasp* had enough. I think that if a machine can
commit suicide, the *Wasp* did, on the night of 22 September
1884 on Tory Island. But even at the very end she gave her crew
a chance to live by grounding on the rocks under the lighthouse.
The only place on the island where there was light enough to
see what was happening.'

I looked at Joyce in stupefied amazement, not knowing
whether to laugh or cry. Did all the effort we had put into our
search for an explanation of the accident, including her own brush
with death, come down to this whimsical nonsense? A ship, of
the Royal Navy, committing suicide? But I knew that I was
treading on very thin ice, as it was only too apparent that she
was convinced her theory was right, and anything I said now
would have to be very carefully phrased indeed if I wasn't to
break down the delicate relationship we had.

I saw that she was waiting for my comment with growing
impatience.

'It's a theory,' I said after due consideration. 'It's not the
official one, as you say. But I suppose it has as much to support
it as the official one has. The locals certainly believe something
like this happened, down to this day, and the official one isn't
based on anything more substantial, since those who would
know what really happened, the officers, were all lost. Unusual,
but acceptable if one goes along with the story of the Cursing
Stones. You may be right, my dear.'

She sat back on the settee, slumped is a better word, and
sighed deeply.

'Those poor sailors. And what an end to a ship that started
out with such high hopes. All lost needlessly.' She sighed again.
'Now tell me what you've been doing with yourself since I've
been out of action. Did you discover anything I should know?'

'I'm afraid not. Nothing at all. But I do have something to
tell you. I've had a letter from Portsmouth and they expect me
back on duty next Monday. That's five days away but I'll have
to travel on Sunday, so I've got four days left. Can you think of
anything we might do to fill the time?'

'Let's go for a walk, I've got some plans I'd like to talk over
with you. Then, after lunch we might take the *Alona* out.'

'Great.' I didn't say anything about certain plans of my own which I wanted to discuss with her. In fact I had to discuss with her, since they involved her. They could wait until we were on board the *Alona*.

10 Tory

George King's mood was sombre as he made his way back to the ship. For the first time he realised the depth of passion that was smouldering beneath the surface of the country he was in. He was beginning to appreciate the undeclared war which Carrington was fighting. The conversation over dinner with Caroline and her father ranged over the whole effect, nationally, of the famine thirty odd years earlier and how it had dragged the population down to its almost hopeless plight.

'I saw some of the hardships the people have to put up with,' he told his host, 'when we delivered supplies to some of the more isolated parts of the coast. It is unbelievable how poor the people are and how short of everything they need, even medicine.'

He told them about the clinics Otway Browne held on the jetty each time they tied up alongside, and how Browne remarked that a dozen square meals would do far more good than all the potions and pills he had in his store. Mulrany agreed with this, saying that he too was trying to relieve his tenants' lot but it was a struggle since he himself had now only a limited income. None of his tenants had been able to pay rent in the immediate past, some hadn't paid anything for up to ten years, so his resources were strained. In fact the whole country was in a mess, thanks to the mismanagement of the politicians. People like Carrigart weren't much help either. Sailing up and down the coast in the luxurious *Huntsman* was making matters worse as it stirred up old resentments, and now that the Fenians had decided to take a hand there was no knowing where it would all end.

The tide was out when he reached the beach and the *Wasp* still sat there, solidly encased in the sand. It wasn't a sight that was likely to cheer him up but as he approached he slowly became aware that there was more activity around the scene than usual. He stopped in surprise.

Sailors were busy under the ship, shovelling away sand under the direction of Bill Hudson. Young Guppy was directing others as they led chains and ropes back from the ship and out into the sea where they were being buoyed. Kerrigan could be seen on deck with the bosun and a small group checking the towing tackle strong points and samson posts.

But most surprising of all, there was a plume of blue smoke drifting from the funnel.

Moving now at almost a run, he made his way to the ship and onto the bridge where he knew the captain would be, if he was on board.

Nicholls was indeed on board. As King stepped off the bridge ladder Nicholls looked up from the tide tables which he had spread out on the chart table and grinned happily at the bemused navigator.

'At last we're getting action, George. I tried to get in touch with you earlier but John told me that you were investigating the *Huntsman*. We'll talk about that later. For the moment let's get the ship ready for sea.'

'What's happened, sir?'

'There was a telegraph message shortly after you went ashore, from Galway to say that the Admiralty tug *Strongbow* will be here two hours before high tide tomorrow. High tide is at 11.13, or so these tables say, which means the tug will be here about 09.00. That doesn't give us a lot of time but we've got to be ready for her. We've been stuck here far too long.'

'I agree, sir. What are your orders for me?'

Nicholls glanced at the chartroom clock. 'The tide is coming in now and it will be dark very shortly. Use the remaining daylight to have a close look at the work everyone has been doing and let me know if you think there will be any problems. Perhaps Bill could do with some extra manpower around the keel? If he does, take the men off the chain party and put Guppy onto something else. I'm sure you'll find something. Oh, and another thing, I want the crew rested, fed and ready for work by 06.00, so tell the marine corporal to have everyone called by 05.30. Off you go.'

With a sudden lifting of his spirits George quickly got into his working rig and set about organising the various groups around the ship. Within half an hour the whole crew was working as one team, instead of as a lot of independent parties. The problems of Lord Carrigart, Carrington and the Irish peasants slipped from his mind, and his cheerful enthusiasm kindled the spirits of everyone else.

By 22.00, with the tide too high for work on the sands, having mentioned it to the captain, he organised a special rum issue for the crew ashore. Everyone was tired and since shovelling sand is hard work, there was a concerted groan when he announced that he wanted them all at work by 06.00. But from their faces he knew that it was more a formality than a genuine protest. Both he and the captain were well satisfied that, with any luck at all, they would be afloat by that time the following day.

The arrival of the hands next morning signalled the start of feverish activity. While most of the sand which had been removed from the keel the previous evening was still clear, some had slipped back into the trench and had to be re-shovelled out. Then a new channel was dug back to the water's edge and all hands were put to this job.

By 09.00, when the tug was expected, all possible preparations had been completed.

By 09.30 there was a definite air of anxiety on the bridge. Nicholls had put two men into the crow's nest to keep watch for the tug but so far they had made no sighting. Guppy was about to hail them, for the fifth time, when John Kerrigan nudged his arm and shook his head in warning. Guppy subsided in silence. King and Nicholls stood silently on the starboard wing of the bridge with nothing to do but wait with whatever patience they had as the water slowly rose around the vessel.

At 09.35 a steward made his way up the ladder with a tray on which five mugs of tea were balanced. He was followed by Bill Hudson, for whom the fifth mug was intended. As the officers gratefully took their mugs Hudson asked the captain was he sure that the tug hadn't been delayed somewhere along the way, but before Nicholls had time to answer there was a loud hail from the masthead.

'Bridge, ahoy.'

All eyes swivelled to the lookouts sixty feet above the deck.

'Bridge. What is it? Do you see her?'

One of the lookouts leaned over the side of the crow's nest and cupped his hands around his mouth.

'A small vessel has just passed Old Head, bearing towards us. Could be a tug.'

As he was shouting his message the second lookout could be seen pointing towards Old Head, then the two stared in the direction of the vessel which was still out of sight from the bridge and deck. One of the men leaned over the side of the nest again.

'Bridge, a second vessel is now passing Old Head. It looks as if two tugs are approaching.'

Nicholls and King looked at each other in surprise. The captain spoke first.

'If someone has had the sense to send us two tugs, our worries are over. Let's hope the lookout is right.'

At the first hail all the crew on board had come on deck and were listening to the exchange with interest. At the news of a second vessel a buzz of conversation broke out to be quickly quelled by the bosun. When the lookout called the bridge again there was dead silence on deck.

'Bridge. It is definitely a second tug, sir. They should be here within twenty minutes. Permission to come down?'

'Very good. Resume your duties.'

As they came down through the rigging like monkeys a cheer went up from the deck and smiles of relief appeared on the bridge. Hudson put down his mug and moved to the bridge ladder.

'I'll go and tend to the fire. You're going to need a full head of steam when the tugs have secured onto the hawsers and I'll see that you've got it.' Without waiting for an answer he went below.

'Right, navigator. Have the gig's crew ready to take me out to the tugs and in the meantime check that we're set up for the tow. Sub, take over the watch. Mr Kerrigan have the deck party standing by.'

For the next half hour or so all were busy as final preparations were completed, so when the captain was being pulled out to where the tugs had anchored a cable off shore he was confident that everything was well and truly ready.

The conference on the tugs didn't take long. Within fifteen minutes of the captain boarding *Strongbow* a line had been brought in and shackled onto the chain which Guppy had buoyed the evening before. This done, the chain was hauled taut, brought aboard the tug and secured to the massive towing post on the after deck. Meanwhile the second tug had taken up station in front of *Strongbow* and passed a line back, over a series of rollers to the same strong point. With everything secured *Strongbow* gave two blasts on her siren.

The tug in front repeated the two blasts, then five seconds later two deep notes sounded from the *Wasp*'s own siren and as the tugs took up the strain the chain came dripping up from the water.

Everyone on deck tried to keep one eye on the boiling sea at *Strongbow*'s stern, while keeping the other on chosen marks ashore to spot when the *Wasp* started moving. Smoke poured from the tugs' funnels and the vibrations of the chain linking them to the *Wasp* could be felt through the deck plates. But that was all. The *Wasp* remained stuck fast.

The pull lasted for about two minutes without result, then *Strongbow* gave a blast on her whistle and the foaming water at her stern subsided. The chain went slack. A murmur of disappointment was heard from the *Wasp*'s crew, then a signaller ran up the bridge ladder to where King was standing.

'Sir, semaphore signal coming in from *Strongbow*.'

The signaller hadn't taken his eyes off the tug as he was speaking. Now without waiting for a reply from King he stepped onto the wing and acknowledged, with his arms, the signal he had read. Then he turned to King.

'Message from the captain, now.'

As the two men watched there was a flurry of flags which the signaller read. He acknowledged and spoke to King again.

'The tug will pull again in five minutes and requests you to get as much weight as you can on to the starboard side before then.'

'Acknowledge, yeoman.' King leaned over the rail and shouted to the bosun.

'Get every available man onto the starboard side, and all the loose equipment you can find. Put the topsail men onto the yards, as far out as they can go, and break loose the baulks supporting us on that side if you have time.'

It was the work of less than five minutes to get the crew organised, then to haul clear the supports using the lines already attached to prevent them floating off. The *Wasp* was now ready to lurch sideways when the pull began again and King crossed his fingers that it wouldn't fall so far over that it couldn't recover. Everyone waited.

Promptly on the five minutes the tug's siren blew twice and the *Wasp* responded. Again the chain came up and tightened. The tugs took up the strain. Suddenly the *Wasp* moved slightly.

It wasn't more than a foot backwards, then it slowly started to heel over. The angle increased and King glanced nervously at the tug to see if it was still pulling. The white water at its stern had died away.

Everyone now waited to see how far over the *Wasp* would go.

The angle of heel increased. Through fifteen, twenty, thirty degrees, increasing quickly to forty degrees as a huge wave rolled out from under her side. Water was now lapping along the edge of the deck and the men clinging in the rigging as tightly as they could were shouting encouragingly to each other to hang on. Then the heeling stopped.

The *Wasp* lay over on her side, supported by the still rising tide. The gamble which the tug captain had taken was that this action would have broken the grip the sand had on her keel, and that now he would be able to pull her sternfirst into deeper water.

Once again he signalled on his siren and once again the chain took up the strain. This time there wasn't any doubt. A loud cheer rose from everyone on board as she slowly slid astern, then at a faster rate as the water got deeper, untill less than a minute later there could be no doubt that she was fully upright and afloat.

'Coxs'n to the bridge,' King yelled. 'Mr Kerrigan, stand by to secure the tow.'

As he gave the orders he rang the engineroom telegraph for Slow Astern, and checked that the chain was coming aboard smoothly to be passed down into the keelson.

The whole operation was over in less than an hour, with the *Wasp* afloat and under her own power after a month's enforced idleness.

Half an hour later she was secure alongside the quay, lying astern of the *Huntsman* which appeared to be totally deserted.

For the following three days it was as if the ship was being commissioned for the first time. Everything had to be brought back on board and restowed. Food, water, coal, equipment, personal belongings, ammunition, sails and cordage, the list seemed endless, but eventually it was completed and a telegraph message sent to Queenstown advising the Admiral that, once more, they were ready in all respects, to put to sea and were awaiting orders.

When a ship has spent a month or so in port, even though unwillingly, the crew and locals form relationships, and the *Wasp*'s crew was no exception. This applied to the wardroom just as much as to the lower deck.

Otway Browne had established a clinic in a disused building on Main Street and there treated patients for several hours every day. He made house calls on most mornings to those too old or infirm to visit his clinic, and as a result his name and reputation had spread widely in the locality. He would be missed.

King, likewise had become almost a member of the family in Westpark Manor, and while nothing definite had been said, it was clearly understood by everyone, except himself, that his relationship with Caroline had blossomed into a state well beyond mere friendship. He knew, without a doubt that she was the most important person in his life and that he loved her dearly, but he couldn't believe that she felt the same about an impoverished lieutenant. He did accept, however, that he would be missed.

Even John Kerrigan had formed friendships, with the family of the vicar, but since he had a girl in Portsmouth, to whom he hoped to become engaged at Christmas, it stayed at a low social level.

Tom Guppy and John Nicholls were no exceptions. Both had been adopted by married members of the Mess in the army barracks in Castlebar, and felt slight twinges of regret at having come to a parting of the ways, but there wasn't anything more to it than that. All of them realised that the sea was their life, their career, their future.

The sailing order, when it eventually arrived on 21 September was like a bucket of cold water thrown over them. Within minutes of the message being opened by the captain every member of the crew knew, by his expression, that it was unexpected and unwanted. Within the hour it was all over the ship that they were to take part in another eviction. Gloom spread from the wardroom to the fo'c'sle and work was done reluctantly and slowly as if to delay the inevitable. Despite that, by mid-afternoon the ship was ready for sea.

From midday members of the local community had been gathering to see the ship leave. Even Mulrany came with Caroline and, with some of the other families who had befriended them, they were invited for a farewell drink in the wardroom. During this break George managed to get Caroline by herself and took her to the cabin he shared with John.

She had often expressed a wish to see where he lived when he was at sea, now he showed her. She was surprised that two people could live in such a small space, her dressing room was much bigger than the cabin and she curiously inspected the drawers and cupboards. Opening one cupboard, which belonged to John, she couldn't help noticing the picture of a young woman which was fixed to the inside of the door. She studied it for a few seconds, then asked George who she was.

'Her name is Priscilla. John and she intend getting engaged

during his Christmas leave. Isn't she pretty?'

'Very. Have you no picture inside your locker, George?'

'You've just seen the inside of my locker. I haven't any pictures, there or anywhere else, as you know very well.'

'In that case I'd better give you one.' She paused and studied the look on his face. 'That is, of course, if we are going to get engaged too.'

He looked at her in disbelief, then crossed the small space which separated them and took her in his arms.

'Do you mean that, Caroline? Not about the picture. About getting engaged. Would you? I do love you, you know, but would you want to marry a sailor? Would you want to marry me?'

She kissed him. 'Of course I will, my darling. I thought that you would never ask me. But let's keep it a secret for a little while yet. I've got to get my parents used to the idea that I'm in love. Can we do that?'

They sat on the edge of his bunk and made plans for the next fifteen minutes or so. This happy interlude might have lasted much longer had a voice not been heard in the companionway outside the cabin door, requesting the presence of King in the wardroom. One final lingering kiss and embrace, then the slightly ruffled and discomposed couple emerged.

In the wardroom nobody commented on their appearance, perhaps because the bar stocks had been liberally dispensed for the previous hour or more, as the ship repaid the hospitality its crew had enjoyed while on the sand. Besides the atmosphere was smoky from the pipes and cigars. But as they accepted drinks from the steward, one of the locals standing with the captain and Lord Mulrany in front of the empty fireplace, saw them and called across the large cabin to George.

'Ah, there you are, Lieutenant. The captain has told us that you were on board the *Huntsman* a few days ago. What did you think of the owner and crew?'

At the mention of the yacht's name, silence descended on all the guests and heads turned to gaze at the couple. It was attention they both could have well done without. Caroline moved to stand beside her father, while George looked at his florid faced questioner.

Not knowing what the captain had been saying George decided, very quickly, that it was time for discretion.

'It's a very fine vessel and my visit was most interesting. But I'm afraid that I can't tell you very much about its owner. I spoke to a gentleman on board, but at the time I didn't realise who he was, and he didn't know that I was from the *Wasp*, so I didn't learn as much as I would have liked. It was much later that I learned who it was I had been speaking to.' He glanced at the captain who nodded, almost imperceptibly, into his glass.

'I see. A pity. Some very curious stories are abroad about the yacht and Lord Carrigart. I understand that she left yesterday for Lough Swilly?'

This time Nicholls answered. 'That's where we heard she is bound. In fact she should be there by now if she was under steam all the way. Now, how about one last drink before we too have to leave. Steward, fill everyone's glass. I want to propose a toast.'

The formalities and leave taking didn't take very long. Twenty minutes later the last of the visitors went ashore, pausing to watch the crew fall in and take up stations for leaving habour. Lines were cast off and to the sound of the whistle and many waving lace handkerchiefs ashore, the *Wasp* slowly moved out into deeper water. As the captain saluted his visitors from the wing of the bridge, behind and to one side George managed a surreptitious wave to Caroline, standing beside her father at the very end of the pier. Both waved back.

Bill Hudson and Otway Browne stood together beside them, waving farewell also. They were in civilian clothes because they were to catch the evening train to Dublin and then continue to a well earned two weeks leave at home. They had been reluctant to go but Nicholls had insisted, since they had been working almost continually since the grounding and he would take no excuses. Standing there with big grins, their baggage at their feet, waving cheerfully, their reluctance seemed to have evaporated and the captain threw them a gesture which was half salute and half wave. Then, leaning over the rail he called, 'See you in a couple of weeks.' All four waved cheerfully back.

Approaching Clare Island, where King had seen his one and only eviction carried out, the captain ordered him to make sail.

The bosun and crew had been waiting and were in action almost before he had passed on the order to the deck and the white sails were quickly shaken out. The engineroom fire was banked and, to everyone's relief, the noise of the engine was silenced. By the time the sails were trimmed and the vessel was settled on her new heading, Clare Island had dropped astern and King had forgotten about it. He took over the watch and prepared for the night ahead.

At 20.00 he was relieved by John and, following a late dinner, decided to have an hour's rest before joining Guppy on the midwatch.

Guppy was quite sure that he was perfectly capable of standing watch on his own, but the captain didn't fully share his confidence and had asked George to keep an eye on him. During the day it would have been difficult for him to get into trouble as either George or the captain were not very far from the bridge. But at night, on his own for hours at a stretch, it was a matter of having the experience to recognise problems even before they arose, and this the Sub was definitely lacking.

At midnight the watch was handed over by Kerrigan and George decided to give the Sub a few minutes to get organised before joining him. So it was about half an hour later that he came up the bridge ladder, walking quietly, to hear an angry voice raised. He stopped to listen.

The voice was that of the Sub who was apparently berating someone for getting him the wrong kind of sandwich.

'When I say I want a beef sandwich, do not bring me one with herring. Do you understand? Or are you a complete fool? Now take this out of my sight and do as you are ordered.'

'But sir, the cook hasn't got any . . .' The voice was interrupted.

'I don't give a damn what the cook has or has not. Do you want me to tell you what you will be without, if you don't do as you are ordered? Now move yourself.'

Guppy's voice had become shrill as he was speaking and King decided that it was time to intervene. As he reached the top of the ladder he met one of the stewards coming at a run to escape the Sub's wrath.

'Stand fast, steward,' he said quietly, stopping the man by putting his hand on his arm. 'Wait here for a minute.' Then he stepped onto the bridge to meet Guppy's eyes glaring angrily.

Guppy's effort to regain his composure was clearly visible. His face paled with shock as he realised that he had most likely been overheard, and he straightened to attention.

'Anything to report, Mr Guppy? What time did we pass Erris Head, or have we not reached it yet?'

'Yessir, it was passed at 23.40 during Mr Kerrigan's watch.'

As he spoke King noticed a red glow on the horizon to starboard. It lasted only a few seconds and he was almost sure that it was a flare. He waited for a lookout to report it but there was silence.

About fifteen seconds later he saw another flare, and at the same time a voice called from the bows.

'Mr King, sir. Flare to starboard. About five miles, bearing north east by east.'

Guppy immediately swung around to face the direction of the flare but not in time to see it as it had been of short duration. He looked back at King. 'I didn't see any flare.' Then he called out to the lookout in the bow, 'Lookout, where's the flare? I'm officer of the watch. There isn't any flare.'

'I'm afraid there was Mr Guppy,' George said quietly. 'Now I suggest that you alter course to investigate and alert the captain. Immediately, Mr Guppy.'

'Aye, aye, sir.' The Sub's face had turned red again with chagrin at having been reprimanded in front of a crewman. But he quickly carried out George's suggestion. Then he noticed the steward still standing at the head of the ladder.

'What are you waiting for steward? Bring me a sandwich. Any kind will do.' He looked at George. 'Would you like one also, sir?'

'No thank you. I don't think we have time to stand around eating sandwiches if someone is in trouble. Don't you think it might serve us better if we started making arrangements to effect a rescue, should that be needed? Or merely giving aid to someone in distress. That's what flares usually mean, you know. Tell the steward to belay the order for your sandwich. You can eat when this is over.'

Once more the Sub's face reddened, but he told the steward to stand by in case food was needed for survivors. The steward moved back from the ladder as the captain's footsteps were heard approaching.

If Nicholls noticed the tension on the bridge he ignored it, saying to George as he automatically looked at the chart, 'What's up navigator? Something wrong?'

'A flare was reported two or three minutes ago. Mr Guppy is just about to log it now, sir.' He glanced over the captain's shoulder to see the Sub move guiltily to the chart table. 'About five miles ahead. The watch has been called to stand by to pick up survivors and I've called down for steam as soon as possible.'

'Very good.'

Thirty minutes later all on the bridge could clearly see the lights of the vessel in trouble ahead, but it was another fifteen minutes before they could identify it as the *Huntsman*. The *Wasp* was, by then, under steam with sails furled, and the captain studied the yacht as King manouvred the gun boat to a position about a hundred yards from the crippled vessel.

'I can't see what is wrong with her. Are you sure that you saw signals, Mr King? This is very odd indeed.'

'Quite sure, captain. Two flares. Shall I send a boat across?'

'Yes. Mr Guppy can take charge of it. Have Mr Kerrigan train a gun on her, just in case there is trouble. From what we heard of her owner in Westport, anything is possible with the *Huntsman*.'

The sea was now rising and an off shore wind had sprung up making it difficult to hear anyone calling from the yacht. Not that anyone was doing so. The oddness of the situation, which had struck the captain, was that there wasn't any sign of life on board the *Huntsman* at all. The decks were lit up, the lifeboats were secured in their davits, there was smoke coming from the funnel, but nobody was to be seen. Not even on the bridge.

Hearing the creak of their own davits both officers watched the cutter being swung out and manned. It was lowered to within a few feet above the surface of the sea and held there, waiting for the Sub to swing down into it. They noticed that he was wearing a pistol in a holster at his waist, but neither commented on this.

As the cutter approached the yacht an officer appeared at the rail. He waited until the cutter was alongside and held a short conversation with Guppy who then motioned to his crew to commence pulling back to the *Wasp*. The captain and George made their way down to the deck to hear what had transpired.

'Compliments of the owner, sir. They have a slight engine problem and would appreciate a tow into Killala Bay. They say that it isn't serious and are grateful for your offer of help. They are confident that they will be able to effect the necessary repairs once they are at anchor.'

'Right, if that's what they want. Mr Guppy, pass their line across and we will bend on a towing hawser.'

As they were speaking a number of sailors had appeared on the deck of the *Huntsman*, and a man — whom King immediately recognised — stepped from the shadows at the back of the bridge into the light. He was accompanied by another man in officer's uniform who raised a megaphone to his mouth.

'Ahoy, *Wasp*. Thank you for your help. Much appreciated.'

Nicholls acknowledged the courtesy with a wave, then without seeming to take his eyes from the activity going on at deck level, spoke to King.

'So that is the infamous Carrigart. Now why do you think he was skulking in the shadows, George?'

'I've no idea, sir. Unless he thought we would leave the yacht out here if we knew he was on board. Some of the Irish gentry, I believe, are a long way from having an easy conscience, and who can say how they feel about having to seek help from common sailors like us. Whom they use as servants when it suits them,' he added after a pause.

'True, very true, George. They aren't all like your friends in Westport, that's for certain. Now please check the tow-line and we'll be on our way.'

The thirty five mile tow into Killala wasn't either difficult or dangerous. Nevertheless King estimated that it would delay them for about twelve hours.

The delay, an unspoken but welcome gift of time, served to put off the evil hour when they would arrive in Moville. This loomed larger in the mind of everyone on board as the *Wasp*, at last, oversaw the yacht securely at anchor in the sheltered water of Killala Bay. Then satisfied that they had done all they could, Nicholls ordered King to set course for the open sea.

By this time more than eighteen hours had elapsed since the tow began, and the weather had deteriorated slightly.

The glass had dropped, but had steadied, and while the wind had risen with occasional heavy showers of short duration, the seas weren't high enough to be troublesome.

What did give Nicholls cause for some concern was that the tow had seriously affected his coal reserves. Steaming for such a long time with the heavy yacht in tow had depleted the level in his bunkers to a point where, he knew, steaming all the way to Moville was now impossible.

When clear of the headlands protecting the bay he left the bridge and came into the chartroom to discuss the new situation with the navigator who was busy plotting position lines on the chart in front of him.

For a moment or two George was unaware that the captain was behind him as he carefully measured off the pencilled line. Then noting the numbers in his notebook he straightened up and looked thoughtfully at the result of his calculations.

'Having problems, George?'

He swung round, momentarily confused, then grinned ruefully at Nicholls.

'Not just us, sir. I'm afraid that the party waiting for us in

Moville is in for a longer wait than expected. We're well behind schedule now, and I estimate that we have another 146 miles to run. That's about sixteen hours steaming in this weather.'

'Not steaming, George. We haven't enough coal to steam all the way. In about twenty minutes we'll be under sail and I'm afraid that it will be sail for the rest of the trip. In fact we should take on more coal before taking the bailiffs and their men out to Inishtrahull, but we can make a decision about that once we get to Moville. Perhaps you could let me have a new time of arrival at Moville.'

'Of course. Mean speed of five knots?'

'That should be about right, navigator. Anything less than that and the bailiffs might give up and return home. That would never do.'

'No, I don't suppose it would.'

As he bent over the chart table to work out the new calculations he quite definitely heard the captain say softly, 'A pity,' as he returned to the bridge.

The change over from steam to sail was effected without fuss when the full effect of the wind from the south-west was felt. King carefully plotted the position as the *Wasp* steadied on a broad reach calculated to take them clear of Rathlin O'Toole Island some thirty miles ahead.

During the following hours there was a further deterioration in the weather, but by dinner time both captain and navigator were confident that the rest of the trip would be routine, at least as far as Malin Head. This they expected to reach by daylight the following morning.

Since this was going to be King's first passage through Inishtrahull Sound and into the narrows at the entrance to Lough Foyle, it was decided by Nicholls that King would take the watch at 04.00, so that he would then have the benefit of the captain's experience in the unfamiliar waters. This meant that John would have the watch until midnight, and once again Guppy would take the short dog-watch, handing over to George.

The advantage of this arrangement was obvious to all. John would have just one course change to make as he passed Rathlin O'Toole Island and Guppy would also have only one change, when he was past Tory and turning for Malin Head. This was considered a bonus privately by George.

With the technicalities out of the way, conversation flagged in the wardroom and dinner was eaten mostly in silence. Thoughts of the hardships to be inflicted the following day by the bailiffs on the islanders had a depressing effect, so when the steward served tea following the meal, the captain picked up his cup saying that he would take it to his cabin where he had paperwork to complete and letters to write. His departure didn't lighten the gloom.

King left the table a few minutes later and went to the bridge to relieve Kerrigan for his meal. When he returned they stayed chatting until the lighthouse on Rathlin O'Toole Island was safely behind them, on the correct reciprocal bearing. Then King decided he too needed a few hours sleep before being called at 03.45.

At this time the *Wasp* was sailing easily on north north east, the course plotted to take it to seaward of Tory Island. The night was clear, but the seas were heavier than they had experienced in Donegal Bay. This wasn't sufficient to cause any alarm.

Had it been serious Kerrigan was sure that the captain would have ordered the engineer who was temporarily in charge in Bill's absence, to raise steam, instead of leaving the fire banked at forty minutes' notice.

Nevertheless, Kerrigan had one slight nagging worry. He felt the wind had veered from south west to west. Checking the compass in front of the helmsman to make sure it was the wind which had changed and not the ship's course, he thought about the problem, then took a bearing on the light being shown by the lighthouse on Tory. To his alarm the angle had changed and the *Wasp* appeared to be heading closer to the island.

After a moment's indecision he picked up the voice pipe leading to the captain's cabin and blew into it. It was answered immediately.

'Kerrigan, sir. Officer of the watch.' He waited.

'Yes, Mr Kerrigan. What is it?'

'I have taken a bearing on Tory, sir, and think the course should be changed. There is a heavy sea and, just now, thick blinding rain. The wind has veered to west. As we have no steam immediately available I felt that you should be told.'

'Quite right. Has the wind increased by much?'

'Not very much. It isn't anything like gale force, it is just that it has veered, as I said.'

'I see. Are you still maintaining the course you were given?'

'Yes, sir. The course was changed about an hour ago to nor, nor east, and it is being maintained accurately. Mr King was on the bridge when the change was made, and I checked it less than five minutes ago. There is no problem there.'

'In that case, Mr Kerrigan, there isn't anything to worry about. Just keep to the course you were given and you'll be all right. Now, good night.'

'Good night, sir.' He replaced the voice pipe and walked over to the helmsman to check, once again, the heading on the compass. It was rock steady, but he still felt uneasy. He looked at the clock on the bulkhead and saw that he would be relieved in fifteen minutes, and satisfied that he had done all that he could, started writing up the deck log for Guppy who would be taking over.

That didn't take long. To keep himself warm he started pacing the bridge and let his mind wander to the eviction to take place the following day. Remembering the find of the rifles two months earlier he thought of the trouble that had caused. He had no reason to think that more illegal arms might be found the next day, but being a gunner he couldn't but hope that some would be, and that this time the captain would persuade the authorities to let the *Wasp* have possession of them for the Navy's use. Following Clare Island he had been sorely disappointed at seeing the find triumphantly seized by the militia from Castlebar.

His musings were cut short by the arrival of a quartermaster who wanted to know should he station a leadsman in the chains to take soundings.

Although able to serve as OOW in a perfectly adequate and responsible manner, some matters of seamanship were quite outside Kerrigan's experience to decide. This was one of them. Dismissing the quartermaster with a terse 'Not at all, the water here is much too deep to worry about that,' he then paced the bridge from wing to wing at a faster rate, while he belatedly reconsidered his decision.

Before he had time to come to any conclusion there was the sound of footsteps on the ladder and Guppy appeared, ready to take over the watch. One redeeming feature which the junior officer possessed was that he was punctual, and looking at the clock John saw that he was being relieved two or three minutes early.

Usually when this happened with one of the others it led to chaffing and hoary old jokes about insomnia, but on this occasion Kerrigan wasn't in a mood to exchange badinage. He was worried, and he decided to discuss his fears with the young officer, taking advantage of the few minutes in hand in that way.

Guppy, however had other ideas. He was in one of his un-
pleasant humours, arrogant and uncooperative to those whom he
considered to be less than his equal, and he dismissed Kerrigan's
worries with a casual resignation which infuriated the gunner.

Controlling his anger with difficulty, Kerrigan picked up the
deck log and handed it to Guppy, using the formal affirmation
which signified that he was handing over the watch. To this Guppy
replied, equally formally, and without another word Kerrigan
left the bridge.

For the next two hours Guppy alternated between crouching
in the shelter of the spray screen and prowling the deck, seeking
out members of the watch who might be slightly less than one
hundred per cent efficient. Even the sight of a sailor yawning
would be enough to bring down coals of wrath on the unfortunate man's head, followed by a charge of wilful neglect of duty
in front of the captain the following day. But the duty watch
had learned how to deal with Guppy and there was very little
likelihood that any would be so careless as to be caught unawares.

The senior rating on duty was Andrews, the second captain
of the fo'c'sle who had over eight years experience, four of them
on the *Wasp*. He had had several tongue lashings from Guppy,
and while there was no love lost between them, he treated the
young officer with a wary respect. Every order he was given he
made sure to carry out to the very best of his ability, but under
no circumstances would he volunteer advice or make a suggestion
which Guppy would more than likely reject with contempt.

The result of this understandable lack of cooperation was that
although he was fully aware that the course was to have been
changed during the watch, he didn't feel that it was his responsibility to remind the OOW, and since Kerrigan hadn't reminded
him either, the need to change course never occurred to Guppy.

Fully two hours before the end of the watch at 04.00 the lookout in the bow saw land ahead and advised Andrews of the sighting. Looking towards the stern from the fo'c'sle Andrews saw
Guppy come down the bridge ladder and called out 'Land ahead.'
Guppy heard the warning and quickly approached the lookout
and PO Andrews, to see for himself where the danger lay.

'Where is it? Where is the land, Andrews?'

When the petty officer pointed ahead and slightly to starboard
it took the Sub quite a few minutes to see Tory. When he did he
scornfully told Andrews that the *Wasp* could easily weather it,

and that he was an old woman to be nervous as the ship was following the course designated by the captain, and was perfectly safe.

Andrews merely replied, 'Of course sir. Very good, sir,' and climbing down from the fo'c'sle, made his way aft to ostensibly check the stern running light.

However, despite his apparent acquiescence he was very worried. He knew that no allowance had been made by the OOW for the changed wind or local currents which he knew, from earlier visits to the island, could be strong and dangerous. He could only put this down to either plain stupidity or over-confidence. He took up a position from which he could clearly see the bridge, listening for any orders that might be given for course changes or shortening of sail.

Most of the time he couldn't see who was on the bridge because of the angle he was watching from, and because whoever was there was taking shelter behind the spray screen. The heavy showers were keeping everyone on the bridge under cover. But by 03.30 the rain had eased and an occasional head, covered with an oilskin sou'wester hat appeared for brief periods. He devoutly hoped that it was the OOW he was seeing on these occasions.

Conditions had improved by this time. It was clear and starry, and in addition, the light from Tory's lighthouse was now so close that the whole deck was illuminated by the beam every time it swept past. The sea was still rough however, and the ship was rolling as the waves swept under her from the north west. But the fact that the lighthouse was now on the port bow, coming nearer, yet being totally ignored by the bridge, was so frightening that his attention switched rapidly between the light and the bridge, in the forlorn hope that one or the other would cause some remedial action to be taken which would get them out of the desperate situation they were heading into.

He moved closer to the bridge to be better able to pass on whatever order might be given which would extricate them from the terrible danger. Then came the cry he had feared, from the lookout in the bow.

'The ship is on the rocks.'

Glancing over the side as he raced for the bridge he clearly saw the foam and spindrift blowing off the rocks on either side and knew the situation was past help. He took the steps, three at a time, and dashed across the bridge vainly looking for the

OOW, but the only person there was the helmsman, white faced and in shock as he vainly turned the wheel this way and that, as the *Wasp* struck.

Suddenly the bridge was full of people. The captain, in his nightshirt shouted 'Brace Up', while Lieutenant Kerrigan grabbed a megaphone and repeatedly called 'Clear lower deck, ship on a reef.' Lieutenant King came from the chart room, holding the useless charts, and looking around in bewilderment when a huge wave rolled over the deck, as a dozen off-watch crew poured up from the ladder leading to the mess deck below. When the wave had passed the deck was empty.

Recovering from shock King and Kerrigan raced for the fo'c'sle and pulled half a dozen or more sailors out, directing them into the rigging. 'Brace Up' was still being shouted from the bridge and within seconds the foresail, the topsail, and the top gallant were braced up and secured. But it was too late and too little. The ship struck again, coming to a stop so suddenly that the main mast toppled over, being held at an angle by the shrouds. King and Kerrigan made their way back to the bridge and attempted to get one of the weather boats free from its davits. Chopping the ropes holding the gig, one end fell free, then another mighty wave hit it, smashing the gig and whaler into a million pieces.

Petty Officer Rattenbury, who had been in his hammock when the ship struck and had tried to clear the lower deck before it became impossible, now raced to the bridge in a vain attempt to take over the wheel. With the captain shouting 'Hard a Port' and the OOW shouting 'Hard a Starboard' he realised that nobody was in effective control any longer, and grabbing a life belt made his way to the rigging. He was less than ten feet above the deck when the next big wave hit, swept across the bridge, and when it had passed the bridge was empty.

Stunned, all he could do now was cling on fiercely and hope for the best, but moments later another wave hit, bringing the mast crashing down. He couldn't hold on any longer and was forced to let go, and as he was swept over the side he saw the incorrigible Dunn, who had saved the padre on Clare Island from humiliation, go past with blood streaming from his torn hands but with a fierce grip on the marine, Styles. Then he lost consciousness.

The *Wasp* struck the rocks at approximately 03.40 am on the morning of 22 September 1884, about forty yards from the lighthouse. Despite the fact that it was aground for a further twenty minutes, or so, before it slid off into twenty two fathoms, it was daylight before the lightkeepers realised that a tragedy had taken place and came to the assistance of the survivors.

Of the total ship's company of fifty eight souls, one rating who was sick in Westport escaped, and six others were saved. Fifty one, including all the officers on board, were lost.

The officers who died were Lieutenant John Nicholls (Captain), Lieutenant George King (First Officer and Navigator), Sub Lieutenant Thomas Guppy, and John W. Kerrigan (Gunner). Surgeon Otway Browne and Bill Hudson (Engineer), who were on leave, escaped.

The survivors were;

PO	Richard Rattenbury	Quartermaster
PO	Philip Andrews	Second captain of the fo'c'sle
Cook	John Hutton	
AB	William Dunn	
Pvt	Alfred Broomhead	RMLI
Pvt	William Styles	RMLI

When the news of the tragedy reached Derry word was passed to HMS *Valiant*, then lying at Rathmullen, to proceed to Tory to pick up the survivors. Captain Marrack, in the absence of Captain Knowles, was in command, and he reported that on his arrival at the island he couldn't do this for more than twenty four hours because the weather was very rough and the state of the sea 'appalling'.

The survivors said at the court-martial that the night of the tragedy was clear but high seas were running. On the occasion it was raining quite heavily, but the light on the island was clearly visible for about two hours before the ship went aground. No survivor said that there was a change of course during the middle watch, nor any change in wind speed and direction, but sail had been reduced when King was advised at eleven o'clock that night that the light was bearing off the port bow, and the course left by Nicholls at eight o'clock in the evening was not altered.

Lieutenant Nicholls was familiar with Tory, having visited it five or six times before without incident. Sub Lieutenant Guppy may have thought he could weather it and miscalculated the strength of the current.

The *Wasp* was under sail, with the engine at forty minutes notice of steam, a fact which gave rise to the most singular circumstances needing to be explained by the court-martial, but which were not. That was not simply how the gunboat came to be wrecked on a rock, the position of which was clearly indicated by a burning light, but how a vessel which was fitted with engines having more units of power than she possessed tons of displacement, came to be navigating a dangerous coast, on a lee shore, in the midst of strong currents, at three o'clock in the morning with a stiff wind blowing, wholly under sail at the time, with her fires banked up.

The court-martial, held on 6 October 1884, in Portsmouth, to establish the cause of the loss decided that it must be 'attributed to the want of care and attention in the navigation of the gunboat.'

Following the loss, the Catholic priest on the island, Fr Michael O'Donnell, seized the so-called Cursing Stones and put them in a location known only to himself. This may have been at sea.

To this day their location is unknown.